The Azalea Assault

This Large Print Book carries the
Seal of Approval of N.A.V.H.

The Azalea Assault

Alyse Carlson

THORNDIKE PRESS

A part of Gale, Cengage Learning

Detroit • New York • San Francisco • New Haven, Conn • Waterville, Maine • London

A Garden Society Mystery.
Thorndike Press, a part of Gale, Cengage Learning.

Thorndike Press® Large Print Mystery.
The text of this Large Print edition is unabridged.
Other aspects of the book may vary from the original edition.
Set in 16 pt. Plantin.

LIBRARY OF CONGRESS CATALOGING-IN-PUBLICATION DATA

Carlson, Alyse, 1966–
The azalea assault / by Alyse Carlson. — Large print ed.
p. cm. — (Thorndike Press large print mystery)
"A Garden Society Mystery"—T.p. verso.
ISBN-13: 978-1-4104-5238-2 (hardcover)
ISBN-10: 1-4104-5238-7 (hardcover)
1. Gardens—Virginia—Roanoke—Fiction. 2. Periodicals—Fiction. 3. Photography of gardens—Fiction. 4. Public relations—Fiction. 5. Murder—Investigation—Fiction. 6. Large type books. I. Title.
PS3603.A75275A99 2012
813'.6—dc23 2012026791

Published in 2012 by arrangement with The Berkley Publishing Group, a member of Penguin Group (USA) Inc.

Printed in the United States of America
1 2 3 4 5 6 7 16 15 14 13 12

For Elizabeth Spann Craig:
Thank you for holding the door.

ACKNOWLEDGMENTS

Writing a book always requires a ton of eyes and a lot of help, but a first book is especially challenging. There was a steep learning curve — crossing all the Ts, dotting the Is, and learning the ropes. So I have a list of people I'd like to thank for their help at various stages of this project. I will surely miss somebody who helped me out, and for that I apologize. But for feedback at various stages of this manuscript, I want to thank: Stacy Gail, Shaharizan Perez, Leanne Rabesa, Natasha Ramarathnam, Mari Salberg, and Stefanie Winter.

And I especially want to thank the trio I think of as the three Es. Ellen, Emily, and Elizabeth. Ellen Pepus is my fabulous agent who connected me with this opportunity and has been wonderfully patient with this newbie. Emily Rapoport is my amazing editor who has taught me so much and has been so kind through a variety of challenges, all of my making. And in particular, Elizabeth Spann Craig, my friend who first recognized in me the "Cozy Voice" and pointed me at all the resources I needed to make this journey.

TO: *Roanoke Tribune,* Living Section
FROM: Roanoke Garden Society
RE: PRESS RELEASE: National Media Event in Roanoke

This Thursday afternoon, the Roanoke Garden Society welcomes *Garden Delights,* America's premiere magazine for gardening enthusiasts. The magazine's staff will be in Roanoke to prepare an eight-page feature on the city's most spectacular garden, for the June issue. Central to the feature will be the photography of world-renowned photographer Jean-Jacques Georges, who has won several international awards and captured noteworthy spreads ranging from international swimsuit models to African wildlife.

Mr. Georges is scheduled to conduct a three-day photography shoot at the historically registered gardens of La Fontaine off of Blue Ridge Parkway. He and the *Garden*

Delights staff will be hosted by Samantha Hollister, Roanoke Garden Society president, and Neil Patrick, RGS founder and owner of La Fontaine.

The magazine release is slated for June 3.

CONTACT: Camellia Harris
camharris@rgs.org

Chapter 1

"Incoming!"

Cam Harris pushed off her kitchen floor, propelling the wheeled kitchen chair she was sitting in to the sliding panel that hid the dumbwaiter. She opened it a hair and yelled to the kitchen upstairs, "Ready!" and shut it again, knocking off the "Over the hill" magnet her sister had recently given her. She heard her neighbor and best friend, Annie Schulz, lowering her treasure, which was how Annie referred to anything she lowered via dumbwaiter, then tramping down the back stairs to Cam's apartment.

The turn-of-the-century house, gifted to Annie when her grandmother had moved to a retirement home, was split into two apartments, upper and lower. The living arrangement was a perfect compromise for the yin-yang best friends. The two had tried to live together before, but Annie's free-form approach to order drove Cam crazy; she'd grown tired of photos drying over the bathtub and finding every bowl in the house dirty because Annie had a wild hair and tried out four new cupcake recipes at once. In the current living situation, they got all the bonding time they wanted, but with absolute boundaries about whose space was whose.

Annie let herself in, as was her habit, and plopped into a chair opposite Cam.

"Caffeine?" she asked, blowing a stray curl out of her face.

Cam rolled her eyes, stood, and poured coffee into a travel cup for Annie, then walked over and opened the dumbwaiter to inspect the goods. "Frazzled morning?"

"Just a little wrestling with the juicer Petunia left. First batch was too pulpy, and I had to take apart the stupid thing to clean it."

"I thought all you had to do was bake and deliver," Cam said.

"Yes, but juice squeezed yesterday would not be fresh-squeezed, would it? No cream?"

"Do I ever have cream? I've got that nonfat hazelnut stuff."

Annie made a face. "You, my friend, are missing the point of cream. It's about texture." They had an ongoing disagreement about coffee supplements. "Are you ready?"

"I am. Just one more load?"

Annie nodded and stood. "But let's get this to the car first." She went to the dumbwaiter and grabbed the first of the food.

Annie was helping Cam, albeit indirectly. Cam's sister, Petunia, was catering a several-day event Cam was coordinating for her employer, the Roanoke Garden Society. Petunia's restaurant, Spoons, bought sweets from Annie's cupcake store, Sweet Surprise, and Petunia had convinced Annie to trade delivery assignments. Petunia would transport the desserts that went with lunches and suppers if Annie would deliver breakfast, since a baker needed to begin work early anyway.

Cam would have done it, but she needed delivering herself. She was saving for a new Mustang, but purchase was at least six months away. Normally she rode her bicycle, except when she needed to look professional, which was the case with this painstakingly orchestrated feature for *Garden Delights* magazine. For the next several days, she'd be begging rides from Annie, Petunia, and her boyfriend, Rob.

Cam helped Annie load the breakfast goods into Annie's Volkswagen. The car was not really suited to catering, since all Annie normally delivered were cupcakes, cookies, and special fancy desserts. After Annie's return upstairs for the rest of the food, they finally accommodated the juice, coffee, fruit, and bagels, but the only spot for the tray of spreads was Cam's lap. She wasn't sure if she was more concerned about the garlic and green onion or the salmon, but she was fairly sure she'd be wearing one of them, given Annie's driving.

As Annie pulled out of their neighborhood, Cam spotted the giant neon star atop Mill Mountain, just visible through a sea of blooming dogwoods. She breathed in the scent of honeysuckle, laid her head against the headrest, and smiled. The dogwoods always made her happy. There was nothing better than pink trees.

She had never been sorry to return to Roanoke, "America's Most Livable City," according to her PR peers at the chamber of commerce. Cam couldn't have agreed more. She'd lived here twenty-seven of her thirty-two years, leaving only to attend graduate school at Northwestern and then work at a public relations firm in Chicago for a couple of years. When her mother died, Cam returned because she worried about her father. She was glad she had.

Cam had to use a towelette to dab a spot of cream cheese from her gray linen slacks when they arrived. The Ann Taylor silk blouse, though, would have been far less salvageable, and it had survived unscathed. Cam felt it was a victory.

"Cammi! There you are! You look lovely!" Neil Patrick stepped onto the porch to greet her. He was host of this event, founding member of the Roanoke Garden Society, and a perfect blue-blooded Southern gentleman. Cam adored him in all ways but one: he insisted on calling her Cammi. She would have thought, given his love for flowers, he would prefer Camellia, her full name. She preferred that to Cammi herself, though she liked Cam best. She chastised herself. Most men her father's age got a free pass, but Neil's young wife, Evangeline, had changed her charitable attitude. A man married to someone born in the same decade as Cam should be more attentive to her preferences, but, as usual, she bit her tongue.

"Mr. Patrick, it's wonderful to see you. Have you met my friend Annie? She's helping Petunia with some of the catering."

"Oho!"

Mr. Patrick looked as if he'd never seen anything quite as outrageous as Annie. Cam felt a little defensive, though Annie probably should have known the nose ring wouldn't fly with this crowd. Her clothes were actually rather conservative, so far as Annie went — a gypsy skirt, Birkenstocks, and a peasant blouse.

Fortunately, Annie was unfazed by anyone else's judgment. She'd decided as a teen she didn't care for anyone's approval who judged on first impressions.

"Where would you like me to set up breakfast, Mr. Patrick?" Her smile was straight and sincere, and it had the effect it always did. Mr. Patrick's short white mustache twitched in a smile.

"There's a tent off the patio, just through there." He gestured and Annie began to carry the various trays through the house, leaving Cam to Mr. Patrick.

"You have a lovely home, Mr. Patrick." It was true — classic Georgian architecture, perfectly decorated. "The magazine crew should be here in an hour. I hoped we could make a list of 'can't miss' features before they get here. Does that sound good?"

He nodded, smiling, less shy than usual, probably because there was no media spy pestering him about his marriage to the youthful former Miss Virginia.

"Let me show you something."

He looked like a boy with his hand in the cookie jar. His blue eyes twinkled as he held out his elbow for Cam. She allowed him to guide her up the stairs, realizing halfway up how it might be misinterpreted if a photo were snapped. When she reached the top of the stairs and saw all the natural lighting through the French doors, though, she pushed ahead of her host into a room with a full wall of windows. It was a drawing room of sorts, but the focus was obviously the natural beauty behind the glass; the garden below spanned an acre, at least. When Cam threw open the other set of French doors and gasped, Mr. Patrick chuckled.

She looked down on his property and the majestic background.

"I've never seen such a thing. It's amazing!"

Mr. Patrick led Cam onto the balcony.

At the center of his garden was a fountain with streams of water shooting up like stamen; the yellow water lilies floating in the fountain's pool looked, from a distance, like the pollen at the center of a flower. The arrangement radiated outward, a pattern of flowers that, from this height, created a perfect mural of a stargazer lily. Whites, reds, and pinks were perfectly distributed, allowing the bushes and smaller plants to create a breathtaking illusion.

Cam was surprised, then, when Mr. Patrick leaned forward over the rail, pointing to a near corner, not part of the magnificence at all. "That trellis over the sundeck was built by none other than your daddy."

"Really? I didn't know you knew my father." Now that she'd noticed the trellis through the lush wisteria, she could see the beautiful craftsmanship; it had just been humbled by the extravagant floral display.

"I don't, really, not well. He built it when my father lived here."

Cam admired it a moment and then focused on the main garden again.

"We're lucky it's been an early spring. This is a lot more advanced than normal for April, isn't it?"

"It is."

"We'll definitely need shots from here, probably at several times of day, as I'm sure that view changes with the sun."

"Oh, that's true. It's spectacular at sunrise. You don't suppose that fancy photographer would come for sunrise, do you?"

He looked so hopeful that Cam couldn't bring herself to answer honestly. "I'm sure he'd be delighted."

The truth was, it was a huge coup for the Roanoke Garden Society to have lured Jean-Jacques Georges to do the photography shoot. It was an effort somehow managed by Samantha Hollister, the current RGS president, but Cam had heard he could be a bit difficult.

Garden Delights was the premiere national magazine for garden lovers, and Cam had been courting them for seven months. Jean-Jacques was exactly the enticement they had needed to believe RGS had a package worth presenting. A famous photographer would do nothing to hurt their circulation, so they agreed to come to Roanoke for the feature. Cam was sure it would be worth it.

"Show me 'Summer.' " She smiled at Mr. Patrick. One of the reasons the Patrick estate, La Fontaine, had been chosen for the shoot was a row of three greenhouses kept in specific conditions to display the region's finest foliage of all four seasons, with the fourth displayed outside — a full year of Virginia's glory on any given day.

He led her down the stairway at the side of the balcony that allowed access to the gardens directly from the upper level. The house had definitely been adorned with all the details to allow maximum garden enjoyment.

As they approached, Cam could see none of the greenhouses had a spot of discoloration, though the "Summer" house did have the telling haze of humidity gathered on the roof. The greenhouses always held samples of in-bloom flowers for each season. It was labor-intensive, but Neil Patrick had a fabulous gardener. Mr. Patrick also helped maintain the grounds. He loved gardening, and he spent time pruning and preening almost every day. Cam doubted he spent much time weeding, though. His nails looked too well manicured for that.

After the greenhouse tour, a woman approached them. "Monsieur, the magazine staff have arrived."

"Thank you, Giselle."

Cam frowned as Giselle walked away. The woman's Southern drawl was not French, whatever pretending she tried. "She's not really a Giselle, is she?"

"No. Sally, I think. I find the staff is more content if they feel they're playing a role." He smiled indulgently. "It was Evangeline who taught me that," he said as he led her in.

Cam smirked at how adoring Mr. Patrick was of his young wife. She supposed she was happy for them, no matter how odd the age difference seemed to her.

"You're here! Wonderful!" Mr. Patrick bellowed a few moments later as he met the new arrivals in the foyer. "I've got you in the servant's house!"

The servant's house was opposite the greenhouses, and quite nice, but Cam could see the magazine staff was a little put out, so she added, "It's beautiful, and closest to everything you'll be shooting. You'll love it." She hoped they would believe her, then realized she needed to introduce herself. "I'm Cam Harris, the RGS public relations representative."

The taller man wore his hair in spikes that were bleached at the ends. He held out his hand but didn't smile. "Ian Ellsworth, photo editor." He then introduced his lighting man and his assistant. Cam wished he at least had the courtesy to make eye contact with Mr. Patrick.

"Mr. Patrick, would you like me to do the tour?" Cam asked, feeling it unwise to pit artistic arrogance against privilege.

"Do! Do!" He shooed them away. "I've got three board members arriving soon, so you kids go ahead and get to work."

Cam gave a reverse-order tour, thinking the mosaic of flowers from the balcony was a wonderful finale. She explained the seasonal greenhouses as she led them on a sweep through, pointing out the highlights. "Winter" included several varieties of berries on decorative bushes and evergreen shrubbery; "Autumn" held caryopteris, scotch heather, and witch hazel; and "Summer" had such variety that Cam felt lightheaded from the brightness and aroma just entering.

She addressed the highlights she and Mr. Patrick had discussed. Ian largely ignored her, never acknowledging her suggestions. He pointed out other items of interest, though "interest" seemed the wrong word, based on his bored expression. The assistant, Hannah, made copious notes while Tom, the lighting man, just squinted and alternately nodded or frowned, mumbling about the amount of work needed to put various selections in optimum lighting.

They exited the last greenhouse and began walking the "lily leaves" of the garden, Cam stopping at the collection of rhododendrons and azaleas. The areas of brightest coloring had rhododendrons at the center, surrounded by the azaleas, which then tapered toward the white of tulips, hyacinth, and assorted flowering ground cover.

Hannah, the assistant, was drawn farther up a tributary, so the rest followed her.

"It's too bad we can't do scratch-and-sniff photos. This is heavenly!" she said.

Cam agreed, explaining that the most fragrant flowers had been segregated. She and the magazine crew now stood among the sweet olive, a deep green bush with small, wonderfully scented white flowers.

"It's so visitors can enjoy each, rather than having their senses saturated to the point where they don't notice the fragrances anymore."

As she shared the information, she guiltily thought this had only been a rumor. She would double-check with Mr. Patrick later. Unfortunately, the photo editor and lighting man didn't seem to share their girl Friday's fascination with aroma.

As noon approached, Cam decided it was time for the finale, so she led them up the outside stairway to the balcony. They followed diligently, though the lighting man now looked as bored as his boss. As they reached the top of the stairs, though, Ian threw his arm out, stopping the rest, and went to the balcony rail alone. Finally, after what seemed a long time, he looked back at Cam.

"That's spectacular."

"Isn't it? Mr. Patrick said it's best at sunrise, but I think it's *always* spectacular."

"I'd have to agree. It's high noon, and though the white reflects too much to photograph right now, it's still phenomenal."

Cam asked about getting a sunrise shot,

and Ian, without refusing, confirmed her fears about Jean-Jacques Georges and how prickly he could be. Tom, though, pointed out a true artist knew the magic of timing and would surely cooperate. It was the most she'd heard him say — out loud, at least.

Hannah looked vaguely adoring, and Cam wondered if the mousy girl had a crush on this odd, quiet man.

Ian spoke hesitantly, breaking the moment. "I don't know . . . Jean-Jacques is used to fashion models and artificial settings." It was the first break in Ian's confidence she'd seen.

Cam bit her lip. "Can't hurt to ask?"

Tom nodded and Ian shrugged. Cam could tell the request fell to her. She had been hoping for an ally, but Ian looked afraid.

When they went downstairs, her sister, Petunia, was bringing in lunch. Petunia seemed all elbows as she maneuvered trays. Cam was thin, but Petunia was positively skinny. Fortunately, she was stronger than she looked.

Several tables had been set up on the back patio under the shade of the balcony, and to the side was the tent with fans to keep the area cool. It was furnished with a buffet table. A handful of Garden Society members milled about, filling plates or holding drinks. After curious glances at Cam and her guests, they went back to their conversations.

As they reached the back patio, Hannah sniffed deeply again, returning to her scent heaven. "Another fragrance!"

Neil Patrick walked out just then and smiled. "Just so! Don't get too close. The bees love the wisteria, but did you know it was Cammi's father who built that trellis so that seventy-year-old tree could continue to thrive?"

Joseph Sadler-Neff, the RGS historian, who'd been sipping sweet tea and watching from the edge of the patio, launched into a long lecture on the year, the building materials, the time it had taken to construct, and the history of the tree. This was common for Joseph. Most people who knew him only half listened, though they were polite colleagues, so at least they faced him and pretended. Cam quickly explained to the magazine crew who he was and why he knew so much.

Ian, listening to neither Joseph nor Cam, gave the trellis and wisteria his full attention.

He circled the structure with an artist's eye. "It would be great to get a shot of the builder next to the trellis. Most well-meaning builders do some damage to the tree, but this looks perfectly executed. Is he still alive?"

"Yes, but he has a busy social life," Cam answered uncomfortably. Cam's father seemed to unintentionally become the center of any gathering he attended, and she wanted this to be a Garden Society event. She was vetoed, though, when Neil Patrick spoke.

"Oh, Cammi! You've got to invite him to the party tomorrow night. We'll convince him to do the photo shoot! It's a wonderful angle."

"Um . . . I'll see if he's free."

Petunia, who'd just deposited a dessert tray that appeared to be her last, met Cam's gaze, an eyebrow raised under her blonde bangs. Cam knew her sister read her thoughts, but there was no helping it. She would have to invite her father to the festivities and hope he was busy. Cam mouthed "thank you" as Petunia turned to leave. When Petunia reached the door, Evangeline Patrick emerged, making a beeline for Joseph. Petunia scowled, or maybe it was only a face caused by the difficulty she was having balancing, since she was removing the breakfast remains as she left.

Evangeline and Joseph began bickering, but in a moment their tone was cordial again.

"Don't mind them, hon." Samantha Hollister put a hand on Cam's, mistaking her frown for a response to the bickering. "Evangeline wants progress, and Joseph feels called to preserve history. They're both right in small doses, but they sure have trouble finding balance. They get into it all the time."

That would have made sense, had Petunia's scowl not left Cam with the distinct feeling she was missing something.

That afternoon the magazine crew began testing the lighting in the various locations they had discussed, a task that would take the next day and a half. Cam made notes. When the photographs were complete, she wanted to be able to hand off a press packet with the information about the plant types and their origins, including the history of the particular plants in Mr. Patrick's collection, to the reporter. Jane Duffy was rather prestigious in gardening circles and would interview the Roanoke Garden Society members. It was Cam's job to make sure the background details were easily accessible so Ms. Duffy could concentrate on the story.

When Petunia brought in supper for the house guests at six, she gave Cam a ride home, and Cam got to work at her computer, composing the various press packet pieces. Cam had extensive files on area plants, some from her own education and interest, but more of them from the historic files she'd gotten from Joseph Sadler-Neff. It was more an organization project than writing from scratch, so she cut, pasted, and proofed until she heard the rattling of the dumbwaiter. Some "treasure" was being lowered.

Two minutes later Annie came from Cam's kitchen with a tray that held a bottle of wine and two tiki cups shaped like shrunken heads. Cam glanced at her computer screen clock and saw it was a little after nine. She'd not gotten to her own garden all day, but it was too late now.

"All work and no play makes Cam a dull girl."

"Pooh! I'm a baseball widow, remember?" It was true. Her boyfriend, Rob, played baseball for a city league, which had recently begun practicing for the season. It meant he was busy at least three nights a week, and

Cam used that as an excuse to work too much.

"I remember when you could out-party Theta Chi."

Cam laughed. That had been many years ago. "You know I cheated, only pretending to drink half the time."

"You hush. You'll lose me my reputation as the evil twin."

It was an old joke. They'd been best friends since seventh-grade science, when the study of genetics identified them as the only two girls in the class with indefinable hair color. "It's not red enough to call red, not blonde enough to call blonde, but it certainly isn't brown." Annie had been the one to declare it the "uncolor," and Cam had laughed and given her a thumbs-up. They had moved their desks together and become science partners and, within weeks, best friends. Of course, twin jokes aside, hair color was where similarities in appearance ended. Cam was tallish and slim, with straight, stylishly cut, shoulder-length hair. Annie was shorter and curvier, with a broad friendly face, unruly curls, and an instant huggability Cam sometimes envied.

"You know people have been permanently silenced for revealing smaller secrets," Cam said, getting back to her cheating at the

Theta Chi drinking games.

"You're threatening murder? I'm stung!"

Cam eyed the cups. "Not murder, head shrinking. Unless . . . will you go to the RGS welcoming party tomorrow night?"

"You honestly think I'd fit in at that high-society thing?"

"Okay, don't take this wrong, but I need some middlers. We've got the blue-blooded Garden Society, and then we have the helper types — the gardener and his son . . . Petunia . . ."

"You better not be saying I'm classier than Petunia, because that's blasphemy! I got no class, Cam Harris, and if you say I do, I'll come in here when you're sleeping and shave your eyebrows!"

Cam broke into giggles; a single glass of wine was enough for her to fall under her best friend's silliness spell. Annie was the daughter of a former senator, though he held title under a political party Annie swore she would never vote for. Annie had been fighting the "stigma" thrust upon her since middle school.

"I swear I'm not saying you're classy. I honestly just need some help. They're making me invite my dad."

Annie nodded, finally getting the picture. Annie and Mr. Harris had a longtime understanding that was far more honest than what went on between father and daughter. Cam didn't mind. She didn't want to know. But she was glad someone she could count on was in the loop to help prevent anything unexpected.

"I suppose your eyebrows are safe for now."

CHAPTER 2

The next day was much the same, except that without the Garden Society meeting, the mood at the house felt significantly milder, like a subtle, sweet-scented garden, instead of the heady, drunken one of the day before. When Cam and the camera crew got to greenhouse three, "Summer," and past the very excitable Barney, Evangeline's Jack Russell terrier, they met Evangeline herself, holding a seated yoga pose underneath an ashoka tree.

"Oh, I'm sorry, Mrs. Patrick," Cam said as Barney jumped onto his mistress's lap. "Should we come back?"

The woman disentangled herself and rose, snatching up the dog with fluid grace, her rather perfect figure apparent in her tight top and yoga pants.

"Not at all. I was done." Her smile was serene. Obviously meditation was effective. "I'm sure all the spiritual properties of the ashoka are relevant to this article. Wouldn't you think?"

Evangeline had moved close to Tom, who looked near to passing out. Hannah frowned irritably.

"I'm sure I covered it in the press packet," Cam lied, promising herself she'd add it soon, in case the woman checked. She may have been a beauty queen, but Evangeline Patrick was no dummy — she'd gone to Brown with her Miss Virginia scholarship. "Ultimately, it's up to the editor."

"I'm the photo editor," Ian added, thrusting his jaw forward.

Evangeline took his arm and led him closer to the little tree Cam knew was Indian, not American, and certainly not native to Virginia — she wasn't even sure it would grow here if not for the summer greenhouse. Ian's gullibility irritated her, but she had plenty of time to set him straight without offending Evangeline.

After that, they continued their route through the greenhouses and gardens, though they seemed to have picked up a canine obstacle. They'd registered on Barney's radar. He'd been fine the day before, but today each time they found him, he growled and blocked their path until Cam managed to calm him. At their final greenhouse, Evangeline once again intercepted them.

"Barney! Shame on you! Here, boy!" She tossed a bone she'd picked up on the walkway. Cam glanced around and realized there were bones in half a dozen places within her vision. Distraction was apparently relied upon often with the little dog. To test this theory, she picked up the nearest bone and tossed it. Barney dropped the bone in his mouth and chased the new one.

The crew broke up before five because there was a reception just a few hours later at Samantha Hollister's home, the crowning glory of which was its English garden. The reception promised to set the magazine feature off to a fabulous start. Cam thought Samantha hoped to raise doubts in the minds of the camera crew as to the location they'd chosen, but she didn't think that would be possible after two days of hard work at La Fontaine, so Cam concentrated on just making sure all had a wonderful evening.

Cam had her boyfriend, Rob, drop her off at Samantha's at six o'clock. He would then change, pick up her father and Annie, and return at seven with the other guests.

Petunia and her husband, Nick — the primary chef at Spoons — were already in the kitchen when Cam arrived. Nick and Petunia had been married almost three years. About a year into their marriage, Nick had helped Petunia achieve her longtime dream of opening a restaurant. Spoons specialized in gourmet "one-pot" meals. The restaurant had seating for only about forty people, but the large kitchen allowed them plenty of room to cater, which was their primary source of income.

Petunia had always been a collector of strays: dogs, cats, and people. Nick was no exception. He had a lot of tattoos, including one that looked like barbed wire around his neck, and he talked like a gangster, according to Cam's imagination, anyway — he was certainly a Yank. She'd never been to New Jersey, but if she closed her eyes when Nick talked, she could picture a dozen gangster movies she'd seen. In his favor, he treated Petunia like a treasure, something of a novelty in Petunia's experience, so Cam had warmed to him quickly, tattoos and all. She'd been the maid of honor at their wedding.

Nick kissed Cam's cheek when she entered. "Hey, sis, you ready for this shindig?"

"Ready as I'll ever be. Glad to have allies

in the kitchen."

"We're glad you send us some fancy business now and then — good for our reputation." He grinned.

"Of course I do. Y'all throw an elegant table."

Nick gave his single bark that was as much laugh as anyone ever got out of him. He always looked sort of sheepish when he received a compliment.

At that moment, Evangeline barged in. "Jack! I thought I heard you. Nice to see you." She clutched Nick's bicep as she passed. "Anyone have a towel?"

Cam handed Evangeline a towel, and the woman left again.

"Jack?" Cam asked quietly.

Nick shrugged as if he'd rather not get into it.

"Who'd you rob to get that?" Petunia finally turned to Cam, after putting the finishing touches on a fancy lasagna and sliding it into the oven. Her studied lack of expression told Cam she was agitated. She pointed at Cam's dress, her tone strange.

"I didn't have to rob anyone. It's rented, if you must know."

"They rent dresses?" Petunia's face registered disbelief.

"They do, and for a hundred dollars, I get

to wear a five-hundred-dollar dress I'd only wear once, so wouldn't be worth buying."

"Heck, if I even had a one-hundred-dollar dress you'd never get me out of it again."

"Oh, I'd get you out of it," Nick muttered from the corner. That was more like the Nick Cam knew, and she winked at him.

"You behave!" Petunia snapped him with a kitchen towel, but she was laughing, the tension dissipating completely. "Rob coming?"

"Yeah, he's picking up Annie and Daddy. They'll be here at seven."

"Couldn't convince Dad this wasn't his thing?"

"I didn't try. That photo editor seemed set on some shots of Dad with that trellis and wisteria at the Patricks'. I thought maybe a mint julep or two might work a little magic convincing him to pose."

"That's true. Did we bring mint, Nick?"

"I bet Samantha has fresh mint in an herb garden," Cam said. "In fact, I'd be surprised if she doesn't have a plot somewhere specifically devoted to cocktail condiments. I'll ask her."

Cam left the kitchen and found their hostess, who led her to the herb garden. The two collected mint and some Italian parsley to garnish the lasagna. Samantha envisioned herself as a local celebrity — platinum coif, bejeweled fingers, and all. Cam would never have ruined that illusion for her. She also saw herself as a mentor for Cam, pushing high manners and tastes that, in Cam's opinion, were a little too extravagant to be truly classy. Samantha had exaggerated arm gestures, designer dresses, and an intimate familiarity when talking about the local politicians, but she was always gracious, a perfect hostess.

She also had an amazing garden, which Cam was seeing for the first time. The grounds were subtly choreographed, leading a wanderer through gorgeous curves of flowers, all set to look as if they had happened by accident, which of course was a great deal more work than something that looked planned.

Cam knew, though, they'd have only forty minutes or so of daylight after the guests arrived, so after extensive compliments, she suggested cocktails and appetizers in the garden and then supper inside. "We'll avoid the bugs that way. The scent from your jasmine should still be lovely through the screen."

"You're right, of course." Samantha wasn't the type of woman to give away when she was disappointed, but Cam thought she was.

Samantha directed a few hired hands to shuffle tables, and Petunia and Nick began arranging snack trays as two of the brutish helpers wheeled the bar outside.

Cam assisted with the appetizers, and as she came out of the house carrying a warmer of little meatballs, Samantha stopped her. "Do you mind if Petunia keeps bar? Only I'm . . ." Samantha trailed off, but it wasn't Cam's first encounter with snobbery where Nick was concerned.

Fortunately, Nick preferred the kitchen, so Cam could honestly say, "That's already the plan," and force a smile.

A short while later, the Roanoke Garden Society members and guests began arriving. The influx set Cam into hostess mode, and she brought people drinks and made sure they were comfortable. When Rob, Annie, and her father, Nelson, arrived, she began formal introductions.

"The trellis builder," Ian exclaimed excitedly when he heard Cam's father was among them. He came forward to shake Nelson's hand, the first smile Cam had seen on him. She wanted to laugh at her father's confused expression.

"The trellis at the Patricks', Daddy." Cam hadn't gotten around to warning him why his presence had been requested. She'd intended to get over to his house that afternoon and do a little work in her mother's garden. It was a regular habit: Cam gardening and her father chatting and bringing her sweet tea. Times like those were when she usually made requests of her father. Having her mom's spirit so close seemed to make him more agreeable. Today, however, had just been too busy.

Several people were looking their way now.

"Well, yes . . . I did several trellises, though that one in particular is the best, I think, because that wisteria was such a grand thing to work with. But I'm just a carpenter. It was my wife who wanted me to get into all that flowery stuff."

"That flowery stuff" was how her dad looked at all of this, but somehow he said it with enough charm that everyone seemed enchanted rather than offended. "My wife even insisted we name our children after flowers, Camellia and Petunia." He shook his head, laughing, as if it were an insane indulgence he'd granted. Cam noticed Samantha smiling giddily like a schoolgirl.

Cam managed to keep from rolling her eyes and went into the kitchen. "I can't take him anywhere."

Petunia gave a sympathetic nod. "Who's

in love with him now?" She hadn't even had to ask.

"Samantha."

At every event he attended, her father collected a new admirer or two.

"Oh, that's all we need," Petunia muttered under her breath.

Cam frowned but knew she couldn't speak too loudly for fear of being overheard. "For your information, Dad could do a lot worse. She's a nice lady."

It wasn't that she heard wedding bells exactly. Cam didn't think Samantha was her father's type, but there were times her sister's reverse snobbery drove her nuts. Her father could obviously do worse than a beautiful, rich widow. In Petunia's mind, however, anyone with wealth, education, or breeding was unworthy, and the only people who deserved Petunia's admiration and sympathy were pity cases who had led hard lives or made bad mistakes. Petunia just nodded back at Cam sadly, as if Cam were the deluded one. Cam looked to Nick for help, but he had immersed himself in grating Parmesan for the salad.

"You need this?" Rob had snuck up behind her and put one arm around Cam's waist. With the other hand he held a wine spritzer. He knew she wouldn't drink anything stronger while she was working, but just having a glass in her hand would help her stress level. She smiled gratefully and went back out to the garden with him.

The other guests trickled out, a dozen in all, as did Henry Larsson, the gardener for several of the RGS members, including the Patricks and Samantha Hollister. He and his son, Benny, looked strangely out of place without their denim work shirts. Then at nearly eight o'clock, the guests of honor arrived together. When they stepped out into the garden, Samantha announced them and all eyes turned: Jane Duffy, premiere reporter for *Garden Delights,* and Jean-Jacques Georges, famed photographer. They were a study in contrast. Both were angular, but Ms. Duffy was a petite redhead, impeccably dressed, while Jean-Jacques was tall and lanky, with a slight hunch to his shoulders and a studied crumple to his clothes. That, with his dark locks that had been gelled back only enough to partially hold, made him look carefree and roguish, though Cam thought perhaps he was trying too hard.

Cam had had a handful of telephone conversations with Jane Duffy to convince her the Roanoke Garden Society merited a feature, so she made her way forward to introduce herself.

Jean-Jacques didn't make eye contact with anyone. He looked around upon entering the garden and immediately sidled up to the bar. Cam heard Petunia's familiar, "I'll bring it right over," just as Cam reached Jane Duffy.

"Camellia, it's lovely to put a face with your voice. I wish we'd beaten the darkness — it smells heavenly out here. I bet it's beautiful."

"It is. I'm sure you'll get another chance, though. Nice to meet you, Ms. Duffy."

"Please, Jane."

"I'll try, Jane. You'll find in some places old-fashioned manners die hard. Anyway, welcome to Roanoke."

"Thank you. Jean-Jacques showed me a little of the area on the way from the airport."

Jean-Jacques sauntered over from the bar, clearly bored but drawn by the mention of his name.

"Really? Have you been here before, then, Mr. Georges?"

"Oui. Il était une froid."

Ms. Duffy looked at Jean-Jacques with a raised eyebrow, as if he'd said something strange. Cam, however, having studied Spanish instead of French, didn't know what. Jean-Jacques's hazel eyes gave nothing away.

Petunia arrived with his cocktail — a Long Island iced tea, if Cam were guessing — certainly something tall that carried a powerful waft of alcohol.

"Merci." Then, as Petunia spun to return to the bar, Jean-Jacques swatted her bottom.

Petunia, Cam, and Jane all froze briefly, and then did what any thinking, polite society women would do when wishing to not offend a world-famous photographer: they pretended nothing had happened. Petunia scuttled away and got back to work, though she wouldn't meet Cam's eye.

"And what did you see today?" Cam asked Jane, avoiding a look at Jean-Jacques in case she couldn't stop herself from scolding him.

"There is a History Museum, and . . . what was it, Mini Graceland?"

"History Museum?" Cam asked, confused as to what they could have seen.

"In One Market Square," Jean-Jacques clarified.

"Really?" Cam asked. It was a tiny little thing — barely more than a hole in the wall.

Jean-Jacques nodded with a smirk, finally showing amusement.

Cam gave a plastic smile. "I'm sure that was lovely. I hope you'll let one of the

Garden Society members show you a few more . . . treasures, while you're here."

She didn't want to offend Jean-Jacques, but the tour he'd presented had about as much class as a butt swat given to a stranger. She hoped she could get across to Ms. Duffy, without words, that not all Roanoke was so tacky.

"It's all this village has to offer," Jean-Jacques muttered, stealing a canapé from a tray as it passed, popping it in his mouth midsentence, and chasing it with a long suck on his drink straw. His accent, when he spoke English, was odd.

Cam tilted her head at Annie, who was talking to the rest of the magazine crew across the brick patio. Annie spoke both French and Italian, having had many opportunities to travel. Annie saw Cam's gesture and shook her head, but a more insistent tilt finally brought her over.

"Annie Schulz, this is Jane Duffy from *Garden Delights,* and Jean-Jacques Georges, famous photographer. Jean-Jacques, what part of France are you from? Annie spent a year of college in Marseille."

"How splendid. Will you excuse me?" He didn't wait for a response before darting away.

He found the magazine crew, and Cam,

feeling wrong-footed at his hasty retreat, covered by introducing Ms. Duffy to the Patricks. She and Annie then worked their way back across the garden, Annie holding Cam's arm.

"If he's French, I'll eat Mr. Tibbles, there."

Cam stifled a snort. She hadn't even noticed the large, squash-faced cat watching the guests from a stair railing that went to the deck. "Mr. Tibbles?"

"Doesn't he look like a Mr. Tibbles?"

Cam rolled her eyes. "I think you're right, though. Not French. Still, I've seen some of his work, and he may be a French fraud, but he's a photography genius."

"Good subject matter and pro lighting guys. I could do that."

Cam frowned again and glanced over at Jean-Jacques. He and Ian were arguing in hushed voices; Ian looked angry. It wasn't like Annie to be snotty about anyone's work, especially artwork, including photography, but the argument was even more unsettling. Ian hadn't mentioned any issues. She hoped it wasn't about the sunrise shots, and more important, that it didn't bode poorly for the next few days.

"Never mind," Annie said. "Rob needs a grope, and if you aren't going to oblige, I might have to."

"Hint taken. I'll go pay attention to my boyfriend for a minute. Why don't you . . ."

"Help Petunia. I'm going to help Petunia." In spite of the relative privilege of Annie's birth, she was ashamed enough of it that she and Petunia got along well, the two of them often siding together to mock Cam's more traditional values.

"You didn't get along with the magazine crew?" Cam asked.

"Which one? The jerk, the silent one, or the annoying one? Besides, they're talking to the guy who just ran away from me."

"You take some mean pills tonight? You're not like yourself at all." The comment had been snarky, even for Annie, but Annie just raised an eyebrow.

Cam found Rob and pretended she needed to speak to him for a minute. Samantha had a few strategically placed trellises supporting clematis and trumpet flowers. Cam pulled Rob farther into the garden and under one that was blanketed with a well-developed orange trumpet vine.

"I just needed a moment of sanity." She hugged him and then squeezed his bottom, mostly so she could tell Annie her mission had been accomplished.

"Hey, you think I'm easy?"

"I know you are."

"Okay. I guess I'll give you that. You know I'm going to have to reciprocate, though."

"I know." She started to sneak away playfully, teasing Rob, but then heard angry voices and pushed herself back into him, forcing them both into shadows again, and swatting his wandering hand.

Rob held her around the waist, taking her hint to be quiet, though ignoring the swat. She listened.

"I know you're hurting, and I'm sorry, but you can't . . ." Samantha pleaded.

"I'm not one of your boy toys, and you have no say in what I do!"

"I think you know I have quite a lot of say! It's time to shape up."

Cam watched Samantha storm away after the argument. Jean-Jacques lingered, lighting a cigarette, but after a few puffs he threw the butt into some iris and slunk back toward the crowd.

"You don't think . . ." Cam started.

"That she has boy toys? Sure I do. It would explain a lot." He nuzzled his nose into her neck.

Cam pulled away with a serious expression. "No, I mean the two of them . . . you know . . ."

"I don't know. I was just thinking that accent of his disappeared fast. Never seen somebody acculturate so quickly."

"How does a sports reporter know a word like 'acculturate'?" Cam teased.

"I know stuff. You act like I'm just a nice set of pecs."

"Can you blame me? It *is* a nice set of pecs."

She ran her fingers across his chest longingly, but removed herself before he could do anything about it. Rented dress or not, it would be obvious if she'd been manhandled. She rejoined the others just as they were retreating into the house for supper. She noted Joseph had been the one to call supper, possibly responding in distress to the fact the hostess seemed to have disappeared.

Cam hoped someone had heard whatever preceded the bit of argument she and Rob just witnessed. She was dying to know if some illicit romance was behind the strings Samantha had pulled to get Jean-Jacques Georges to Roanoke — not that Cam was a gossip, but the need to know was a prerequisite in her field. If she paid attention to whispers, she could anticipate trouble that might come up, and anticipating meant damage control. Unfortunately, it made her always want to know, even when it wasn't pertinent. Rob, a reporter with the same instinct, was the first boyfriend she'd had who not only accepted but also shared the inclination.

At the moment Cam thought the only likely repercussion of the argument was the degree of difficulty it added to coordinating between the photographer and the Roanoke Garden Society, a challenge that would undoubtedly fall on her.

She rushed to help play hostess, realizing Joseph was probably right. Samantha would be somewhat distraught. In every pair or trio she approached to suggest seating possibilities, she heard whispers. When she reached Rob, she pointed out seats but asked him to do a little listening, too, as she couldn't contain her curiosity. He was happy to oblige, so she went back to her own eavesdropping.

". . . can't believe he'd be so rude!"

"Well, you *know* how the French are!"

"Her husband was *right there!*"

"I would have punched him if it was *my* wife."

"That had to have been the most disrespectful . . ."

The only pair that looked content was her dad and Henry Larsson. From the way Henry was laughing, she suspected her dad had just told one of his jokes. The rest of the room, though, was a bundle of nerves.

Apparently Cam had missed quite a scene before Jean-Jacques and Samantha had wandered out farther into the garden: suggestive comments, terrible manners, and Jean-Jacques had had the nerve to complain to several people how boring flowers were compared to Heidi Klum and Adriana Lima. He claimed to have given up a photography shoot for a prestigious fashion magazine to be there, and acted as if they should all be grateful to have him, though when pressed, he admitted Klum and Lima were not to be involved. That was when Samantha had called him over to talk and they'd wandered out into the garden. Jean-Jacques was now seated next to Evangeline, chatting amicably enough, as if unaware of the havoc he'd wrought.

By the time supper was served, conversation elsewhere was uncomfortably stifled, and people began to leave soon after the meal, many not even staying for Annie's famous mud pie. Jean-Jacques was among the first to leave, and Cam couldn't help but notice the tension left with him.

As people left, Cam's father came inside from the garden with Jane Duffy. The two were laughing, Jane hanging on to Nelson's arm. Petunia gave Cam a scolding look.

"Oh, Camellia, your father just showed

me the swings he made in the garden. They're beautiful! Though I'm feeling a little seasick after that last one."

"Keeps you young," Nelson began, but Cam cut him off.

"Yes, Daddy has a great many talents. So does that mean you'll come for some pictures, Daddy?"

"Pictures?"

"They want you to pose with the trellis you built at the Patricks', for the magazine?"

"Magazine?" He looked shocked, and Cam rolled her eyes.

"You have heard me talk about this magazine shoot . . ." she reminded gently, knowing he was just being a tease. "The one Jane is here for . . ."

"Oh, well in that case . . ."

Jane giggled like a teen, and Cam was reminded of a dozen other older women who'd spent a little time with her father. She knew after age sixty, women greatly outnumbered men, but she wasn't sure why her father felt obliged to single-handedly try to make up for that.

"I suppose I should get back to my hotel," Jane said girlishly.

"Let me drive you."

"Daddy, Rob drove *you.*"

"Oh, right."

"But I'd be happy to give you both a ride," Rob volunteered. "Then by the time I swing back for you girls you'll be about done."

Cam wasn't sure whether she was annoyed or grateful. Rob encouraging her father and skipping cleaning duty was a little irksome, but then, it wasn't his job; it was hers. Annie still felt free to give him an evil eye.

During cleanup, Cam grilled Petunia for details of what she'd missed while she and Rob were under the trellis.

"That photographer seems to know that snotty Evangeline."

"What do you have against Evangeline?" Cam suspected she knew. Evangeline was a trifecta on Petunia's list of "so good it's bad." She was a Brown-educated former beauty queen, and now that she'd married Neil Patrick, she was rich.

"I just hate her kind," Petunia said, though again, she wasn't meeting Cam's eye. "And that John-Jock kept going up to her and whispering, like they were old buddies."

Nick frowned. He was never cuddly to look at, but usually he did a better job of maintaining a nonchalant, tough-guy expression.

"What did you think of him, Nick?"

"Didn't see him." He had joined his wife

in failing to meet Cam's eye.

"Anyone else scandalized? I want to know how many feathers will need smoothing tomorrow."

"May want to bring a whole goose," Petunia answered darkly, but just then, Rob returned. They were done cleaning, so Cam and Annie helped load the last few things into Nick's van and then left with Rob.

"Shoot!" Annie blurted as Rob's Jeep pulled out of the long driveway.

"What?"

"I forgot one of my good pans at the Patricks' this morning, and I have a mountain of orders tomorrow. Think they're still up?"

Cam called and Evangeline said they were on their way to bed. However, she assured Cam someone would be up and able to give Annie her pan by six thirty in the morning.

Annie nodded at the news, resigned to starting a little earlier than she'd planned.

CHAPTER 3

Rob drove Cam to the Patricks' the next morning, since Annie's busy day required her to be at her shop by seven. Annie had several special orders for the coinciding Vinton Dogwood Festival and a charity bicycle race. Between the two, people had ordered hundreds of cupcakes. Cam's real work would begin today, too, and, after the night before, she had some trepidation about how things would go.

They turned off of Blue Ridge Parkway and rounded the corner. Cam spotted an ambulance parked in the gated driveway of La Fontaine. Rob pulled over to the opposite side of the road and got out with her, concern etched on his face.

Cam's first thought was that Mr. Patrick had had a heart attack. She sprinted across the street toward the front door, barely registering the two police cars. The door stood ajar, so she ran in and hustled up the stairs two at a time, calling for the Patricks.

Cam didn't find either of them. Instead she felt the chilly spring morning air and found a wide open window on the second floor, through which she heard voices. The screen was missing, so she leaned out to see what was going on. Below were half a dozen official-looking people, including police officers and a guy in a plastic suit carefully picking at . . . a body.

Her chest knotted painfully. There was a body sprawled facedown across the azaleas. Her brain kept arguing one didn't die from jumping out a second-story window, but judging by the scene below, that was what had happened.

Behind the official-looking people, a few yards back, was a mass of others, those either staying or working at La Fontaine. They loitered nervously, except Rob, who had joined the official group and was talking to one of the policemen.

She looked more carefully at the sprawled body, noting the slightly rumpled clothes. They seemed so familiar.

Jean-Jacques Georges.

"Miss, you'll need to come down from there. There may be evidence," one of the police officers called to her.

"Oh, right. I didn't touch anything." It

was surreal; she was in a fog.

"Very good. Now . . ."

"Coming!" She finally pulled her brain into focus and her body into motion, which took great effort.

To Cam's confusion and irritation, Rob didn't meet her when she joined the crowd. He kept talking to the police officer who was directing things. It was only then she recognized the officer as Jake Moreno, Rob's friend from his city league baseball team. The man looked different in a police uniform than he did in sliders and a baseball cap, sadly. Then again, Rob looked better in sliders, too. At that thought, she scolded herself. This was a tragedy.

She approached Rob and stood behind him, hoping to catch part of the conversation, morbid curiosity and horror dueling for her attention. Jake diligently kept the bystanders back as the plastic-suited man assessed time of death. "Between oh-six hundred and oh-seven thirty," he said, sounding official. He couldn't narrow it further until the autopsy was done. The other things he said to the notetaker went mostly over Cam's head.

She felt queasy so near what she now knew was a dead body, so she peeked farther around the corner into the backyard and spotted Neil Patrick, who held his arms around his sobbing wife. Jake wasn't saying much aside from the commands necessary to hold back the crowd, and Cam couldn't bear to look anymore, so she made her way to the Patricks. Giselle hovered near the doorway, ready to respond if needed, but she seemed determined to give them privacy. Evangeline had red-rimmed eyes and looked like she'd been rather hysterical until very recently.

"I'm so sorry. Who found him?" Cam asked.

"Benny, poor lamb." Evangeline sounded strangely sympathetic for a woman Cam thought had grown used to a haughty station. Cam didn't really know Benny, except that he was the son of Henry Larsson, an exceptional gardener. The young man, in spite of approaching thirty, seemed to find bodily functions more than a little funny, regardless of who he made uncomfortable laughing about them. Such behavior would have been more normal in a twelve-year-old, but it hardly made him a lamb.

"Do you know *how* Benny found him?" She still wasn't ready to say Jean-Jacques's name.

Neil took over as his wife collapsed further. "They came early to deadhead. No garden can look its best with wilted flowers in there. Has to be done daily, and with the photo shoot starting today . . . Henry went one way and Benny another."

"He was so distraught," Evangeline added, a tear leaking from the corner of her eye. "I heard him shout. When I found him, I called for Giselle to call the police at once, of course, but still . . . poor dear." Evangeline's breath caught and she shook. Cam thought Benny wasn't the only one who had been very upset.

"Where is he now? I saw him and Henry from upstairs, but they were gone when I got down here."

"There's a police officer asking Benny questions in the servant's house. His father's with him," Mr. Patrick said.

"Why's his father —"

"Cammi, you may not know this," Mr. Patrick cut her off quietly. "We don't talk about it out of respect for Henry, but poor Benny's a few bulbs short of a flower box. He might need some help with the questions."

Cam suddenly felt like a giant heel. Mr. Patrick may have been a bit tactless in how he put it, but no wonder Evangeline spoke as she did. She was being nice. It made all Benny's past transgressions vanish. Not being very bright excused a lot of fart jokes.

Rob approached, looking strangely smug, and rubbed Cam's shoulder. "Jake says he's going to need to talk to everyone from the party last night."

"Heavens! Why?" Neil started.

Rob moved in closer so only the four could hear. "When the medical examiner flipped the body over, it had a set of pruning shears through the abdomen."

Evangeline screamed and fainted, nearly knocking over her husband. Cam helped him lower her onto a reclining lawn chair.

"Murder?" Cam whispered to Rob, once the deadweight she was helping with had found a home and Neil had knelt to attend to his wife.

Rob nodded like the cat that ate the canary, or at least the catnip.

"Why does that please you so much?" she whispered, trying to look stern.

"Griggs is clear. Doesn't matter what department you work for, you scoop it, it's yours. This is a great opportunity."

Roger Griggs was the *Roanoke Tribune*'s editor in chief, and he dictated the rules of the paper. Cam had heard this one before, but it had never occurred to her it might leave her sports-reporter boyfriend investigating a murder.

"Rob Columbus, there's a dead man!" Her whisper was now the shouted variety, and Neil Patrick looked up at them in alarm.

"Near as I could see it, it couldn't have happened to a nicer guy. Jake says he'll keep me in the loop, so it's my story."

"I thought you liked baseball, football . . . an occasional hockey game?"

"I live for them. You know that, but investigative stuff is what makes careers. Heck, even a god like Mitch Albom had to write a sappy book to get national fame, and I don't have a sappy book in me."

"It's a beautiful book — all of them are," Cam said defensively, then wrinkled her brow and tried to give her longtime boyfriend a fresh look. She'd always thought as long as he made his living writing about sports, he would be happy. She hadn't recognized ambition hidden in there at all. In fact, lack of ambition was part of why she had not pressed harder toward engagement.

"Well that's great, then. Good luck," she said, though she wasn't sure how she felt about it. Worry was the emotion that kept surfacing most prominently.

Rob smiled and kissed her cheek, then returned to Jake.

"Cammi, we need to make a decision."

Cam turned to Mr. Patrick. Evangeline must have recovered enough to go inside, as she was gone. "Should I start rounding up board members and such, so they're all here?" Cam asked.

"Just the officers. Go ahead and print a list with names and addresses of everyone who was at Samantha's last night for the police. We need to cooperate, but it would just be best if all . . . this . . . wasn't . . . here."

"The photo shoot?"

"The photo shoot." He sighed.

Cam went inside, wondering if the position of Jean-Jacques Georges's body meant he had really been inside and fallen, or if there was some other explanation for the open window and missing screen. She was distracted, but she called all the board officers, explaining only that there was an emergency and she'd like to explain it in person, since some decisions would be necessary. As she worked her way through the list, Samantha Hollister couldn't be reached, either at home or on her cell phone. It struck Cam that this was the first time in nearly two years of her RGS presidency that Samantha had not been reachable, though admittedly, there had only been a half dozen "emergencies."

The argument of the night before came to mind, but Cam swallowed it back. She didn't plan to lie when questioned, but it was really nobody's business except the police's. She may have liked to *hear* gossip, but she wasn't in the practice of spreading it — that would have been counter to her instinct for damage control.

By ten o'clock the ambulance and medical examiner had carried off the body. All of the Roanoke Garden Society officers, minus Samantha, had gathered. Madeline Leclerc and Cam — the key hired staff — were also present. Giselle brought in coffee and leftover muffins and other treats from the previous day's catering.

"We can't lose this photo shoot. It's generated thousands in charitable donations, and is sure to drive up membership," Madeline said. She looked strained.

Cam owed her job with the Roanoke Garden Society to Madeline Leclerc. The RGS had hired Madeline as coordinator, charged with increasing publicity, membership, and revenue, which Madeline swore she could do, but only with a public relations team. "Team" was a bit of an exaggeration, as it consisted of only Cam, but the job combined Cam's three loves: gardening, her hometown, and PR.

"Lose? Madeline, in case you weren't paying attention, there was a murder — a world-famous photographer was *murdered,*" Joseph Sadler-Neff said, looking anxious and tired. Sweat glistened from under his comb-over.

"The magazine staff is already here, and the feature visibility will help us with all our goals!" Madeline's voice was shrill, invoking panic.

It was unnerving to have her unshakable boss so flustered. Cam wanted to calm everyone, but she needed them to vent first so she'd know what she was dealing with. *Then* she could calm them more effectively, or so she hoped.

"But with no photographer —"

"There are other photographers," Madeline insisted.

"Not so talented. That was how Cammi convinced the magazine to come, wasn't it, Cammi?" Mr. Patrick said.

Plans to stall aside, she couldn't ignore the question.

"Yes, sir. His fame. I'm sure there is other talent, but his fame brought them here."

"Where's Samantha?" Madeline asked, seeking the board president for leadership.

Everyone looked around, as if Samantha were hiding in the room. Cam could have sworn Neil Patrick looked under the table.

"I couldn't reach her," Cam said. "I left messages at her home and on her cell."

"It was a distressing party," Joseph conceded, his concern apparent. He seemed near tears, as if overcome with empathy, either for the deceased or, more likely, for the upset hostess. At that moment, it occurred to Cam that Joseph had a crush on Samantha, but she supposed that made sense. Samantha was beautiful, gracious, and single. And as far as Cam knew, Joseph was alone. His emotional display was unusual; normally, he was just terribly proper.

"Maybe she had a breakfast date," Mr. Patrick offered hopefully.

Cam smiled at Mr. Patrick, then looked at Joseph. The man waxed poetic when telling an official story, but rarely said a word otherwise. Cam was glad someone was defending Samantha, though she couldn't help wondering why Samantha needed defending. She stifled the thought that maybe Joseph knew why.

The police had been interviewing the magazine and household staff while the RGS officers held their half-hour meeting. Now, as the meeting broke up, they began their interviews with the Garden Society staff and officers. As Cam left the library, she ran into Nick and Petunia.

"Shoot! I forgot to call you! Well, I guess everyone will still need to eat, and they'll want to talk to you."

"Yeah, what is this?" Petunia pointed at the nervous clusters of people. She then impulsively hugged Cam, picking up the ambient anxiety. Petunia often misinterpreted the cause, but she was good at detecting mood.

When they separated, Cam got her first good look at her brother-in-law. "Geez, Nick. You look like hell warmed over."

"Yeah."

Eloquent as always, but Petunia explained. "We have three different big lunches today, and I will need to work all day long because there is also a supper, so Nick spent the whole night at Spoons, cooking."

"Sorry to hear that. Well, I think if you want to just tell the police where you'll be . . . maybe you can request they come talk to you after all your stuff is done."

"You didn't tell me what this is. Why do they need to talk to us at all?" Petunia's raw anxiety caused Cam to twitch.

"Oh, right. That photographer was found

dead this morning."

"He OD?" Nick asked, suddenly alert. Petunia elbowed him.

Nick had said he didn't know who the photographer was. Cam narrowed her eyes. "If he did, he proceeded to fall onto a pair of pruning shears when he passed out."

"Murder!" Petunia went wide-eyed and covered her mouth. Fortunately, she'd mastered the muffled squeal. "Some husband get ticked he was goosing every woman in the room?"

Her snarky tone surprised Cam. She would have thought "murder victim" qualified someone for Petunia's pity list.

"He didn't goose *me,*" Cam pointed out, one eyebrow up, one down, in a mock leer.

"He goosed you?" Nick scowled at Petunia.

"He's dead. It doesn't matter." Petunia patted her large husband calmly. Cam could have sworn he began to purr. She almost laughed.

"Mighta mattered if I'd heard it last night. I mighta volunteered to kill him myself."

"Shush, Nick." Cam eyed him seriously. "You say that with the police near and you'll have trouble."

Petunia, though, was gazing at him fondly, happy to have a man who wanted to defend her honor. Cam knew she'd had far worse men in her life before Nick. Petunia rubbed his shoulder and smiled, then looked back at Cam. "We'll check in. Then I'm going to call you tonight to see how this goes. Sort of exciting, isn't it?"

"A murder? It's pretty horrible."

"Well, yes, of course. Horrible. But exciting."

"And it couldn't have happened to a nicer guy," Nick added, echoing Rob.

He gave Cam a fond pinch on the arm as he went out the front door, leaving Petunia to check in with Officer Moreno. Seemed like maybe Nick knew Jean-Jacques after all.

Rob had left by the time Cam returned to the remaining photography staff and the couple household workers who were still hovering. She figured he'd gone to file a story with the paper and stake his claim to the investigation. It was then Cam realized that not only did they not have a photographer to complete the shoot they'd been planning, but they also had a potential PR crisis on their hands: this story, if not properly managed, could really hurt the Roanoke Garden Society. She didn't want to ask Rob not to cover it, but at the same time she hoped he wouldn't print anything inflammatory.

She then chastised herself. Rob might be a sports reporter, but he was committed to the truth. Unfortunately, the truth looked pretty bad right now. She would have to talk to him later about how to include information about the RGS.

"Camellia Harris?"

Cam turned with a raised eyebrow at hearing her full name. "Hi, Jake." The people around her, mostly members of the RGS, likewise turned, noting her friendship with the police officer whose name badge read "Joaquin Moreno."

"Thought that was you. Come on over here. It's just procedure. Nothing to worry about." He led her to two facing chairs in a quiet corner of the drawing room.

"Yeah, thanks. My only real worry is I worked hard to set up this big photo shoot and now it looks like it won't happen."

"Well, your worry is understandable. Seems to me, the sooner a killer is nailed and put away, the sooner you can get back to it."

"That's true."

Cam squinted at Jake. She'd never thought of him as smooth before — good-looking, sure; he had that soulful Latin lover thing going on. But strategically convincing a witness it was in her own best interest to cooperate — in a single line? She'd clearly underestimated him. And he was right. Solving this fast would be damage control. There was nothing she liked better than damage control, except maybe damage prevention.

"How well did you know the victim?"

"We shared a room full of people for just over an hour. We were part of one conversation together, in which I learned he'd shown Jane Duffy some of Roanoke. Either he was a poseur trying to impress Ms. Duffy with local knowledge or a very tacky man. Or maybe he had a bone to pick with Roanoke. He tried to impress her with Mini Graceland." She rolled her eyes. "But then I snuck off with Rob for a bit."

"To goose him . . ."

"That squealer! What did he tell you?"

"To say that and see how you reacted." Jake grinned.

Cam raised an eyebrow. "Fine. We snuck under the trellis so I could goose him, and then I heard Jean-Jacques get mad at Samantha. Well . . . they got mad at each other."

"Mad how?"

"Rob didn't tell you?"

"Sometimes women pick up more. They're more perceptive."

Yes, he was smooth. Cam frowned, wanting to be honest but also not wanting to give a bad impression of anyone in the Garden Society. Then she remembered the benefit of a quick resolution and pushed on. "Jean-Jacques said he wasn't one of her boy toys. It was as if she'd told him what to do, then she answered she *did* have a say in what he did. That wasn't like Samantha at all. She's good-natured when I tell her no. But she sure got mad back at him, like maybe they knew each other."

"Huh. And does she . . . have boy toys?"

"Not that I've ever known. I mean she's a rich, beautiful, single woman, but I never heard anything like that. I have heard rumors about her, but those involved politicians or businessmen. If she has boy toys, she's discreet."

"And did you talk to him before yesterday at all? Jean-Jacques, I mean."

"Jean-Jacques? Not really. When Samantha told me he could do the shoot, I sent him a thank-you letter with an agenda and a list of our most promising features, so he could prepare. That was by email, and he sent a confirmation that said something like, 'Got it. See you there.' "

"Samantha made the arrangements?"
Cam nodded.
"You mind if we get that email? Both the sent message and the received?"
"Not at all. Should I forward it?"
"For now, but it's possible we'll need an expert to retrieve it, make sure there was no tampering. I trust you, but if it were needed for evidence or something . . ."
"That's fine. Whatever you need."
"If you were guessing, what would you say might have motivated someone to target Jean-Jacques?"
She described the argument she'd witnessed between Jean-Jacques and Ian, and then the hearsay when she and Rob came inside, mostly related to sexual insults, but that was all she knew. Half consciously, she felt herself suppressing the fact that the first goosing she'd been aware of was the one Jean-Jacques had given her own sister, but she didn't mention it directly. "I'd guess an angry husband or boyfriend, but that's totally a guess. I didn't know anything about him except his photography."
Jake nodded grimly. "That's the main story we've been getting, too. We'll start with that. Did he touch you?"
"No." Cam frowned. She hadn't wanted to be goosed, but now it somehow seemed

her goosability was in question.

"Probably woulda, but you were off with Rob," Jake offered charitably.

She wasn't sure she liked that interpretation any better.

"Well, I know how to find you, so I better get on with the inquiries."

"Can I ask you a question?"

Jake raised an eyebrow and waited.

"Did he fall first? Or did he get stabbed first?"

"The shears killed him. That's as much as they could tell without the full autopsy."

Cam nodded. "Good luck. I hope it's resolved quickly."

"You and me both." He smiled his charming smile. "Say, that friend of yours, Annie — where is she? Rob said she was here last night."

Cam had taken Annie to countless baseball games, but hadn't realized Jake knew who she was.

"She was here to help me out a little — Petunia, too. Annie had to be at Sweet Surprise by seven this morning, though. Busy day."

"You know when she slows down?"

"Usually between one and three, then she gets the after-school rush before closing."

"Why is she so busy in the morning?"

"She's baking. She sells a lot to local markets and hotels, plus works with some caterers like Petunia. Actually, I think she's baking for the Dogwood Festival, the traitor."

"Busy girl." Jake laughed.

It sounded like maybe his interest wasn't strictly professional, and it amused Cam to think of the wayward Annie dating a police officer. She waved as he left to talk to others, and then she went to grab a sandwich.

Madeline Leclerc found Cam as she was taking her first bite. "There you are! *Garden Delights* is trying to cancel! Come quickly." Cam wondered what she could possibly do that the woman hadn't already tried, but she reluctantly left her sandwich and followed Madeline into Neil Patrick's library, where another meeting was underway.

Ian Ellsworth, the senior-ranking magazine staffer present, was explaining the impossibility of staying. "What you have is a visual piece, and with no photographer we can't do it. Besides, this is a huge scandal associated with the shoot, and the magazine doesn't need that kind of publicity."

"Please, Mr. Ellsworth, the accident didn't have anything to do with us. Don't you have a magazine photographer?" Evangeline begged.

He looked uncomfortable under Evangeline's pleading gaze.

"No, as a matter of fact. Our only staff photographer is in Amsterdam for the Tulip Festival. Cam, you remember?"

Eyes turned to her. "It's true. That was why Samantha suggested Jean-Jacques in the first place. Though it's also true that this . . . 'scandal' could sell more magazines, provided it's handled tastefully and the gardening pictures are still really good." It was spin, no doubt about it, but she hoped it sounded plausible.

"Cammi, can you help save this photo shoot?" Neil Patrick begged.

"We can't get out until tomorrow morning anyway, so if you find a replacement photographer today, we can stay," Tom said as Ian scowled. "Otherwise, we'll need to cancel."

It occurred to Cam that Tom might have more clout than it had seemed at first. She also thought Ian was a sanctimonious jerk. Annie's radar had nailed it. Then an idea occurred to her. It wasn't the sort of thing she could blurt out, as it might not work. Best friends were worth more than jobs, no matter how much you loved your job. She thought, though, this might be a winning option for everyone.

"I'll do my best, sir. I think I have an idea."

Chapter 4

Cam forced herself to breathe. It had been so much work to get *Garden Delights* to Roanoke in the first place. She couldn't stand the thought of losing them over something so uncontrollable. If she were honest, which she wasn't always, Cam had control issues. She believed if you put in the legwork you could will something to happen, and she hated it when life didn't fall into line. It didn't just disappoint her. It angered her.

"I'll see what I can come up with, Mr. Patrick. I'll come by later this afternoon to discuss our options. I'll see y'all then."

The Garden Society and magazine staff all waved to her with varying degrees of encouragement, but as she got out the door she realized she had no ride. She felt her blood pressure rising. Cam puzzled at how this hadn't occurred to her, but when stress welled up like this, the truth was she got a little twitchy. She paced manically. Just leaving wouldn't do, because though she had a "what to do" solution, the "how to do it" part had yet to come to her. Normally she gardened to meditate, but when things were this stressful, she needed to get on her bike and ride out of town for a while, hit the open roads, and let her self-created breeze wash it all away. Then she would be able to think. To get to her bike, though, she first had to get home.

She spotted Jake Moreno, also winding up for the time being.

"Um, Jake? I hate to ask, but I came out here with Rob, and he . . . left me."

"Well, that's one idiotic boyfriend, leaving you for just anybody to pick up." He grinned.

"Like maybe even a handsome cop?"

"I've heard of stranger things. You want to do something to get arrested?"

"Hitchhiking count?"

"Yeah, I'll have to take you in for that."

"Perfect!" She smiled and climbed into his passenger door.

"So this probably isn't very good for that Garden Club of yours, is it?" he said.

She bit back a comment about how offended the Garden Society would be at being called a "club." "Not at all. The magazine is threatening to bail if we don't find another photographer today."

"Is that hard to do?"

"I hope not. Annie's actually quite talented."

"Annie? I thought she baked." He licked his lips, as if savoring the idea of baked goods.

"Annie is a virtual ninja of talent. She not only bakes and takes pictures, she sculpts, too. I've even seen her paint, though admittedly, that was with food and I was washing it out for weeks."

"Sounds kinky." He raised a hopeful eyebrow.

"You don't know the half of it," Cam answered dryly, hoping this appealed to the hot cop. Some part of her hoped to live vicariously through her best friend. She eyed him, imagining how a cop might think. "So any new theories?"

"No, but I am annoyed you didn't mention him slapping Petunia's backside when you first met him." He eyed Cam, and she dropped her head.

"Sorry. I think I blocked that. I felt bad for Petunia."

"Just make sure to work harder to remember in the future, okay?"

Cam nodded. To make nice, Jake went on

like he hadn't just lectured her.

"Pissed-off husband or boyfriend still seems most obvious, like you said, but he wasn't a popular man."

"No kidding. You don't have any clue yet, do you?"

"A few ideas, but they are very speculative, and there are a lot of folks still to talk to." Body language, which Cam had learned to read out of professional necessity, said that was a lie. He didn't have a clue, speculative or otherwise.

"Nobody in the Garden Society?" *That* would be a PR disaster, Cam thought.

"Cam, we'll do our best. Don't worry your pretty head about it."

His condescending dismissal annoyed her. She hated chauvinism. It also missed the point. In some way she was responsible for these people. She knew it wasn't rational; she didn't control anybody in the Garden Society, and Jake's obnoxious comment was just Jake being a cop, but it irritated her. She was relieved when he dropped her off at home.

Cam donned her biking shorts, T-shirt, and helmet in record time. She knew a route out of town with only three stoplights, and if she rode her fastest from the first, she could make the other two without stopping. Then she was out into the hilly countryside, green and fragrant, with the newly budding rows of corn and tobacco on the farmland, pines on the not-so-distant mountains, and the sporadic trees, glistening with shiny new leaves, interspersed between the fields. Her favorite was a twisting butternut tree halfway through her ride that looked like an old person who had persevered since the beginning of time, regardless of the land around it being taken over by agriculture. She always shouted hello as she passed.

"Hey, Gramps!"

Her father and Petunia had had fits when they learned her routine. Not far out of Roanoke the houses became rundown. People were poor, and her family insisted she'd get her bike stolen or get in an accident and not be able to find anyone with a phone. But after living in Chicago, she didn't feel frightened by this kind of poverty. People got by, and she'd never been bothered. Plus, she carried her own phone.

Cam didn't think Rob understood what her biking route was like, or he might have protested with her dad. He got his exercise in a gym, a batting cage, or on a baseball field. His road trips were via interstate, and she doubted he'd been this direction on back roads. She was glad — she didn't want to have an argument about it, but she wouldn't give this up for anything. It was heaven and helped her clear her head. Now what she needed was a way to convince Annie about the photography.

Just after she passed Gramps, a devious plan occurred to her. Annie claimed to be an artist — "above" real photography jobs — and she would most likely protest if Cam suggested she try, but if the Garden Society and magazine saw her portfolio first and wanted her, then she would be unwilling to refuse — her snobbery was in the abstract, not the specific. Cam hurried home to shower, and then she snuck into Annie's apartment to grab her portfolio.

She called a cab to head back out to La Fontaine. It was a splurge she didn't normally indulge in, but she figured it was needed for work, and she could catch a ride back home with Petunia when Petunia dropped off supper.

The cab smelled strongly of patchouli, and Cam was relieved to reach La Fontaine and step out of the cab to breathe in the lily of the valley that lined the Patricks' front yard. She was surprised it was blooming already — she thought it almost never did until after

Mother's Day. Neil Patrick was in the yard picking wilted flowers from one of the many bushes. Dressed as he was, in slacks and an oxford shirt, he seemed ill attired for the job. Perhaps he'd just needed some air, Cam thought.

"Cammi! We're glad to see you again."

"Are the officers still here?" she asked, a bit surprised.

"We took a break this morning to make some phone calls to other members, but we decided the full board should meet." He looked at his watch. "In ten minutes. Lazy-head Samantha even arrived!"

"Oh, well, that's good."

He led Cam into the house.

"Giselle! Could you bring tea into the library?"

"Sure thing, Mr. P." Her attempt at a French accent was gone.

Mr. Patrick frowned. "I'm afraid being French has lost favor with my staff."

"It's not surprising. Maybe you can suggest she go by Helga."

"Oh, no! I had a German nanny as a boy. I want helpers, not commanders."

Cam laughed and followed Mr. Patrick into the library.

She waited as the board gathered and the tea was brought in. People smiled or waved, though it was a timid enthusiasm, some having just learned about the murder. Once everyone was seated, Mr. Patrick asked the loaded question.

"Well, Cammi. What do you have?"

She stood and looked at the assembled group, gauging their mood. "For now, I think I have a perfect candidate to replace Jean-Jacques Georges. I hope that tomorrow I can let you know the news is contained, so RGS doesn't carry a stigma from this."

"Isn't that fiancé of yours a reporter?" Mr. Patrick asked.

"Boyfriend," Cam corrected. People were forever assuming engagement. "And yes, he's a reporter, but a sports reporter."

"Can't he help?"

"Well of course I'll ask, but I don't know how much influence he has." Chatter began among the board members, making her feel less guilty for not disclosing that Rob would actually be covering the story for the newspaper. She wished the group wasn't so easily distracted, though; they were like children, really. "Excuse me!" She shouted over the clamor that was escalating. "I will do my best at news containment tonight. In the meantime, we need to let *Garden Delights* know by this evening whether we have another photographer, or they will leave. I believe I've found someone for the job."

Clamor broke out again until Samantha stood and shouted, "Enough! Let's move ahead!" She sat down again, and the board had the decency to look embarrassed as they quieted.

"Go ahead, Cam."

Samantha's eyes were red rimmed. She'd been crying, which renewed Cam's belief there'd been a relationship between Samantha and Jean-Jacques, and she wondered how a class act like Samantha could end up carrying on with a lowlife like Jean-Jacques Georges. Then again, some people were drawn to fame, and that wasn't exactly counter to what Cam knew of Samantha. She must have stood contemplating too long.

"Cammi?"

"Right. Sorry. I've found a talented local photographer who I believe is perfect for the shoot. It will save the magazine feature, and I'm hoping you'll approve suggesting her to Jane Duffy and Ian Ellsworth. They are the *Garden Delights* decision makers, but, before I approach them, I wanted the buy-in of the board."

They all nodded their approval, and Madeline Leclerc beamed. Cam's tight regard for protocol would avoid future problems for their office, should something go wrong.

Cam opened the large portfolio and began slowly flipping pages. Occasionally, a painting or drawing was stuck in, but most of the pages held photographs. The board was impressed. Halfway through, she reached a picture of her father in a rose garden. Cam knew the shot had captured a moment of profound grief, but in that, there was a deep, touching beauty. She caught her breath.

"Cam, who took those?" Samantha asked, clearly moved.

"My friend Annie."

"They're beautiful. She's caught both the subject and the floral majesty very well."

"I didn't realize that picture was in there," Cam said.

"When was it taken?"

"Soon after my mother died. He used to wander in our roses to be near her. I didn't know there were pictures."

"Well, I think Annie's skill is evident, and isn't your father one of the human subjects for our shoot? They seem to have a rapport."

"If you only knew," Cam muttered, thinking about Annie and her father laughing together and then refusing to reveal the source of fun.

"I move Cam present Annie's work to *Garden Delights,*" Samantha said decisively.

"So moved," Neil Patrick said.

Several "ayes" were announced, and then Samantha said, "Opposed?"

Silence followed, though Cam wasn't sure Joseph had voted. Still, no one opposed, and Joseph could be disengaged that way.

"Good. I'll go talk to Ian now." Cam smiled, gathering the portfolio and leaving the board to the rest of their meeting.

All three of the magazine photography staff members were in the front room of the servant's house, the two men picking at what looked like the remains of a catering tray.

"Look, I met your friend," Ian sneered at her suggestion. He began pacing and wouldn't meet Cam's gaze. "She seems flaky at best. No offense." His tone was even more hostile than his words.

Cam breathed out slowly. Obviously anyone would take offense, and this Ian character was an idiot. "I'm not asking you to take it on faith. I'm asking you to look at the portfolio. Where is the harm in that?"

He walked off as though he had a thousand better things to do, but silent Tom, who'd been watching, sat and gestured for

Cam to lay the portfolio on the coffee table in front of him. She obliged and then started to follow Ian, but she'd only gotten a few steps when it occurred to her she just needed to appeal to the other *Garden Delights* decision maker. Jane Duffy would have at least as much say as Ian Ellsworth.

"Tom, do you know where Ms. Duffy is staying?"

"The Hotel Roanoke. Probably easier to call her cell, though. Ian has the number."

Ian was the last person Cam wanted to ask for anything at the moment, especially as her goal was to undermine him. She took out her cell phone and was about to search for the number for the Hotel Roanoke when she thought of somebody else who might have Jane Duffy's cell phone number. She pressed her speed dial and stepped out front for some privacy.

"Daddy?"

"Well, hello, sunshine! Are you all right?"

"I take it the police have talked to you?"

"They have. What a hassle!"

Cam thought he sounded as secretly excited as Petunia. She wondered if there'd been some mutant morbidity gene that had skipped her, but she managed not to ask, because she needed a real answer, not a joking one.

"Listen, Daddy, it's awful, but it's also awful because the magazine might leave if there's no photographer, and the photo editor won't even look at Annie's portfolio."

"What? That's outrageous! She's a talented girl!" Cam smiled at what a fan her father was of Annie.

"Exactly, but the other person with a say is Jane Duffy. You didn't happen to get her phone number last night, did you?"

"Of course I did, but I can do you one better. I'm picking her up for supper in half an hour. Why don't you meet us at Arzu for a glass of wine and show her Annie's work? Then she and I can eat supper."

"That's perfect! Thank you, Daddy!" Arzu was a nicer restaurant with Mediterranean food, one of her father's favorites. She thought this was a sign he thought highly of Ms. Duffy.

Cam went back inside to collect the portfolio.

"This is great work," Tom told her as she zipped the case.

"Beautiful," Hannah concurred.

"Any idea what Ian's issue is with Annie?" Cam asked.

Tom looked away, so Hannah braved it. "He said something about a psycho ex-girlfriend. I think she reminds him of someone. But then when he talked to her, Annie called his bluff on a few things, which he also doesn't like."

"Ian said it was a good thing they'd gotten Jean-Jacques to be the photographer, because a dump like this couldn't possibly have any talent of its own," Tom admitted. "Then Annie rattled off a dozen or so names — a few I knew. I didn't know they were from here. It just set Ian off. He likes to be the expert. It almost seemed like they knew each other."

"Well, I doubt that. Anyway, Jane's going to look at the portfolio tonight. Does she trump Ian?"

"She will when we point out he never even looked at the work," Tom said. Hannah edged closer to Tom, putting a hand on his shoulder. Cam wondered if this was a romantic getaway for the pair. They seemed to want to stay.

Hannah wouldn't meet Cam's eyes now, but Tom looked sincere.

"Okay, so the trial is with Ms. Duffy. I'll call you, or ask her to, when she says yea or nay, so you know what's coming," Cam said.

She took their numbers and then went to tell the board the decision was in Jane Duffy's hands and she would see the portfolio that night. Cam was hopeful. "Is anyone headed back to town in the next half hour?" She preferred not to wait for Petunia. She hated having things unsettled.

"I can give you a ride," Samantha offered. "I have an appointment in a little bit and it's on my way."

Things seemed to be lining up perfectly, except for the new mystery about the tension between Annie and Ian, but surely that wasn't too big a deal.

Samantha's Jaguar had the softest leather seats Cam had ever sat in.

"Thank you so much. I really need to buy that car I have my eye on, but I'm still a few thousand dollars away from the down payment."

"Oh, honey, it's no trouble. Far better to hold off and find what you want than to settle." Cam thought the statement wasn't about cars.

After an awkward silence, Cam asked the question that had been nagging at her all day. "Where were you this morning, Ms. Hollister?"

"Sleeping like the dead!" Samantha gasped, realizing what she'd said. Tears sprang to her eyes, and her knuckles went white on the steering wheel as she clutched it, but she didn't comment for what seemed a long time. "You know I haven't slept that hard since after my last husband died, and that was with the help of sleeping pills."

"But you didn't take any last night?"

"No. After the party I thought I might need one. You *know* it didn't go well." She looked at Cam earnestly and kept driving. "Joseph stayed for a nightcap. He does that now and again. We debated old movies and the true meaning of chivalry. He loves old fantasy books and movies full of knights and dragons and princesses — he joked about a duel with . . . but . . . never mind. Seems so awful, now. It calmed me, though. Joseph has some very old-fashioned ideas about honor, you know, but to me he's like an old shoe — not all that attractive, but worn to a perfect fit. Neil stopped by, too, after Evangeline went to bed, just, well . . . you know . . . to see how I was — we've been friends a long time. He stayed for a drink and then left. Then, when I was alone again, I had a cup of tea and was out soon after."

"So you slept what? Ten hours?"

"Almost eleven. I know it's shocking, but Francine was here from six o'clock this morning and knows the truth of it."

"She's your housekeeper?"

"Cook, mostly. Though she does some other things. She says she tried to wake me at eight and I just mumbled to her through the door. I didn't get up until after eleven."

"Samantha." The woman's first name felt strange on Cam's lips, and caused Samantha to turn toward Cam, even though she was driving. "There isn't anybody who'd want you to sleep that hard, is there?"

Samantha paused, staring, but finally realized what Cam meant. "Do I think someone drugged me? Heavens, no! Who would? Not Joseph. Certainly not Neil. Nobody else was . . ."

Cam wondered what idea had interrupted Samantha's thoughts. Samantha seemed to have missed Cam's reasoning, but that was just as well. "You didn't happen to save that cup of tea, did you?"

One eyebrow went down in thought. "It may still be in my room. Normally I leave it in the kitchen sink, but I fell asleep too quickly."

"I don't want to alarm you, but it sounds like someone might have wanted you asleep all night, and . . . well . . . if you can prove someone slipped you sleeping pills, then if anyone thinks you're a suspect that would help prove you couldn't have done it."

"Oh! Do they think I did it? I wouldn't!"

"I don't think so, no. But not coming to La Fontaine or answering your phone this morning is suspicious, where . . . your teacup would cancel that out. See what I mean?" She hoped she was reassuring, even if, had she been the investigator, Samantha would be near the top of her list. She thought an angry lover was as likely a suspect as a jealous spouse, but she knew Samantha didn't know she'd overheard the fight. Besides, as part of RGS, Cam preferred to keep Samantha out of the limelight unless there was real evidence.

"What should I do?"

"Call Jake Moreno. You got his card, right? And tell him what you think might have happened. Don't touch the cup again. Let him get it, and tell him what I suggested and why."

"Oh, Cam, you're wonderful. Thank you!" Samantha then slyly changed subjects. Cam thought she'd had enough of the dark topic. "So how did you meet Rob?"

Cam grinned. "At a Young Media Professionals meeting in Chicago. He worked for the *Sun* but was stuck in Classifieds. It's hard to move up in big markets when there is so much competition."

Samantha smiled happily. "So you brought him back here with you?"

"All I had to do was dangle that Roanoke sports reporter position in front of him."

Cam grinned at the memory. Rob had accused her of outplaying him, which had always pleased her, given how important games were to him, but the move had been good for both of them — personally and professionally.

When Samantha dropped her off at home, Cam wondered again if it was possible Samantha actually *had* killed Jean-Jacques Georges, but the idea felt so foreign that she pushed the thought aside. She put on a skirt more appropriate to evening, slightly shiny, fitted, and black, and walked the dozen blocks to the Historic Market District and Arzu Restaurant. The bulky portfolio and heels made going a little slow. Her dad and Ms. Duffy were already seated at a cozy table when she arrived, and her dad ordered her a glass of merlot. Cam sat and flipped through the portfolio for Ms. Duffy.

Jane was suitably impressed with Annie's work and promised to call her colleagues. Once Cam pressed, Jane left the table and called the magazine staff immediately, though Cam thought her own unspoken threat to stay until it was done had a large part to do with her urgency. Ms. Duffy was looking forward to a little alone time with Mr. Harris, something that seemed even dearer now that she'd seen, from the photos, how deeply he could love.

As Cam stood to leave, she looked at Jane Duffy curiously.

"You know . . . last night, when Jean-Jacques was speaking French, you frowned like you heard something odd. I don't speak French. What did he say?"

"It was just . . . well, a beginner's mistake, but he's about as French as I am. He meant to say 'once upon a time,' but what he said was, 'It was a cold.' The words sound similar, but only a person relatively new to French would do that."

"So he was . . . pretending to be French." Cam was thinking of Giselle and wondering if there was a connection. Mr. Patrick said Giselle's accent and name had been Evangeline's idea, and Jean-Jacques and Evangeline appeared to have been friends. She nodded and waved good-bye. There was no need to trouble her dad and Jane Duffy further, and she was pleased to have the photographer task handled.

Cam went outside and called Rob, hoping to spend the evening with him. She had a lot she needed to sort through, and talking it out helped.

"Jake and I were just ordering a pitcher of beer," Rob responded.

"Where are you?"

"Martin's." Martin's was a sports bar on First, only a few blocks from where she was.

"I'm at Arzu. I stopped to show Jane Duffy something. Would you mind if I joined you?"

"Not at all. It's perfect, actually," Rob said.

"See you in ten or fifteen minutes."

It was just starting to get dark, but it was a lovely night and downtown was alive with activity. She hoped she'd spot Rob's Jeep so she could put the portfolio in it, but thinking about that reminded her she really needed to inform Annie she'd just found her a job. She pressed the speed dial for Annie's number on her cell phone.

"Hey, Cam," she answered.

"Do I have a special ring tone or something?"

"Of course you do! You're my best friend!"

"What is it?"

"That *was* it. 'You're My Best Friend.' Queen."

Cam laughed. "How long have you been waiting for that exact joke?"

"Month or so."

Cam snorted. "So what are you doing?"

"I'm naked!"

"I think you missed that — I said 'What

are you doing?' not 'What are you wearing?' With you, naked could mean just about anything."

"It's true, but sadly, it just means I'm getting in the shower. On my thirtieth batch of cupcakes today, I ended up in a wrestling match with a package of Dutch cocoa, and I think I have chocolate up my nose."

"Tasty. You need a beer to balance that? After you've showered, that is?"

"Duh!"

Cam passed on details of where they'd be, deciding it was better to spring the photography job on her in person . . . and with witnesses. When she hung up, she made her way west on Kirk, then wove her way to Martin's Downtown Bar on First Street. There she found Rob and Jake in a surprisingly quiet corner, looking at a legal pad, in spite of wearing muddy sliders and cleats. They'd clearly come straight from practice.

"Am I interrupting?"

Instead of simply scooting over, Rob stood, allowing Cam to slide between him and Jake. Men could be ridiculous, Cam thought.

"Not at all. Griggs is thrilled with the story I filed today, so Jake was just walking me through the standard investigation process."

"Cool." She was interested in that herself, but her own professional interests took precedent. "You didn't, erm . . . How did the Garden Society come out in your piece?"

"Not mentioned. Jake says we keep specifics out of the paper for a while in case it's important to the investigation."

Cam let out a deep breath and relaxed back against the booth. Rob slid back in after her.

"Thank you for that." She smiled at Jake, thinking maybe he was slanting his information to the rookie reporter to make his own job easier, but it also helped her. "Annie's meeting us in a little while." She smiled smugly. She could see Jake was pleased as punch. "So any new info?"

Suddenly Rob looked away, which wasn't like him, but Jake seemed unaware anything was amiss.

"The offended-boyfriends-and-husbands angle may be panning out; it's thrown up a lead or two."

Cam nodded, still not understanding Rob's response.

"Er . . . Cam?" he finally said, looking around the bar nervously.

"Yeah?"

"Did you know Nick was an ex-con?"

"Nick?"

"Nick."

"I'm sure he's been arrested. He was wild when he was younger . . . punk rock or something . . ."

"He did five years in Brunswick."

Cam's jaw dropped. Brunswick was a state prison near Lawrenceville. It was a far cry from a night in a city jail, which was what she'd been imagining.

"Seems he's our likeliest suspect," Jake said calmly, possibly not knowing how close Cam was to her brother-in-law. He took a sip of his draft and sat back. Rob had taken out a pen and was studiously coloring on his coaster to avoid her gaze.

"Look, I know Nick." She turned from one to the other, feeling closed in. "He's a pussycat."

"Cam, it doesn't look good," Rob said gently.

"Maybe not at first glance, but there's a lot more to look at."

"Of course there is. Nobody is stopping there. He's just the current favorite." Jake sounded uncomfortable, finally, which cheered Cam up, but only slightly.

Cam promised herself if he stayed a favorite, she'd find the killer herself. She would rather a Garden Society member did it than Nick! She couldn't take the idea of Petunia's Prince Charming turning into a toad without a proper look for the real culprit. She stared into her glass, tired of both Rob and Jake at the moment. She wished Annie would hurry.

CHAPTER 5

"So . . . I thought you'd be drowning your sorrows or something." Annie appeared to float up to their table in waves, her long, iridescent skirt balanced by her casual tank top.

"We are." Annie's smart-aleck ways aside, Cam was very glad to see her.

"With beer you can see through? How humiliating." She gave an exaggerated shiver.

Annie waved over a waitress and before anyone could protest, ordered a pitcher of Snapping Turtle, a local India Pale Ale. Cam was glad Jake seemed amused. She and Rob had an unspoken rule about calories, but she knew not everybody lived by it. Jake stood and allowed Annie to slide into the booth next to Cam, then slid in behind her. Cam was more entertained than anything else, so she decided to turn to more pressing matters than Annie's beer critique.

"Annie, I have a proposition."

"And I keep telling you — of course, as long as the ratio is at least balanced."

Cam rolled her eyes. It was a joke about threesomes and Rob not being man enough for both of them — in reality it was just Annie trying to get a reaction from Cam, which she didn't, because Cam already knew the joke. Rob wasn't aware of it, and Cam preferred to keep it that way, but he looked at Cam questioningly. She shrugged, feigning cluelessness, then turned back to Annie.

"I have a job to offer you."

"Cupcakes with little flowers for a fundraiser?" Annie teased.

"Photos for a national magazine."

Annie was intentionally obtuse. "You're offering me magazine pictures?"

"I'm offering you national recognition for taking magazine pictures."

"Okay, remember the eyebrow promise? All bets are off. Why would I want all that commercial noise?"

"Because one-point-three million people would see the gorgeous photographs you took."

"One point . . . Holy cow! Do that many people care about gardening? Why do that many people care about gardening?"

Cam stifled a snort and ignored the jab. It

was just Annie being a pill. "Between the print and web circulation, yes."

Annie had bitten the inside of her cheek and was looking at each of them suspiciously. Cam could see she was torn, and loved this part.

"You could do a couple arty ones, in addition to the regular fabulous ones you do," Cam offered.

Annie frowned more deeply. Cam knew her best friend well enough to know she was irritated she was yielding. She didn't want to want to, but she did want to. The temptation of a huge audience was too much.

"And so this shoot involves what?"

"Three days, probably thirty locations within the Patricks' gardens, but you know better than I do how many shots that means."

"All outdoor?"

"Outdoors and the greenhouses."

Annie nodded, calculating lighting, then scrunched her face. Cam knew Annie was about to bring up the magazine crew led by the giant bonehead, so she diverted.

"And you can get Daddy better than anybody else."

"Your dad?"

"He built the trellis, remember?"

Recognition crossed Annie's face and she

scowled. Cam thought she had her.

"The terms are generous," Cam said. "Jean-Jacques cost a fortune, so I'm sure you'd clear more in three days than you do in three weeks at the bakery."

"Fine. Because I like your dad. Not because I like you, because at the moment I'm mad at you!"

The waitress had just brought the pitcher of amber beer, its hoppy odor wafting at them as she set it down. Annie poured a pint, drinking half in one long draught, then covered her mouth and burped.

She giggled. "Sorry. I was distraught for a minute there."

"You're better now?" Jake asked cautiously.

"I'm sorry. I'm being rude. Here you are investigating a murder, and I'm upset because someone wants to pay me to take pictures."

"Yes, well . . . I signed on for my job," Jake said.

"Traitor," Cam mumbled.

Rob and Jake laughed.

"Okay, fine. We've all had a good laugh," Annie spurted, but her humor was back. "So who dunnit? You've solved it, right?"

"Hardly."

"Well hurry! Cam's job hangs in the balance!"

Cam looked at Annie, knowing this was the first phase of revenge.

"So what *have* we learned?" Cam asked diplomatically.

"Two sets of prints on the weapon, neither a match with our files, but the ones we took today aren't in the system yet."

"Well, then they can't be Nick's, can they?" Cam said.

Rob put his hand on hers, but it was patronizing, so she pulled hers away.

Jake just ignored her and went on. "Nothing on the victim but wallet and keys to a car registered to . . . wait, I shouldn't tell you this . . ." Jake stopped himself.

"Why not?"

"It's part of the investigation."

Annie scooted around, nearly on top of Jake. Cam was pretty sure her hand was on his thigh.

"Please." She batted her eyelashes.

It was a teasing flirt, not an outrageous come-on, but Jake still seemed moved.

"Fine. You'll hear tomorrow anyway. It was a car registered to Samantha Hollister."

This only seemed to be news to Annie, who, when she saw Cam and Rob nod together, frowned at having been left out of the loop.

"Some friends you are," she muttered. Jake went on. Cam thought it was to distract Annie.

"My interview with Ms. Hollister isn't until tomorrow morning, so I have no idea what it means," Jake said, his head lowered uncomfortably.

"Did they ever narrow the time of death any further?" Cam asked.

"Between six thirty and seven thirty, according to the coroner."

"Holy crap! He was being murdered while I was picking up my pan?" Annie asked.

"You were there this morning?" Jake asked.

"Yes. I'd left my best pan and had a lot to do today, so I needed it. I picked it up around six forty. I could tell something was weird. When Giselle opened the door, she looked ready to kiss me."

Jake frowned, and Cam thought a subject change was in order.

"Did he fall out that window?"

"Cam, I don't think — . . ."

"Come on, Jake."

"If he did, he was dead already. There wasn't any bruising consistent with a fall like that."

"But they don't know?"

"A lot of stuff they can't tell."

Cam acted more irritable about this than she felt. In reality she hoped she was distracting them from Samantha and Annie. Nobody took the bait, and Annie seemed intent on encouraging Cam to just drink a little more so she'd calm down.

"Was the car at the scene?" Annie asked as she poured Cam some of her heavier beer.

Cam stepped on her foot, but Annie was still annoyed enough with Cam to ignore it. She pinched Cam's leg under the table, and soon there was an almost silent pinching war going on; the men watched in amusement.

"Close enough. He parked a few houses away, maybe just to be considerate of residents."

"Not likely," Cam and Annie chorused.

Jake looked back and forth, unused to mind-melding friends.

"So you think two houses down is hiding, rather than considerate?"

Annie and Cam nodded in unison, suddenly back on the same page, but it was Cam who elaborated.

"Jean-Jacques didn't know the definition of 'considerate.' He was certainly no practitioner."

"That means he probably wasn't just making an early start to his workday, either."

"I'd gotten the impression, and Ian basically confirmed it last night, that Jean-Jacques always acted too big for his britches and pushed for a ten-to-three schedule, if not forced to do otherwise. I know I wasn't expecting him until nine. In fact, I expected him to be late," Cam said. "It's possible Ian asked him to show up early — we talked about the view at sunrise and hoped to get a shot, but Ian would have to tell you whether or not that came up when they talked. I really doubt it, as Ian struck me as a giant wuss."

"Wuss, yes, but sunrise? That's awfully early," Annie said.

Cam looked at Annie in disbelief. "Says the woman who *bakes* for a living?"

"Well, I just thought later hours might be a perk of the job."

Cam rolled her eyes that Annie was already complaining about hours. "We'll look at the weather when we get home, pick a day, and the other two you can sleep until eight."

"Woo-hoo!" Annie said with exaggerated enthusiasm.

"Cam?" Rob looked timid again, which meant bad news. "A front comes in tomorrow night. I don't know how long it will stay."

Sometimes she hated that he paid attention to the news. A little oblivion could do a lot for her mental health.

"Great — speed photography tomorrow outside, so we can take our time in the greenhouses."

"At least part of it was planned for the greenhouses," Annie offered.

"That's true."

"Well, if I might have to start first thing, I need to make sure cupcakes are covered." Annie pushed at Jake to let her out of the booth and left the table with her cell phone.

"So, Cam . . ."

Cam turned to look at Jake.

"A couple of these personalities don't quite make sense. I was wondering if you could help me out."

"I can try. A lot of them don't make sense to me, either."

Rob ran his hand up her thigh in appreciation. She appreciated back, but would have preferred not to be interviewed.

"Benny Larsson?"

Cam sighed. "Henry Larsson, Benny's dad, is chief gardener — Master Gardener in fact, an earned title, not easy to come by." She leaned in. "Benny, I just found out today, is officially, um . . . challenged? Learning disorder or something . . ."

"Do you know why he and Jean-Jacques might have gambling debts with the same bookie?"

Cam paused, taken aback. She couldn't imagine any scenario where that would be true, or even how Jake would have learned it.

"Well, I wouldn't think it would be wise for . . . I imagine the bookie is taking advantage of Benny. Is he local?"

Jake nodded, but that only brought up a more confusing point, which Cam was eager to point out.

"I guess the bigger question is what Jean-Jacques was doing there, with the local bookie, I mean. He's *not* local. Why would a local bookie lend him money? Though I don't think you should be above pressing them about this boy with the disability!"

" 'Boy' is a little bit of an exaggeration. Benny is twenty-eight. And I'm going to ignore the fact you seem to know how bookies work. Benny's disability isn't obvious, really. I mean, he was a little slow, but I thought it might be nerves."

"Any idiot gets how bookies work. I watch movies. And as for Benny . . . it doesn't come across as a disability — you're right.

He just seems . . . inappropriate."

"Which a lot of perfectly capable people do. Look at Rob over there."

Cam snorted, choking on the drink she'd just taken.

"Low, man." Rob took a sip of his beer and acted disinterested.

Jake's grin was sheepish and timed perfectly for Annie's return.

"What did I miss?" Annie asked, sliding in next to Jake.

Cam couldn't breathe; she was laughing so hard. She fell over onto Rob's lap.

"It isn't *that* funny," Rob grumbled.

"In the middle of a police interview it was."

"Whoa. Police interview?"

"Just about some of the people who . . . seem off."

"Oh, well, I see where Rob fits there," Annie said dryly.

"What is this, pick on Rob night?"

"No, this is only *practice* for pick on Rob night," Cam said, kissing Rob's cheek sweetly.

Rob muttered for a minute, then kissed her back more intensely than was probably appropriate at a table with other people.

When Cam came out of the home-run kiss she slapped the table, took a swig of her beer and said, “Okay! Who’s next?”

“Maybe tomorrow would be better,” Jake suggested, looking from Cam to Rob with concern.

“Are you asking me on a date?”

“Cam,” Rob asked quietly, “did you eat today?” He gazed at her with concern. “You didn’t, did you?”

Cam slapped her hand to her mouth, realizing it was an uncoordinated gesture. “No! I tried, but I never got back to it. It was his fault.” She pointed at Jake.

Rob nodded to Annie, who ran to the bar to order a snack.

“We’ll do it tomorrow, okay, Cam? What time is good?” Jake asked.

It seemed to require a lot of effort to remember, but finally Cam told Jake she was flexible from ten until about one.

“I’ll come to La Fontaine to talk to you. You’ll be at the Patricks’?”

Cam nodded, only partially catching it.

“Jake is meeting Cam at ten tomorrow. Will you remind her?” Rob asked Annie as she returned and sat back down.

Cam frowned, irritated at being babysat, but she forgot it quickly, as Annie went into rare form.

“As long as Jake promises to dance like I

like." She eyed Jake, who blushed but answered.

"Name the time."

Annie grinned. "Maybe fifteen, twenty minutes?"

"Here?"

"Is this dance music? Of course not." Annie pulled Jake out of the booth, then took his arm, whispering to him as they left. Cam thought it was probably about sticking Rob with the bill.

Rob winked at them as they left. Cam observed it through her too-little-food haze, amused Rob still hadn't gotten the joke, though she knew he probably would have offered to pay anyway, since Jake had been helping him. Then she realized she had lost some detail.

"Where are they going?"

"Annie is going to make him dance like she likes," Rob said cautiously.

Cam snorted again. "Oh, that boy won't know what hit him."

"Why? How does she like to dance?"

"I can't tell you, or then I'd have to kill you!" She broke into giggles and fell onto his lap again.

"You're drunk."

"Maybe."

■ ■ ■ ■

The waitress delivered the quesadilla Annie had ordered, and Rob made sure the majority of it got into Cam. After that she felt a little more human, but infinitely more sleepy, so Rob drove her home.

Merengue music floated from Annie's upstairs window.

"That," Cam said, glancing upward, "is how Annie likes to dance."

"Oh." Rob stared at the dimly lit window. "Maybe we should dance like that."

"Sure," she said, but as Rob got her inside, he had to help her into pajamas and seemed to give up on the idea of dancing.

She rallied enough to brush her teeth, in spite of a bit of vertigo. She never skipped toothbrushing, but that was as much as she remembered.

Chapter 6

The alarm went off at five the next morning, and when Cam reached for snooze, she found her clock had been moved across the room. Normally it sat on the table by her bed, and even before it registered that her head hurt, she identified it as foul play.

"Freaking Annie," she muttered, sliding out of bed and running her tongue over the apparent socks on her teeth.

She had to move a note that had been propped in front of the alarm clock to turn it off. It read, "Possibly the only day for sunrise shots. We leave in an hour." She cursed at the clock as if it would pass the message on to Annie.

Cam brushed her teeth, showered, and dressed, debating for too long over her contacts but finally forcing them in. Then she ate a piece of peanut butter toast, knowing it would help. By the time she heard Annie barreling down the stairs, she was alert, for the most part, and over her irritation.

"Give me a hand with the stuff?" Annie asked.

The camera equipment was too fragile for the dumbwaiter, and foot delivery would have taken Annie about four trips. It was more reasonable for the two of them to do it.

"You need more drinking practice," Annie said as they carried the second load down.

"And you need to hide it better when you get lucky," Cam scowled, finally finding a home for her repressed annoyance.

"Luck nothing. That, my friend, is art."

Cam couldn't help herself. She laughed, then winced.

"Besides, I drink."

Annie made an "L" shape with her thumb and forefinger on her forehead. "You're the world's biggest lightweight."

"Only when I don't eat."

"And what kind of real person doesn't eat for, what . . . ten hours?"

Cam looked away. She hated it when Annie had a point. Food just wasn't one of her biggest priorities, especially when she was busy.

"Well, if we're doing this little project together, I'm going to make sure you eat. I need you in drinking shape!"

"Fine."

They drove in relative silence and then pulled up to the Patricks'. Cam let Giselle know they were taking some shots from the balcony, and Giselle insisted they come through the house instead of carrying all the equipment around. As she led them through, she kept muttering about the "ugly business" at the side of the house, a fact Cam had somehow willed herself to forget, though it made her glad they were going through instead of around. Cam looked more closely at Giselle and realized she looked like she hadn't slept well. She was pale and disheveled, when normally she was tidy and proper.

When they reached the balcony and Giselle left them, Annie began to set up. Cam, feeling useless, suggested she fetch the magazine crew.

"Can you wait? I have an hour, maybe, of shots here. Please don't subject me to Ian yet."

"Yeah, why does he think he knows you?"

"He's a deluded idiot?" Annie said as she fixed the legs of her tripod into place, jiggling them slightly to make sure they held tight. Annie didn't look at Cam, but given her concentration, that didn't seem unusual.

"You need anything?"

"Coffee?" Annie asked.

"Shouldn't be a problem. I'll be back in a minute."

"With cream or half-and-half, unless these folks are insane like you." Annie had shot a few preliminary pictures already. She still wasn't looking at Cam, but Cam knew now she was avoiding Cam's eye roll.

Cam found Giselle and made her request. In minutes she was loaded with a tray that included a coffee thermos, cream, sugar, and packets of fat-free creamer. For some reason it irritated Cam that Giselle knew her reputation where coffee was concerned.

She poured Annie her coffee, then sipped her own.

"This really is a magnificent view," Annie admitted as she continued shooting.

Cam sat back on a chair and vowed not to be hungover the next day. That was the only flaw in the current setting: the dull throb that kept threatening to turn into a headache. She should enjoy working with Annie, and she decided she would if it killed her — though that unfortunate thought caused another stabbing sensation in her forehead, as it reminded her of the very flaw she was trying to suppress.

After about half an hour Annie finally

pulled away from her camera for more than just a drag of coffee. Three rolls of film had been deposited in her bag, and she'd taken many more shots with her digital camera.

"So what all do we need to get today? This bird's-eye view ought to help us map the order."

"You sound . . . organized."

"Camellia Erin Harris, artistry and organization are *not* mutually exclusive!"

"I know, I know. I've just never *seen* it before. No need to bite my head off."

Annie head-butted Cam in the shoulder to show she was teasing, then held out her hand expectantly.

Cam scrunched her eyes against the pain this caused her head, then looked at Annie's hand.

"What?"

"While art and organization don't have to be mutually exclusive, I happen to know *I* don't have to be organized, because *you* are. Where is your list?"

Cam mock glared, then pulled out her notebook and rested it on the rail to show Annie the features she'd noted in the garden; she pointed to various areas as she explained.

"Hannah's got another list — Ian's list, but this was mine."

"Ian's a jerk-off who can bite me."

"Feeling's mutual."

Annie and Cam spun together; Cam was mortified. The *Garden Delights* crew had joined them on the balcony. Annie looked unfazed.

"We ready?"

"Let me look at the plan," Ian said.

"No, you show up late, you can catch up as we go."

"Annie, they aren't late. This is when we said. We just started early for those sunrise shots, because of the weather front."

"Front? You should have called." Tom scuttled forward, concerned and eager to get on the same page.

"What for? We won't need lighting until the greenhouses."

Cam elbowed Annie. There was no reason to be rude to Tom. Fortunately, though, he had missed the signal.

"Because I have a list of shots."

He pulled out the list that was indeed in Hannah's writing. Annie and Ian dived at the list, then began fussing immediately, each tugging to see it first. Cam had never seen Annie respond so irritably toward anyone and wondered what had happened two nights earlier to set off this dynamic.

Tom finally used his fingers to give a loud

whistle, then pulled the list to his own chest.

"If Cam's right and there's a weather front coming, we need to keep moving. We'll have to get all the outside shots today, which means we don't have time for whatever this is." He swept his hand in a gesture to show he was referring to the Ian-Annie struggle, then he took the lead.

As they moved down the stairs, Cam shuddered when she eyed the azaleas where Jean-Jacques had been found.

"You okay?" Hannah asked. She seemed genuinely concerned.

"I just don't like seeing where someone died."

"He didn't die there."

"What?" Cam slowed down, providing a little distance from the rest of the crew, and Hannah slowed with her and leaned toward Cam.

"I'm sure he didn't. Azaleas don't smell all that strong. When I identified him, I had to get close because they didn't want to move him yet. He smelled of jasmine."

"Why did you identify him?"

"I don't know. I saw the police arrive. Giselle directed them to the spot and I was out here. They asked if I knew who it was."

Cam had all but forgotten Hannah had been asked to identify the body.

"And you think he died in the jasmine?"

"Either that or he rolled in it and then died. Died in it makes more sense to me."

"Did you tell the police?"

She frowned. "They didn't ask me anything like that at all — I mean, I only identified him initially. Then later, none of the questions were about that — they were about the last few days up until the police arrived — not after."

"I think it would help if they knew. I doubt any of the official people have your flower expertise. I'm meeting with Jake later this morning, so I can tell him, but he might have more questions."

"You know where I'm staying. So does he, I guess."

Hannah's pleasantness and concern were such a nice contrast to the Ian-and-Annie war that she didn't want to return to the others, but they had to. Tom periodically had questions on direction, as he had spent less time in the garden than Cam had.

Cam took one brief break from them when she spotted Henry Larsson tending to some rhododendrons. She wanted to make sure she knew where all the jasmine was, though she didn't let him know why she was asking. She quickly returned then to the crew, as she worried they'd never get done without her peacekeeping.

Tom and Cam, on alternate urgings, managed to push Annie and Ian through a handful of locations, but their bickering got louder and more annoying as they moved. Finally Cam blew up at Ian.

"What the hell is your problem?"

Ian turned and, surprisingly she thought, looked Cam in the eye.

"Why don't you ask Miss Crowbar here."

The force of venom made Cam step backward. She looked at Annie, who blanched.

"What are you talking about?" Cam asked, though less confidently.

But Ian had turned to Annie.

"You remember Paul, don't you? Psycho."

Cam had never seen Annie so ready to crumble. She knew Annie had dated a Paul, but it was when Cam lived in Chicago, so she didn't know anything about how it had ended except that it had been sudden. She could see Ian's words had really upset Annie. She knew Annie too well, though, to take what Ian said at face value. It was time to defend her friend.

"You just back off! I've known Annie for twenty years, and if there really is some story under your hot air, I know she was in the right, but I think you're mistaken. So back it up a notch and just do your damn job!"

Both Ian and Annie fumed, but Cam was glad Annie looked less haunted than she had a minute earlier. They managed to make it through three more locations before they found themselves in the jasmine.

Annie got to work, ignoring Ian, working with Tom — a strategy they'd used successfully for the last three spots. Cam, feeling disaster had been averted, let her eyes wander. She looked for a bush with a lot of blooms knocked off. It took a while. There was a lot of jasmine — it smelled too good for a gardener not to be tempted to plant a lot of it.

Finally, she spotted a disheveled shrub and approached, examining it more closely as Annie ignored Ian and snapped photos. Tom and Hannah chatted amicably, and Ian acted superior.

Cam crouched, not certain why she was so interested. She'd avoided the azaleas where Jean-Jacques had been found, so why now the curiosity in the place he'd probably died? But she couldn't seem to help herself.

And then she spotted it. Resting in the branches of the partially squashed jasmine bush was a charcoal glint that, on closer inspection, was a cell phone.

■ ■ ■ ■

Cam looked either way, feeling suddenly guilty for her find. She was nervous but excited. She had the foresight not to touch it with her bare hand, but not the willpower, once the phone was retrieved, to not look at who Jean-Jacques had called last. She immediately regretted looking.

The last call made was to "Vange." That was undoubtedly Evangeline Patrick — there just weren't that many people who could be nicknamed "Vange." "Sam," the second-to-last contact listed, was a little more ambiguous, but Cam instantly recognized the associated number. She had dialed it herself repeatedly the day before, until she'd finally plugged the number into her own contacts, though the recipient had failed to answer any of the calls. It was Samantha Hollister. Cam paused a moment to catch her breath and then pressed buttons to look at each contact again. Samantha had been called the night before the murder, but Evangeline had been called the morning of the murder at six thirty.

She dropped the phone in the pocket of her satchel, hoping nobody had seen, then looked at her watch.

"Shoot! Jake said he had questions for me at ten and it's ten after. If I leave you four, is it possible you won't kill each other before I get back?"

"Not funny," Hannah muttered. She edged closer to Tom, who remained oblivious.

Cam felt a little guilty leaving. Ten was the earliest Jake might appear, and she actually thought he'd come find her, but she needed a break from the bickering and didn't have the patience to dawdle. She wanted to get the phone to Jake and find out if he'd learned anything else. She also had a small part of her trying to forget the cryptic accusations Ian had thrown at Annie. What the heck was she supposed to make of "Miss Crowbar"? And how was that related to Paul? She tried to convince herself it wasn't even the same Paul. It might just be a coincidence.

She searched her memory for what she had heard about Annie's Paul. Cam had been in first an internship, then a very busy job in Chicago, swept up in a brand-new relationship with Rob and not only busy but also distracted. She remembered Annie dating Paul — Annie felt it was getting serious, but then it was just over. All Cam heard was, "He wasn't who I thought he was." She could hardly draw conclusions from that, though. Every person who'd ever ended a relationship in the history of time could say that. Nobody broke it off without feeling a little that way.

Surprisingly, when she reached the house, Jake was already there. Seeing Jake reminded Cam that Annie had moved on and felt no lingering sadness. It had been a few years, after all, and while Annie hadn't had another serious relationship, she had seemed content until now with the field of men at her disposal.

"Hey, Jake. How were the dance lessons?"

"Great! We taught each other some new moves."

"I bet."

"What? No! Not like that! I mean —"

"I've been Annie's best friend a long time. I'm sure you *tried* to be a gentleman."

He blushed and then caught sight of his clipboard, which seemed to pull him back to the task at hand.

"I have some questions about a few people."

"I remember. But I think you'll want something first. Do you have . . . one of those gloves or something? And a bag?"

"Evidence?"

Cam nodded.

He reached into his satchel for a tissue-sized box and then grabbed the wrist edge of a latex glove, handing it to Cam. He helped Cam slide it on, but then he had to retrieve an evidence bag from his car to put the phone into. While he was gone, Cam pulled out a few extra pairs of gloves — they seemed a handy thing to have.

When he returned, Cam held the tip of the cell phone antenna with her thumb and pinky. He had his own gloves on by then, but he neglected to hold out the zippered bag toward her.

"Did you touch it already?"

"I had a tissue, so not directly."

He frowned, but then nodded.

"Where did you find it?"

"In the jasmine. Hannah said when she identified the body, he smelled like jasmine, even though he was laying across an azalea by the house."

"And she never said anything during questioning. So he must have died somewhere else."

"It sounded likely, so I looked out in the garden while we were shooting pictures, and there is a squashed jasmine bush. In the branches I found —"

"I guess that explains the lack of blood with his body." Jake had cut her off. He pulled out his own cell phone and called to get the forensic team back.

"They'll be here in ten minutes. And you can show us where?"

She nodded. "The phone . . ."

He held up a hand and called somebody else, apparently his supervisor, then looked back at Cam.

"Can you meet me here in fifteen minutes? I need to check on something."

Cam nodded, dropping the cell phone into the bag Jake had finally held close enough for her to reach. There was no point arguing. Her watch said it was ten thirty, so she decided to see if there was still coffee somewhere.

To her surprise, Joseph was hovering near the kitchen.

"Joseph! What are you doing here?"

"I was just checking on things for Samantha. She's so distraught."

"Why's that?" Cam hated playing dumb for a Garden Society member, but things with Samantha just seemed so fishy.

"She's just waiting for the police to come. They still need to look through Jean-Jacques's things."

"His things? You mean he was *staying* at Samantha's?"

Joseph's eyes went wide. "You didn't

know? I thought . . . well, as you were coordinating . . ."

"I just had his cell phone number. He didn't tell me where he was staying."

"Oh. Well, maybe I shouldn't have . . ."

"It's fine. I won't say anything, but I'm sure, if Samantha's worried, they'll know soon. It sounds like she's planning to tell them."

Joseph shifted uncomfortably, adjusting his bag, but his expression wasn't any different than he'd worn the past few days, so Cam excused herself to get her cup refilled.

Evangeline was in the kitchen filling her own cup and stepped toward Cam, giving her an unexpected hug.

"What would we do without you? You're a lifesaver."

Evangeline's hug suggested firmer parts than a woman in her late thirties was supposed to have, and her chemically held hair almost made Cam sneeze, but the spontaneous gesture was sweet, even if it unbalanced Cam, who was only a hugger with her closest friends.

"Really, it's just my job."

"But it's not. I can tell how much you love it, and we're all grateful."

"I just hope this gets solved quickly. Even with great pictures, the magazine won't take a chance on us if we're mixed up in an open murder investigation."

Evangeline shivered.

"I hope they catch them, too, but it may be hard. Jean-Jacques had no shortage of enemies."

"You were friends, weren't you?" Cam asked. She was guessing, but it was an educated guess.

"Oh, I guess I thought we were once, but I've learned a lot of terrible things since then."

"You were talking pleasantly at the supper."

"I was not making waves, as this event is important to Neil and Samantha."

Jake came in, breaking the moment.

"Cam, you ready to show them? Forensics is here."

"Forensics?" Evangeline jumped.

"I found evidence Jean-Jacques was killed out in the garden, not by your room."

Evangeline looked, if anything, relieved, but Jake hustled Cam out of the kitchen before she could learn why. She also wondered when Evangeline and Jean-Jacques had been friends. She'd only been referring to the amicability of the supper conversation, but Evangeline had suggested that that cordiality had been an act, that their friendship had ended long ago. Jean-Jacques and Evangeline had nothing but age in common. Cam also felt a little guilty for not sharing that Evangeline's number had been in the phone she found, but she supposed it helped the investigation to keep it secret. In fact, she probably was not supposed to know herself.

She was glad she'd kept quiet once she and Jake started walking.

"You didn't mention the phone to her?" Jake asked in a tone that implied she should have known enough not to have mentioned it.

"Only what you just heard — evidence he was killed elsewhere," she answered irritably. "You could have told me not to, though, if you wanted to be sure."

"Sorry. I was just excited to have it and didn't think about you running into her. Usually the people who find evidence aren't friends with . . ."

Cam was sure "suspects" was the missing word, though he didn't finish. Cam wondered why Evangeline was considered a suspect, since the police obviously hadn't had the phone information earlier.

"How do you find your way out here?" He stared dumbly at the flowers and forks in the path, clearly not able to tell one path from another.

"I know these plants the same way you know a fingerprint or a sample of DNA. It's what I studied."

Jake nodded appreciatively and grinned at her, trying to make nice again.

"You know how to get things across to people."

"As do you, Officer." She didn't expand on his smooth talking of the day before. She just let the compliment hang as she led him and the forensics team. They finally reached the jasmine. "See how the rest of the blooms are sort of uniformly distributed? Some are wilted, but those are all spread out. And see how they're pruned to a pleasing shape?" She pointed out a number of jasmine bushes, and Jake nodded. "And so you can see how that one caught my eye?" She pointed at the one where she had found Jean-Jacques's phone. There was a dent at the center and a lack of flowers where a large, heavy mass had clearly crashed into it.

A photographer began snapping pictures, both of the normal and the abnormal bushes.

"Show me where the phone was," Jake said.

Cam went to the bush and crouched,

pointing at the trine of branches that had held the cell phone off the ground.

"Those, I think. Very close to those, anyway."

The forensic assistant ducked in and, using gloved hands, tied a small yellow ribbon to the middle branch. He then wrapped yellow crime tape around the whole area, and the three mysterious men with large kits moved in. To Cam, their actions looked random; they seemed to take a sample of this and a sample of that, but she was too far away to know whether it was a hair, fabric, leaves, grass, or some other substance they were gathering as evidence. She froze as she watched them. It was fascinating. It occurred to her how private and secluded this part of the garden was. Why would the killer have wanted to move the body, clearly risking being seen in the process?

"Okay, Cam, we can go back. They're looking for blood in the soil and such — they'll probably want prints from your shoes and those of everyone else who was here — maybe you could list who was with you, to see if any other prints can be found. It's boring to watch in the best of circumstances, and I hear we have a storm coming, so they'll need to hurry."

She raised an eyebrow at Jake. They'd

heard about the storm front together the night before. She wondered if he just compartmentalized so much he had forgotten that detail. "That's why we were trying to rush the outside photography."

A look of recognition crossed his face and his mouth twitched. "How's Annie doing?"

His grin couldn't hide his infatuation.

"Great, if she doesn't kill Ian."

She regretted it as soon as the words left her mouth.

"What do you mean, Ian? What's wrong with Ian?"

"He's an arrogant fool who is bossy and seems to have it in for Annie. Hey, I've got a question," she said, partially as a diversion. "Why would a killer move a body from a hidden, quiet place to a busier place?"

Jake's face elongated as he thought. "Normally it's a statement, though it's also possible, maybe more likely in this case, that it was done to make somebody else look guilty."

"Like Evangeline?"

He eyed her uncomfortably. "He was found under her window. So that would be my guess — unless we figure out a message, I mean. Anything meaningful about jasmine or azalea?"

"There's all sorts of flower lore. I'll bring

you a few pages of highlights later if I find anything." She doubted there was anything related to bodies left in an azalea bush. She left it at that.

"Are you seeing Annie again?" she asked, changing the subject.

"Supper tonight, I think. It's a little up in the air because of the investigation."

Cam smiled bigger. "I hope it works. And don't let her claim cops are too straight for her. I think you'd be good for her."

It was Jake's turn to frown.

"Oh, she didn't say anything." She tried hard to reassure him. "I just know. Rules aren't her strong point."

Jake sighed. "And she'll be worried I'm all about rules."

"Maybe. Aren't you?" Cam hated it when she stuck her foot in her mouth. She was usually a better navigator of conversation, but Annie's waters held a lot of obstacles.

Jake looked determined. "Not necessarily. I mean . . . some rules. But I'm not a goody-two-shoes. So what do you suggest?"

"Maybe something a little wild and avant-garde?"

"So being the gentleman last night totally played into her worries?"

Cam turned and stared. Annie had never said the word "gentleman," nor had she expressed dissatisfaction about the night. That meant Annie had either misled her or was lying about what she liked.

"Can I get back to you? I'm getting mixed signals."

"What?"

But Cam darted from Jake, hoping she hadn't just screwed things up for Annie. She decided she should get back to her job.

The photography quartet was yelling quite loudly, so once Cam focused her attention, they were easy to locate. She headed in their direction.

"Cam, wait!"

She turned back to find Jake still on her heels.

"I still have people I want to ask about."

"Right."

"Let's have a bite of lunch — official business. Then I can ask all the questions."

Cam sighed, then nodded. She had to do it eventually. She just wished her first "reveal" had not been to expose her best friend, or that she'd at least have time to give Annie a heads-up.

Jake drove Cam to 419 West, a nice, middle-of-the-road restaurant that could be dressed up or down, depending on the night and mood.

"I wanted your opinion on whether Annie would like this. I . . . well, it's not as arty as she is . . . but they have live music next weekend."

Cam smiled encouragingly. "It's good food. You can't go wrong. Annie will pick arty places if she wants arty places. It's more a need for spontaneity now and then that I was warning about. And I'll write you a list of the places that are too arty, if you know what I mean."

Jake laughed at that, and then they ordered food and Jake began his more official questions.

"So, Evangeline. What do you know?"

"Former beauty queen. Went to Brown. Married a rich, much older man. I'd like to say that made her a bitch, but evidence runs contrary. She actually seems like a nice lady."

"You don't know how she *met* this rich older guy?"

Cam shook her head. "They were newlyweds when I started with the Garden Society, but I've never heard the story."

"Do you know who her friends are? Or were before?"

Cam shook her head again. "I've only seen her with the Garden Society, and all those people are on your list already."

"Does she know anyone you know? I mean, besides the Gardening . . . thing?"

"She might. She's only five or six years older than me, and we're both from Roanoke originally, so I guess it's possible we know some of the same people, but . . . not that I'm aware of."

"So no other friends?"

Cam's frown became a sneer. "Like who?" Jake seemed to be after something, but she had no clue what.

"Calm down. I'm just trying to get some background information."

But Cam no longer felt like that was it. She felt even less comfortable sharing information with Jake as the interview continued, and decided to stick to an "answer only" mode.

"Tell me about your brother-in-law."

"Nick is the first man I've ever known who really treats Petunia like she deserves," Cam said defensively.

"So she's been treated badly before?"

This was a subject Cam could go on and on about, but realized how it looked — like Nick might feel Petunia needed protecting. That was a sentiment likely to backfire.

"In the past, but really, nobody has done it since Nick came into her life. It's like he's a guardian angel, and so long as he's there, nobody does anything mean."

"Are they scared of him?"

"No!" She was annoyed, now; she realized she'd shouted when people at the next table turned to stare. She lowered her voice. "They just know she's married and to stay away."

"Calm down, Cam, I get that he's family. I just want to get a feel."

"He looks rough, and he was in a punk band, so I'm sure his youth was a little wild, but the whole time I've known him — more than four years now — he's been very sweet and calm."

Jake nodded but didn't look convinced.

"He bought Spoons for Petunia! Her lifelong dream and she'd never had a hope!"

"Okay! Nick is a sweetheart. What about Samantha?"

Cam breathed again, suddenly glad to throw some light on Samantha, after feeling so boxed in about Nick. She detailed her thoughts of the day before, though she volunteered nothing until she was asked — she was rather annoyed with Jake and couldn't make herself cooperate any more than she absolutely had to. She instinctively felt a little protective of Samantha, but it was a very detached protectiveness compared to what she felt about Nick. It was much easier to reveal what she'd seen and what she knew about her colleague than it had been to speculate about her brother-in-law, and a guilty sense of relief washed over her when Jake seemed to find her theory about Samantha having a history with Jean-Jacques plausible.

"When do you talk to her?" Cam asked as the questions seemed to wind down.

"I go there next, though a couple of evidence boys went this morning — Jean-Jacques was staying there."

Had Cam not just learned that herself, she might have been shocked.

Jake looked at his watch and must have decided it was time to hurry, as he jumped back into questions Cam had thought he was done with.

"Does Evangeline know your brother-in-law?"

Cam started to shake her head, then remembered the "Jack" episode and finally thought she understood what Jake had been getting at earlier.

"Maybe, but at the party at Samantha's she called him Jack, so . . . not well. She acted like she knew him, but she used the wrong name. Nick didn't really answer. He seemed uncomfortable, like maybe it was a mistake."

"Or maybe he didn't want you and Petunia to know they knew each other?"

Cam frowned, remembering Nick's expression.

Jake asked a few more questions about Evangeline but then went on to other Garden Society members. He asked about Neil Patrick, whom Cam praised, then Joseph Sadler-Neff, who was a little harder to put into words.

"He's brilliant, knowledgewise, but a little socially inept. There is something a little off. I mean he's polite — obsessive, in fact, about manners. But he doesn't really relate to people, so he's hard to know."

"That explains some things."

"Like what?"

"Just . . . odd behavior seen by some of the others."

"What others?"

"Cam, I'm not at liberty . . ."

Cam rolled her eyes irritably. Joseph's awkward social skills did explain a lot, so the "odd behavior" that "the others" had referred to could be any number of things, but Cam wasn't happy about Jake's evasive answers.

She was relieved when Jake finally put his notebook away, drove her back to La Fontaine, and left for Samantha's house. She hadn't liked being questioned about people for whom she felt so responsible.

"Cam, there you are!" Madeline Leclerc rushed at Cam as soon as she arrived.

She'd almost forgotten her boss in the chaos.

"Hi, Madeline. What's up?"

"Just . . . I'm *sure* nobody in the Roanoke Garden Society had anything to do with this. It's *very* important any questions you answer support that!"

Cam stared at Madeline, thinking she was supposed to read between the lines of what her boss had just said. She thought back to Madeline's demeanor at the previous day's meeting of the Garden Society officers, at how desperate she'd been for the photo shoot to go on, and it occurred to her that Madeline would just as soon she made stuff up.

"I certainly would never make anybody look guilty on purpose."

"Camellia, you and I don't have jobs if there is no Roanoke Garden Society."

Cam had worked that much out on her own, but she suspected Madeline thought a single guilty party among the RGS members was a condemnation for the lot of them — something *she* didn't believe.

"I swear I won't point any undue fingers."
Madeline pursed her lips.
"No fingers at all. RGS needs to come out of this smelling like roses."
"Fine. I'll do my best."
Cam thought a cover-up had far greater chances of backfiring than any truth, but at the moment, since nothing was known, there was no need to argue yet. She was just glad Madeline was leaving for the time being.

Chapter 7

Cam was relieved to finally get inside. Just as she found a quiet corner to breathe for a minute, however, she heard the sputter of Petunia's minivan. It backfired, as it did more often than not when it stopped, announcing Petunia's arrival. Curiosity got the better of her, and under the guise of helping with lunch, Cam went out to assault her sister with questions.

"You having a dry spell in there?" Petunia eyed her suspiciously.

"Oh, there's plenty to do, but you're more important at the moment."

Petunia pulled her head out of the back of the minivan and stared at Cam, disbelief etched on her forehead.

"There's a first."

Cam pushed her way forward and grabbed the salad bowls as Petunia seemed to possess the only hot pads. She followed Petunia through the house to the patio, food in hands.

"Oh." Petunia looked at Cam as she set the bowls down and rolled her eyes. "That was heavy."

"Everything else was hot. What was I supposed to do?"

"Get towels from the passenger seat."

"And I would know those were there, how?"

Petunia rolled her eyes again, but Cam followed her back outside anyway. She grabbed two towels from the front seat and helped with the rest of the hot food, though now Petunia complained that the drinks were the heavy part and Cam was slacking by not helping with those. Cam persisted, however, and followed Petunia back out again when lunch was deposited.

"What?"

"Sheesh, don't have kittens. Towels?" Cam handed Petunia back her towels.

"You would have stopped me on the back porch if that was all. What is it?"

Cam felt tongue-tied but finally just spit it out. "Did you know Nick was an ex-con?"

Petunia's eyes flashed with fear, not surprise. She looked around, then swore. While Cam swore like an off-duty school teacher, Petunia swore like an off-land sailor. Cam didn't even recognize some of the words. "How'd you find out?" she finally asked.

Cam moved closer and lowered her voice, then explained what she'd heard, without mentioning Nick was the current favorite suspect. There was no reason for Petunia to get worked up if it didn't end up going anywhere.

"I bet that damn Evangeline started this!"

Cam was startled, as Jake had only recently tried to connect Nick and Evangeline.

"What would Evangeline have to do with it?"

"They knew each other in Providence . . . worked together some. Shoot!"

"What is it?"

"We just don't need this. It's just her type of drama!"

"Okay, why are you being so cryptic?" Jake's questions had at least made sense, Cam thought with growing frustration.

"Because I'm annoyed. Look, tomorrow is just a cold lunch. I can deliver early. Will you come home with me then? I can explain better there."

Petunia's behavior was mysterious and annoying, but Cam agreed at once. It sure sounded like there was a deeper story, and Petunia clearly wasn't going to tell it here.

■ ■ ■ ■

Cam felt off center that her sister had knowingly married an ex-con and not told her. What's more, she thought, waiting until the next day to hear the full story might very well kill her. She was not made for this kind of sustained tension!

She sought Annie, who was leading Hannah and Tom back to the patio for a late lunch, Barney trailing happily behind.

"You trained the beast," Cam said, indicating the dog.

"He's my best friend, aren't you, buddy?" Annie picked him up, and he wiggled and licked her face.

"How'd you do that? I thought he was a one-woman dog."

"Trade secret." Annie smirked.

Hannah shrugged, though Cam thought it was a "sworn to secrecy" shrug, rather than an unknowing one.

"Where's Ian?"

"Hell if I care," Annie said.

"He went for some aspirin. He'll be over in a little bit," Hannah added.

Cam steered them all toward the buffet table of taco fixings, with choices for either traditional tacos or taco salads with beef, chicken, or beans. She was full from her lunch with Jake, but the unanswered questions swimming in her head were making her nuts and she thought they'd be less likely to walk away from her if they were eating. She pulled back on Annie's elbow.

"So what *was* that with Ian? You've never met him before, have you?"

"Of course I haven't. He's insane. But I'm starved, and because I was annoyed, I only gave permission for half an hour for lunch. Can we talk after I fill up?"

"Sure." Cam yielded and let Annie fill her taco shell with lettuce, tomatoes, beans, and a wide variety of condiments Cam normally avoided, some of which she couldn't even identify. Annie then seated herself with Hannah and Tom. She obviously preferred to avoid being grilled. It annoyed Cam for only a moment, though, before she shrugged it off.

"Cammi!" she heard as the doors to the patio slid open and closed.

"Oh, hi, Mr. Patrick."

"And how's everything going?"

"Seems to be well." It was only a little white lie.

"Ms. Duffy has interviewed a few of us today and feels the mood might improve if we have another little party. I'm happy to host — tomorrow night?"

"Sure. Even just knowing it is planned should help."

"I know your friend is busy with pictures, but Samantha says she makes the best brownies in town."

"That's true. They're wonderful."

"Do you think she could make some for the party?"

"I'll see if she can fit them in." Cam smiled. Heck, she'd borrow Annie's recipe and bake them herself if it would turn this shoot around.

By the time she sat back down with Annie and the magazine crew, they were finishing; Ian was still nowhere in sight.

"Is it at all possible to make brownies for twenty for tomorrow night?"

"See, that's what I love about you, Cam . . . give, give, give. Never asking for anything in return."

"Annie, I'm sorry. Samantha specifically mentioned *your* brownies! It's not my fault they're so fabulous!"

Annie looked around, "You, me, Rob, Jake. We'll bake them tonight — the special red wine variety."

"What?"

"You heard me."

"What time?"

"Eight, at the shop. You bring the wine."
"You're on!"

After the camera crew left, Cam checked on Jane Duffy. The interviews were going relatively smoothly, but Jane reiterated the down mood she'd observed.

"I know it's normal after what happened, but I would hate this to be the face that goes out to the public."

"I totally agree, and we're having another dinner party. We just can't . . . call it a party. It would be really inappropriate."

"Oh, yes — I agree with that, but these people need a little fun!"

Cam wasn't sure "fun" was appropriate, either, but she agreed with the assessment that without an intervention, the Garden Society was a darned gloomy set of people, incapable of putting on a public front that would sell, whether it was seeking membership or donation money.

Instead of finding her photographer, who at the very least had full information to keep going, Cam spent the afternoon with Evangeline, planning a menu.

Evangeline rattled off the list of what they'd served and what they hadn't in the last few days. Cam tried to steer toward items Spoons served.

"I'm sorry, Cam. I love Spoons' food, but we've sort of exhausted them, haven't we? And think how rude it would be to add on so much extra work last minute. I was thinking . . . well, in order to be good Southern hosts, we should have a good old-fashioned Southern barbeque — barbequed pork with North Carolina barbeque sauce, beans, corn muffins, corn on the cob — a real feast, Southern-style. I know the weather isn't cooperating, but we could have it catered."

Cam sat down to make calls.

Two hours later she slammed the phone down, exasperated.

"Nobody!"

And nobody was right. Not a single person heard her cry of frustration that nobody was available to cater a big Southern barbeque the next night. Evangeline had gone on to domestic or recreational matters out of earshot, and Cam suspected the servants were avoiding her. Nobody took on extra drama voluntarily, and Cam was sure that was what this looked like in their eyes. This photo shoot had brought nothing but extra drama.

But it was fine. She'd always been able to fall back on her scrappy practicality, no matter how elegant some event was supposed to be. Here, elegant didn't quite fit anyway

— the more personal it seemed, the better.

Her first step was to make a series of relatively large takeout orders at different places not far from each other for the next afternoon. No one restaurant had the capacity to do it alone, but all of them could do some portion of it, so she split up what they'd need. One place had no trouble at all with the large order for barbeque, but they didn't sell sides as takeout because they needed them for the "full suppers" that they sold in-house. Another sold beans and slaw sides, and a third sold trays of cornbread. She also made a note to herself to have yet another difficult conversation with Petunia. She might not need Petunia to cook, but she'd need a number of her warming pans if this was to "appear" catered.

Finally, at nearly four, she set out to find the photography crew again.

"Remind me to buy that man a tiara," Annie muttered when Cam asked where Ian was.

"He said he had some things to look into." Hannah trembled, unhappy with being messenger, particularly for a coworker who was acting so inappropriately.

The crew was progressing through the list of outdoor locations well, so Cam, uncomfortable babysitting the crew when Ian was being such a pill, helped for just half an hour before claiming she needed to catch Petunia when she delivered supper. Before heading back to the house, however, she decided to reconfirm the evening's plans with Annie.

"We still on for brownies tonight?" she asked Annie.

"You know we are," Annie answered without halting her photography, so Cam felt at least her friend was on her game, regardless of how anyone else framed it.

Back on the patio of La Fontaine, Cam tried to organize the lunch dishes so they were easy for Petunia to retrieve. Softening the blow was in her best interest. She also considered it might not *be* a blow. Petunia and Nick had been busting their butts for several days now. Maybe they'd welcome the break, or rather the lack of an additional burden. She tried to convince herself that was the case, even if she never began to believe it.

"You want to what?"

Cam couldn't believe how she'd deluded herself — not that she actually had. It had been wishful thinking to expect that her sister would willingly offer her equipment to serve someone else's food. Petunia appeared to be steaming, though the steam was actually from the tray of chicken cordon bleu behind her. It was still a powerful illusion.

"I'm sorry, 'Tunia. We've served all your styles now and just thought something different was a good idea — and this is . . . well, what people expect when they come to the South."

"We? That's it! This was that Evangeline's idea, wasn't it?"

Cam couldn't contain her sputter, so Petunia knew the truth. Cam tried to mention late notice and unfairness, but Petunia was having none of it. Nick stood silently, knowing better than to get between bickering sisters.

"Right through here, Officer."

Cam, Petunia, and Nick all turned together. Neil Patrick guided an unfamiliar police officer out onto the patio.

"Are you Jonathan Nicholas Conroy?"

Petunia gasped. Nick squinted and then nodded.

"You have the right to remain silent . . ."

The next few minutes melted together. Petunia shrieked, and Cam caught her as she sank to the ground, fighting off Cam's efforts to help her. Nick, strangely, was trying to comfort his wife by saying it was okay because he hadn't done anything, though it didn't look to Cam like he actually believed in the justice system for which he was advocating. He looked scared, which unnerved her and seemed to unhinge Petunia.

Garden Society members began peeking outside, and Cam sprang into the house, pleading with the police officer behind her to take Nick around the side. She didn't care so much about the Garden Society at the moment but was very concerned for Nick's humiliation, and by default, Petunia's.

Cam talked the arriving Garden Society members into the library and managed to track down Giselle to bring in wine.

"Was that the killer?" Joseph asked hopefully.

"I really doubt it," Cam answered. She managed to stop herself from glaring but knew she didn't have a poker face when she felt strongly. She could lie well only by convincing herself of a degree of truth, and at the moment she was too upset to convince herself of anything.

"Why, Cam?" Samantha asked.

"Because I know him. He's not a killer."

"But they wouldn't arrest him if he

wasn't," Neil Patrick said. "I can't believe we've had the killer catering!"

"No, Cam's right." Evangeline had stepped forward, taking her husband's arm. She looked everyone in the eye, speaking slowly. "He's a kind, gentle man. He wouldn't hurt anybody — not like this anyway."

Confused but recognizing an ally, Cam asked Evangeline to keep everyone there until the spectacle was over. Evangeline was strangely cooperative, and though Cam vowed to find out why later, feeling instinctively suspicious of the rumored friendship between Nick and Evangeline, for the moment, she was extremely grateful.

She rushed back out to the patio and around the corner of the backyard, where Petunia clung to a handcuffed Nick.

"Sis, are you okay?" Nick asked her. "They can't have anything solid. I didn't do it. And it's not like I haven't seen the inside of a jail before."

Cam was sure Nick thought he was saying comforting things, but she could see it wasn't working on Petunia. She wanted to ask him why he'd been in jail, but the police officer urged Nick up the side of the house toward his car. Cam had to hold Petunia back as she cried and tried to keep hold of Nick.

" 'Tunia, stop! Look at me! We'll make sure they know Nick didn't do it, okay? I'll help you; I swear it. No matter what it takes."

Petunia focused on her for the first time since the police had shown up. She squinted and looked a little angry, staring into Cam's eyes with a slightly mad sheen.

"Swear it?"

"I swear it! I love Nick, and I love how he treats you. I'll figure out who really did it if that's what it takes."

"Swear on Dogwood Village?"

Dogwood Village was a magical place they'd made up when they were little — always beautiful, and the good guys always won. The boundaries had actually been defined by the rows of roses in their back-yard, but each spring a fabulous dogwood bloomed and put everything else to shame.

"I swear on Dogwood Village."

Petunia collapsed into her chest, muttering about Evangeline and how she'd framed Nick. Cam doubted that was the case but knew this wasn't the time to say so.

Cam excused herself from supper with the camera crew and Garden Society board to help get Petunia home, as she thought

Petunia might be too upset to drive. She called Rob but got his voice mail, then remembered he was having burgers with Jake for supper, something Annie had grumbled about when Cam had last seen her. The case gave the two men a lot to talk about. Cam figured, though, she would see both of them later at Sweet Surprise. She helped Petunia into her town house condominium in a newer subdivision of Roanoke and suggested Petunia might need company until it was bedtime.

Petunia pulled out a bottle of tequila and a lime and slammed them on the table, claiming she had company, but Cam wasn't sure that was the best idea.

"Don't you think you need to be top-notch tomorrow? In case Nick needs you?"

Petunia looked annoyed, but the raised brows were opening enough for Cam to see she was at least half listening.

"One shot of tequila for the misery, okay?" Cam conceded. "Maybe a glass or two of wine while you watch a romantic comedy to distract you, then bed?"

"It's six o'clock."

"All the more reason to start with soft stuff, or commit to bed now."

"Nick has some sleeping pills."

Cam's neck prickled.

"He does? Why?"

"The occasional midnight shifts have messed with his sleep cycle. He doesn't have to do the late shifts too often, but often enough that when we go to bed around eleven or earlier, he can't sleep . . . which we can live with, unless there's a lunch thing, which means we have to start really early — so he got the sleeping pills."

"Geez, Petunia. That sucks. Isn't there something you could do differently?"

"Not without a lot of preparing ahead and freezing stuff, and Nick is pretty anal about everything being fresh."

It was hard to picture Nick being anal about *anything,* but she supposed if he was, it would be about his cooking. Then it occurred to Cam that this left Petunia without a cook.

"Shoot. Are you okay for the next few days? I mean if he's in jail?"

Petunia looked up at Cam, her eyes watering.

"Not really." Tears filled the corners of Petunia's eyes. "We got two new lunch orders this afternoon — a hot lunch and then a huge sack lunch order."

"What are you going to do?"

"Well, at least we don't have *your* thing tomorrow night." Petunia's voice dripped with sarcasm.

"Seriously? At least is right! Look, I'll help. Dad will help. If Rob and Annie need to, they'll help."

"Dad." Petunia paused, a faraway expression on her face. "Dad could probably do most of it."

Before the sentence was completed, Cam had speed-dialed their father. He was clearly upset about Nick and expressed the outrage she would have expected, but he rallied at Cam's plea for help.

"Well of course I'll help! I'm no slouch in the kitchen, you know, so long as someone tells me what to do!"

Cam relayed the message, which got a wet laugh from Petunia, so that was something.

Shot of tequila taken, arrangements for cooking and catering assistance made, Cam urged Petunia to take the sleeping pill, then took her sister's catering van. She vowed to return first thing in the morning. First, though, she had to get through the various obligations of the night.

"Shoot!" she shouted as she started toward home to change for brownie making. She'd forgotten the front that was expected, but now pictured her seedlings, barely peeping above the soil. They were fragile when they were so freshly sprouted. The same thing would be true at the plot she maintained at her dad's house.

Cam spent the next couple hours frantically staking the stronger plants and putting tents over the least hardy of the younger ones, in some cases covering the seedlings completely with a tarp, and in others, using a mesh that allowed water through but blocked the pummeling of driving rain. After all her efforts at the two gardens, she was tired and sweaty when she arrived home to shower, but she needed to hurry because she was running late for the brownie party.

CHAPTER 8

"Nice of you to make it," Annie snapped. Rob looked up gratefully from a mixing bowl that appeared to hold the dry ingredients for brownies.

"Where's Jake?" Cam asked as she put three wine bottles she'd grabbed from her own stock on the counter. She figured she'd have at least two or three glasses, so for four of them, three bottles might be necessary if she counted what went into the brownies.

"Couldn't be bothered," Annie said, tossing her thick ponytail via head flip. She was clearly pissed.

Cam looked at Rob. He wore an apron already covered in flour, but he shrugged innocently, as though oblivious to the reason for Annie's mood. Cam could tell he really knew what was going on.

Annie went to her back room, and Rob moved closer.

"He backed out on me, too. I think he

really had work to do, but explaining that doesn't seem to help at all. She was really angry at him when I got here, and what I said only made it worse, so I dropped it."

Cam nodded. They'd get to the bottom of it. Nothing like a little baking with wine to get Annie to open up.

Annie came back and tossed Cam an apron just as Rob pulled the first cork from a wine bottle.

"Are we allowed to?" Cam asked. "These aren't actually . . . for the brownies?"

Annie didn't even let her finish before she'd poured three glasses and taken a pull from the fullest one.

"A little goes in the brownies — half a cup or so. Other than that, have to keep it out of the work space, but between batches, cooks indulge. Though you better not sue me."

Rob started to laugh, but Annie's glare silenced him. He looked at Cam. Annie set the wine bottle on a back counter and put her glass next to it. Cam and Rob nodded agreement, then took much smaller sips and followed Annie to the main work space, washing their hands on the way. The hand washing Cam remembered from helping in the past, but Annie's leer would have made them aware of the rule anyway.

Because Cam had helped Annie before, they set Rob at the mixer, while Cam retrieved ingredients and Annie directed. They got the first batch mixed and in the oven, and the second mixed before Annie began swearing at Rob about Jake.

"Why didn't you freaking tell me he was married?"

"What?"

"I was at Mick or Mack for more cake flour and eggs this afternoon, because this was unexpected." She paused to leer at Cam. "So I didn't order for it, and in comes Mr. Two-Timer with his wife and kid!"

"He's not! I'm sure he's not! He doesn't wear a wedding ring. He's never said . . ." Rob was clearly flustered. Cam knew infidelity didn't sit well with him for personal reasons, and he'd never knowingly enable it.

"Well, then it had to be a longtime girlfriend — one who *does* wear a wedding ring! The kid was feeding him — fingers in his mouth and he was doing the loud . . . munching thing, nom, nom, nom!" Annie's mimicry would have been comic if she weren't so upset. "That is *not* casual friend behavior!"

Rob sputtered but decided to change topics, in his typical cowardly fashion.

"You had a hard day, too?" he asked Cam.

She'd hardly said a word, but being late was clue enough for the two people who were closest to her to know it couldn't have gone smoothly. Cam was never late.

"They arrested Nick."

Annie dropped her wineglass, sending fragments flying. Cam grabbed paper towels to wipe up the spill and pointed Rob toward the broom. She felt a small sense of relief that Annie was as shaken up by the news as she had been. And maybe a little additional relief that Annie had stepped outside of whatever insanity she was submerged in.

"Why?"

"They didn't say, but I'm pretty sure it was murder. I took Petunia home and got her to bed — she was a wreck."

"I bet — poor girl. Poor Nick." Annie stared around in a daze for a moment and then swore about Jake being stupid as well as a cheater.

Cam walked over to Annie and hugged her, glad for some solidarity on the Nick front, before she picked up a new wineglass and filled it for Annie.

"I think I know why," Rob confessed as he swept the glass into a dustpan.

Cam rounded on him. "Why?"

"Well, a couple things — it looks like

maybe Jean-Jacques was harassing Evangeline."

"Because of the phone call?"

"How'd you know about that?"

"I'm the one who found the phone."

"Oh, right. Though I don't think you were supposed to look," he smirked. "And there's more, but I don't think it's public yet."

"That's not related to Nick, though." Cam responded to the issue of the calls, ignoring the fact she shouldn't have looked for now. She also didn't mention Petunia blaming Evangeline. It seemed premature and biased. She did want to hear the new information, though.

"Apparently . . . Spoons . . . the loan . . . was cosigned by Evangeline Patrick."

"What?" That threw Cam off balance. It was the last thing she'd expected.

"There has to be something big there for her to back him up on a loan that size. Jake didn't tell me how large, but restaurant start-up is huge."

Cam was about to protest, but the buzzer went off, indicating the first batch of brownies was done. Rob excused himself to pull the pan out, sensing Cam's annoyance.

"Did you know there was a connection?" Annie asked. Her face was etched in disgust.

"No."

"That bastard better not have cheated on Petunia!"

"Annie, I don't think there was anybody cheating on anybody. There's an explanation."

"Oh, somebody was cheating on somebody," Annie said. Her dark expression didn't flatter her.

Rob returned in time to hear that and opted once again for the coward's way out, in Cam's opinion.

"Hey, did you know Samantha is Jean-Jacques's aunt?"

Fortunately for Rob, this new tidbit had the desired effect.

"What?" Cam and Annie asked in unison.

"Jake got it from her today."

That was a misstep on Rob's part.

"Jake! What the hell does he know?" Annie drank the contents of her fresh wineglass, rather a lot for one swig.

Cam frowned.

"Why didn't she just say so?"

"They'd had an agreement. I guess . . . he'd borrowed money or something from her when he was first starting out and hadn't paid it back, so she used it to pressure him to come, but she gave him a place to stay and lent him the car. Admitting they were related, though, would have blown that

French artist thing."

Annie tutted, letting them both know she hadn't been fooled.

"I guess now we know why he called her," Cam said.

"Exactly," Rob replied.

"But not what he was doing at the Patricks' so early."

"Jake thinks he was there to pester Evangeline."

"And what does Evangeline say?"

Cam felt newly defensive for Evangeline. She'd shown herself to be helpful and sympathetic earlier that day, and Cam wasn't eager to put her in a negative light.

"Please!" Annie interrupted with as snotty a tone as Cam had ever heard Annie use. "Jake doesn't need to *talk* to Evangeline! He can just stare at her . . . at her . . ."

"Annie, Jake has never been like that, at least not that I've seen," Rob said.

Annie wasn't having any of it. "Like you'd notice." She'd poured another large glass of wine and was drinking it too fast.

Cam looked at Rob helplessly.

"Tell you what, Annie. I'm meeting Jake for a while tomorrow. I have to — for the police investigation," Cam added defensively. "I will find out the scoop, because I'm sure he's not married. He can't possibly be as horrible as he seems right now."

"Bastard probably wouldn't marry her! Even with that cute little boy!"

Cam went over and hugged Annie again, letting Annie cry tears of frustration onto her apron.

"He just seemed like one of the good guys — and I know y'all wouldn't steer me wrong. I was so sure I wouldn't get burned again!"

"Again?"

Annie sniffed. "Oh, geez, I snotted on you. You have to go change aprons or be banished."

Cam eyed Annie. She knew this was avoiding, or at least stalling, but Cam was also pretty repulsed with the snot on her apron, so she went in back to change it. By the time she returned, the third batch of brownies was in and Annie and Rob had both slouched down to the floor, each holding one of the brownies from the first batch.

"Get a brownie," Annie ordered.

"I'll have a few bites of Rob's."

"No you won't. Get your own brownie!" he demanded.

Cam laughed. Rob didn't have much of a sweet tooth, but if he demanded his own, he loved what he was having. She retrieved a brownie and sank down with the two people she loved most, aside from her family.

Rob ate a bite of brownie, then nuzzled Cam's ear.

"Ick! You're getting brownie in my hair!"

"I am not, but so what? I know you'll take a shower first thing when you get home anyway." He sounded amused, which helped. Then he blew it. "Cam, I think you need to get used to the idea Nick might be our guy."

She scowled and used her legs for leverage against the wall. She pressed herself to a standing position and walked away.

"I wouldn't believe it was Nick if you found him with the body in his trunk. I'm that sure." She finally took a bite of heavenly brownie to show her confidence.

"But Cam, the evidence . . . His past conviction, Petunia getting . . . grabbed. The loan from Evangeline and Evangeline being harassed . . ."

"The evidence is really incomplete right now, so I'll thank you to keep that particular opinion to yourself!"

Rob sighed.

"I hate that! Don't you patronize me! I'm right on this! Annie?" Cam was glad Annie seemed to be standing guard with an "I told you so" expression.

"Nick's a good guy, Rob," Annie said, "even if you have to take it on faith."

That wasn't quite as strong an endorsement as Cam had hoped for, given Annie's posture. She looked at Annie more closely.

"Geez, Annie, are you okay?"

"When do I shoot your dad?"

"What?" Rob sputtered, confused, but Cam got it.

"Late morning. I'll have to look."

"Good. I could use a talk with him. He's a good listener," she said. She sounded a little bit drunk. Then, after a pause, "Listen, I need to clean up."

"We can help."

"No, really — dishes and Jane's Addiction will clear my head better than you two or sleep ever could."

Cam was worried, but also not inclined to force herself on Annie when she wanted privacy. And if Annie craved Jane's Addiction, the original "Screamo" band, in Cam's estimation, she'd rather give the space. She'd learned over the years that her friend usually knew when alone time was the answer.

"You ready?" she asked Rob.

He tried to protest, urging her to stay and help Annie, but it didn't take long before he agreed and the two of them left together.

■ ■ ■ ■

Cam was prepared to tear into Rob about his refusal to accept Nick's innocence, but when she got in the Jeep, he offered another tidbit of information that distracted her.

"Print results come back tomorrow."

"Prints?"

"Fingerprints from everybody at the party — so they can match the shears."

Cam grimaced. Somehow being fingerprinted had been humiliating, even though she knew she hadn't done anything wrong.

"That's good," she said, though she knew her tone didn't match her words.

Rob frowned. "Don't you want to know who did this?"

"Of course I do! I just don't want it to be somebody I care about. And for your information, Rob Columbus, there is nothing wrong with that!"

She threw her arms across her chest and stared out the passenger window.

"I didn't say there was."

"Then why are you so determined to pin this on my brother-in-law? Do you have any idea how badly other creeps have treated Petunia? How wonderful Nick is by comparison?"

"No, I had no idea." His tone was sarcastic. "I might have known more, had you bothered to tell me. Though, honestly, I'd be an idiot to know Petunia for three years and not have gotten the same idea."

He was as riled as she was. That hadn't been her goal. She wanted to vent. Now, though, a fight was inevitable, and she couldn't stop herself from diving in.

"It doesn't take much! All you'd have to do is meet the guy!"

"I've met the guy. He has freaking prison wire tattooed around his neck!"

"Physical stuff isn't everything!"

"Says the woman who won't even splurge for a brownie!"

"I ate a brownie."

He stopped the car in the middle of the road. She looked behind the Jeep, panicked, to make sure no one was behind them.

"You ate a third of a brownie. You are five-eight and weigh a hundred and ten, and you can't even finish a brownie."

"I weigh a hundred and seventeen."

"Excuse me while I move you from underweight to nearly healthy!"

Cam was stung. "I thought you liked how I look."

Rob put his hands on his face.

"I do, babe. I love how you look. I just

wish you'd allow yourself some splurges. You deserve them and have plenty of wiggle room. I'm sorry. I just got frustrated."

When he put it that way, it was almost sweet. She was still mad and wrestling with herself. Part of her craved contact — connection with the part of her life that was okay, as much of it seemed to be flying off-kilter, but part of her couldn't let it go.

Cam considered spilling her worries, explaining to Rob that her fears about Petunia losing Nick were causing not only anxiety but guilt, too. She wished she'd never brought Jean-Jacques to Roanoke. She also worried about what had been dredged up about Nick. Even if he was proven innocent and released, it still had come to light that Evangeline cosigned on the Spoons loan. That wouldn't make Petunia happy. And it was now semipublic that Nick was an ex-con — that might be bad for business. Cam just wished she could make things right for her sister, but it looked unlikely.

Normally she would have invited Rob in, but when he started to get out of his Jeep, she stopped him, as much out of irritation with herself as him.

"I'm really tired. I'll see you tomorrow, okay?"

He looked annoyed.

"If this is about you being skinny —"

"No, it's not about that. It's about working from seven in the morning to eleven at night. That's all."

"You sure?"

"Positive."

She leaned in and gave him a very tender kiss.

"Yeah, like that makes me want to leave."

She rolled her eyes and got out, waving as she ran up the steps.

Chapter 9

It was heavenly to sleep until eight the next morning, even though it was only seven hours of sleep. Cam stretched and glanced at the clock at seven fifty-five, pleased she didn't have the jolt of the alarm to ruin the end of her sleep.

On the other hand, Annie, who arrived as Cam finished her makeup, looked like something Davy Jones had dragged in. Davy Jones was a neighborhood stray they fed from time to time, and his taste in gifts left something to be desired.

"Geez, Annie."

"I don't wanna hear it. I need coffee, a drive-through breakfast with some grease, and Excedrin if you've got them."

"You do straight shots or something after we left?" Cam asked as she retrieved ibuprofen from her medicine cabinet.

Annie hid her face in her hands. "Not exactly."

"What did you do?" Cam handed her the bottle, along with the water that had been at her bedside.

"Look, I'd rather not talk about it. We've got a long day ahead, looks like we'll be swimming through it, which is a bonus, so let's just get to it." She popped the tablets, chased them with water, and stood, following Cam out the door.

"Okay by me."

Annie had left part of her equipment in a locked closet at the Patricks', so there was only one load to get into the car. They went through a drive-through and got lattes and a sausage-and-egg biscuit for Annie. Cam, on impulse, and in rebellion of Rob calling her skinny, ordered a ham-and-cheese croissant.

Annie stared in disbelief, but all she said was, "Looks like we're all keeping secrets this morning."

Pulling out of the drive-through, Cam noticed the dark clouds to the west and pointed them out to Annie.

"Good thing outside is mostly done for now, though today is the day with your dad and the wisteria," Annie commented.

"Is it?"

They were at a stoplight, and Annie

turned toward Cam, her eyebrows raised.

"Okay, fat and pork for breakfast, I'll give a pass. Honestly, it's shocking it hasn't happened before now. Maybe Rob wore you out last night. But not knowing the agenda? Who are you and what have you done with my best friend?"

"I guess the pressure is getting to me. I forgot to call yesterday to remind him to come today. You know how he is with a schedule, and he's supposed to help Petunia."

"Well, his interview is today, regardless. Jane would have reminded him. We can always get the pictures later — next weekend or something, if it comes to that."

"I guess that's true. Though I doubt by this point there's anything Jane Duffy doesn't know about him. So the interview may be short." Cam worked hard not to make a face. Her dad's dates were a topic she preferred to avoid.

"They are not going to put that he wears boxers instead of briefs in a gardening magazine."

Cam felt her face redden.

"How do you even know that?"

"Hello! Lifetime best friend? Sidekick at laundry duty? Besides, your dad is far too cool for briefs."

"I don't want to think about that."

"Rob wears briefs, doesn't he?"

"Rob looks *good* in briefs."

"He'd look better without them."

Cam shrieked and threw her napkin at Annie just as the light changed to green.

"What? You saying he doesn't?" Annie asked once she'd crossed through the intersection.

"It's none of your business!"

"Oh! You thought I meant *naked!* Pervert!" Annie managed to keep a straight face.

"You *did* mean naked. I know you too well to claim otherwise."

Annie feigned innocence. "I meant boxers, man panties, a thong, a G-string . . . He'd look better in pretty much anything other than briefs, and certainly better in nothing!" But then Annie broke into laughter across her steering wheel. "Got you! Cam, I didn't know you did jealousy!"

Cam felt a little indignant at first, until she realized there was some truth there.

"He's a briefs man, and a briefs man he'll remain."

"Your loss." Annie shrugged, as if she didn't care one way or the other.

Moments later, they pulled into the Patricks' driveway. Cam got out and walked to the trunk, waiting for Annie to pop it open.

■ ■ ■ ■

As planned, they met the *Garden Delights* crew in greenhouse number one, "Winter."

"Should be able to work with the lighting coming in, too," Tom observed. "Looks a lot *like* winter."

Ian hadn't shown up, even knowing there was a deadline. With the current photographer, he was more a hindrance anyway, but Cam couldn't hold her tongue.

"Where's Ian?"

"Off acting strangely," Hannah blurted, then, at a glance from Tom, she looked at the ground and pretended she hadn't spoken. Cam thought now wasn't the time to probe, but she filed it away in her head.

Annie and Tom got straight to work, so Cam went back to the house, hoping to find her dad. She was sure she'd hear about any problems later.

Her father wasn't there yet, so she took our her phone and dialed his cell number.

"Daddy?"

"Well hello, sunshine! I was just heading out."

"For here?"

"Well, no. You said eleven."

"There's a storm coming in. Any chance

it could be sooner?"

"I guess we could get it to go."

"We?" Though she knew. He had obviously been about to step out to breakfast with Jane Duffy. She pretended it was late enough for him to have slept at home the night before and returned in the morning for the shared meal at Jane's hotel.

"Oh, I'm sure you already ate, sweetheart," her dad said, being intentionally obtuse.

"Right. To go would be good. You haven't talked to Petunia, have you?"

"Petunia?"

"Helping out. Remember?"

"Oh! Yes! I talked to Petunia. She said she could handle it and to come after my interview and pictures."

That made Cam feel guilty, that her magazine shoot was why Petunia didn't have help, so she signed off with her dad and called Spoons.

"Is Petunia there?" she asked the girl who picked up on the third ring.

"She is, but she's swamped. Can I take a message?"

"Tell her Cam will come there to help with lunch, organizing, delivering — that stuff."

"She'll appreciate that," the girl said. Cam

thought it was the twenty-five year-old who snapped her gum a lot, but at least Petunia was at work and had help. She hung up a little regretfully.

"Everything okay?" Hannah asked when Cam rejoined the crew.

"Yeah, my dad should be here in half an hour." Cam looked out at the wall of clouds heading toward them.

" 'Kay," Annie mumbled. She'd heard Cam's report, even though Cam hadn't realized she was paying attention. Annie then finished a series of shots and looked up. "Timing works. We should be done with 'Winter' by then — not as much here as in the other ones."

Cam nodded. "I'm going to go make sure everything is set up at the wisteria, okay?"

Annie shrugged as if she didn't care, but Cam knew better. Her friend wasn't having a good day. There was no comfort she could offer in front of the others, though, except to give Annie their nearly forgotten secret handshake as she left.

Annie finally grinned a little. "Thanks. I needed that."

Cam made her way back to the house, assessing the approaching weather front as she went. She figured they had somewhere between thirty and ninety minutes to be done before a downpour hit.

She found Ian standing on the patio like a lump, assessing the storm as she'd just been.

"Come here. We may only have a half hour, and my dad is on his way. What is the 'can't miss' shot?" Being diplomatic was hard, but she thought she'd better try.

"Like she'll listen to you. She won't even listen to me."

"She doesn't *like* you, with good reason, I might add. She'll listen to me." It seemed pretty dense of him to think anyone would listen to an arrogant jerk over a best friend, but she doubted Ian had any friends.

He didn't look at her, just walked ahead of her toward the wisteria.

"The lighting makes that purple way cool."

Cam felt annoyed she'd just thought the same thing, only with better vocabulary — storms could provide very impressive lighting. The sun was still relatively low, and so the yellow tones of its morning rays reflected brightly off the underside of the clouds.

Ian spent a few minutes explaining what he'd found so aesthetically pleasing about the wisteria and trellis, but then suddenly shut up at the sight of a fast-approaching Annie.

"Is he here?"

Annie asked as she arrived, trailed by the equipment-encumbered crew.

"Any minute now. Why don't you set up?" Cam said.

Annie nodded, ignoring Ian entirely, and within moments Cam heard, "I'm here."

Cam turned toward the house to see her father walking their way. "Daddy! Wonderful. Come on over here."

Cam led her dad to the spot Annie seemed to be aiming at.

"Now listen to Annie."

"Do I have to?" He chuckled.

Cam rolled her eyes. He always laughed at his own jokes.

"Okay, Mr. Harris, dance like I like," Annie said. She looked through her lens.

Mr. Harris started singing a really bad rendition of "Walk Like an Egyptian" and moving strangely.

"There you go, baby," Annie said.

Cam broke into hysterics, as did Jane Duffy, who'd just joined them. The rest of the *Garden Delights* crew looked thoroughly confused.

Without changing tone, Annie directed Mr. Harris. He fell back to lean against what showed of the trellis, a content pose, arms crossed in front of him and a satisfied smile on his face.

Cam could have sworn she heard Annie whisper, "Smile like you just got lucky," but she tried to ignore those kinds of interactions. Jane started giggling next to her, which was embarrassing, as Jane must have interpreted it the same way Cam had — but with pleasure rather than discomfort.

After a dozen pictures, Cam got hit with her first large raindrop. Annie effortlessly put an umbrella over her tripod — it seemed to be a part of the contraption, and she kept shooting.

"I'm drowning, Annie," Mr. Harris said.

"No you're not. This is good."

And then the downpour hit.

All of them were instantly soaked, and Annie cackled madly.

"Perfect!"

Cam's dad stood, arms out in a confused pose, laughing rather helplessly. Cam noticed the yellow sunlight was still strangely coming through from the east, even as the storm from the west drenched them.

"Okay, it's a wrap!" Annie yelled over the now-pattering downpour.

Cam ran to help Annie, who had Cam hold the umbrella while she got her things stowed, and then they made a dash for the covered patio to shake off the excess water.

When they finally got inside onto the

sandstone tiles that covered the lowest level of the house, they found Evangeline and Jake sitting at a ninety-degree angle to one another, coffee cups in hand, snacks placed between them on the coffee table. They chatted amicably, which contrasted the chaos entering the room. Evangeline jumped up to fetch towels.

"Annie!" Jake looked surprised.

"Don't Annie me, you —"

"Sorry I couldn't make it for brownies. I really am! Did you —"

"Save it, you lowlife creep!"

Annie came toward Jake, hands on her hips, menace in her voice.

"Watch out. You're almost to the crowbar part," Ian growled.

Cam hadn't noticed him enter behind them and turned to stare, but Annie ignored him.

"You two-timing *married* son-of-a —"

"What? I'm not . . . But you —"

"I saw you! Your little family is very sweet, but don't you dare —"

"But they're —"

"Can it!"

Annie stormed away, and Cam stood, stunned. She wanted to follow her best friend, but at the moment, professionalism contraindicated it.

"I suppose that might have gone better," she said.

After Annie left, Evangeline returned with towels and passed them out. Cam stared at Jake, remembering her own issues with the man, but Ian interrupted her thoughts.

"I knew that nut-job would crack, after what she did to my brother . . . well . . . his car, really."

Cam finally took stock of who was present and realized Joesph and Samantha had just arrived — they seemed to spend a lot of time at the Patricks' — in addition to the *Garden Delights* crew and her father.

She looked carefully at her dad and noticed his somewhat guilty expression. She suspected he knew something. This wasn't the time to get into it, but she was too curious not to try for the short version in whispered tones.

"I can't believe he'd be so awful!"

"He's just acting on the wrong set of facts."

"And what set of facts are those, Daddy?" Cam looked at him intently.

"I'm sorry, sunshine. Those aren't my secrets to tell. You ask Annie."

That wasn't what Cam wanted to hear, and she frowned. She didn't want Annie to reveal her dad's secrets — that would be embarrassing. But she'd never considered her dad knew secrets about Annie that she didn't.

Jake and Evangeline seemed to be done, so Cam approached, ready to give Jake a piece of her mind, but he headed her off with a question.

"Why didn't you tell me Annie had a record?"

"What?"

"I woke up this morning to a pile of garbage on my porch — baking garbage — so I looked. Annie has a record."

"What kind of record?"

"Vandalism — she smashed some guy's car windshield. That's probably what Ian was talking about."

Cam stared, not processing for a moment. It had nothing to do with the Annie she knew, even if it fit with what Ian had said.

"I think that's the wrong Annie."

"I don't think so. She's not as stable as she seems."

"Says the married guy who wanted to date her!" Cam spat.

"You saying you believe that? I'm not!"

"Serious girlfriend, then."

"No, she's my —"

"Save it! I'm done unless this questioning

is official!" Cam shouted, feeling rather content to stomp away in spite of the stares.

She found her dad at the edge of the room again. He hugged her.

"You know, there is a truth in the middle somewhere," he said.

"So tell me."

"I can't. Annie needs to talk to you."

"Then can you drop me off to help Petunia this afternoon?"

"Petunia? That's right. I'm on my way there, too!"

"I'd really rather I did lunch and you could help her this afternoon to prepare for dinner."

"Well, sure. Whatever helps."

She took his arm and steered him out to his car. They sprinted through the rain, and then she spouted her worries as he drove.

Chapter 10

Cam breathed a sigh of relief. Who would have ever thought sitting in the passenger seat while her father drove and she unloaded would be an improvement over . . . well . . . anything? But at least he was relatively calm. He nodded a lot and made pained faces. But he didn't blow up or blame Nick. She knew not all in-laws were so cool.

"I'm heading back out to La Fontaine later — I promised to pick up Jane and take her back to her hotel this afternoon. Do you want me to take you back around three?" he asked. The change of subject was unexpected but also seemed appropriate. Who knew her dad was good in a crisis?

"That would be good. We have lunch to deliver there, but if I could help Petunia with all her lunch deliveries, I'd feel better."

"And then I'll be at Spoons by four to help with dinner, right after I drop off Jane at the hotel . . . You know, this isn't your fault, sunshine."

"Daddy?" She felt her voice ready to crack and knew her father heard it.

"What is it, honey?"

"Have you heard the stuff about Nick? His record, I mean?"

"Not the whole story, and I'm not going to judge him on the little I do know. I don't think we should decide anything until we hear everything. They only have half a story about Annie, and look how that looks."

They had just pulled up in front of Spoons, and Cam's eyes stung, but this time it was in admiration for her father.

"You're the best man on earth, you know that?" she said as she climbed out of the car.

He laughed.

"After the supper tonight, will you come back to my place?" she asked, speaking through the open passenger-side window. "I think Annie might be more willing to talk if you're there."

"Of course I will. I'll see you at ten of three, okay?"

"Perfect. Daddy?" Her dad looked back expectantly. "I'm serious. You're the best."

He made an "aw, shucks" sort of gesture and swiped his hand in front of him, and then he put the car in drive and pulled away.

■ ■ ■ ■

Petunia started barking orders at Cam the minute she entered, but it was nice to be so busy she didn't have time to think. Chop mushrooms. Toss salad. Strain pasta. Help transfer food.

It was almost an hour before they were in the van, but Cam only knew it because of her watch. Time had flown. She was glad Petunia had the distraction.

They had three lunches to deliver: a small one for an office party that the two of them managed in one trip using the rolling cart Petunia had, then the Garden Society, and finally a sack lunch for a group day retreat.

The office delivery went smoothly. The meeting was still in session, so the receptionist helped transfer things to her own cart and then waved them away.

The Garden Society, however, was another matter. Petunia seemed completely offended this group had somehow gotten her husband thrown in prison, so she wouldn't say a word.

Cam helped with the first load but then felt a need to check in with her employers. Mr. Patrick was deep in conversation with Joseph Sadler-Neff at one of the covered patio tables, so Cam waited behind Joseph, hoping for a break in the conversation.

". . . if he'd only signed off — then I could have done that full-time, instead of having to maintain the librarian spot, too. You know, it's really his fault it failed."

As Joseph finished, Mr. Patrick looked up and spotted Cam hovering nearby. "Cammi! What a pleasant surprise!"

Cam could tell Mr. Patrick wished she had not heard them, not that she could make heads or tails of why the conversation was so sensitive, except that it sounded like Joseph had a bruised ego.

"Mr. Patrick, I'm helping my sister, Petunia, just through lunch, so I'll be back at three. How are things here?"

"Fine as far as I know."

"Do you know where the camera crew is?"

"In the summer greenhouse, I think. A lot to do in there, and Evangeline wanted to pose by the ashoka tree."

Cam bit the inside of her cheek to keep from grimacing. "Could you maybe encourage her to also pose by a native plant?" she asked, knowing the request was useless.

He smiled, but Cam was sure he had no intention of disappointing his wife.

"Ah! Sustenance!"

Cam turned to see the camera crew coming toward them, taking advantage of a break in the rain and led by Tom, whose proclamation made it sound like he was starving. Hannah accompanied him, always eager for his company.

A hundred feet behind them Annie and Ian were arguing worse than ever.

"I'm just saying, I have you pegged for the killer! You're unstable."

"I wouldn't hurt a flea! Not that it's any of your business."

"Oh no? Well, you seem to be awfully good friends with a crowbar."

They stopped, realizing the patio was populated. Cam was thoroughly annoyed to see that Ian looked pleased with himself. What she wasn't prepared for was a defense from a totally unexpected front. Samantha had just come outside and stormed over to Ian.

"You have no idea who you're talking to! I'll have you know Annie is the daughter of a former senator, and you are way out of line!"

Cam sighed. She felt like she should stay, but Petunia had started tapping her foot expectantly.

"I'll see you at three," she said on her way out, but she was pretty sure nobody heard.

■ ■ ■ ■

The next delivery was easier but took more time, as they had a hundred sack lunches to deliver to a seminar, so even with the cart, it took three loads, with a fair amount of shuffling at either end.

When they were done, Petunia asked if she could go home to shower.

"That's great. Daddy can pick me up there. Would you mind if we picked up the pans for tonight on the way?"

Petunia rolled her eyes, but they headed to Spoons without an additional lecture. Cam helped load the pans into Petunia's van, and they headed to Nick and Petunia's condo. Nick and Petunia had it on a rent-to-buy lease, and it was decent, as condos went, though Cam never wanted to own something with so little yard. She couldn't imagine containing her gardening in a ten-by-twenty lot.

They left the pans in the van, figuring it was easiest to move them straight to her dad's Camry when he arrived. Petunia headed into the condo for her shower, and Cam followed. As she entered the living room, she instantly saw signs of distress.

Petunia, while not necessarily obsessively

clean, as some accused Cam of being, was still usually tidy. Cam could see, however, there were dishes in the sink, socks on the floor, mail on the table, untouched, and a box of mementos strewn across the sofa and coffee table.

Two CDs for a band called the One-Eyed-Jacks. Concert tickets where the One-Eyed-Jacks were opening for bigger-named bands. Publicity photos of a trio, all with eye patches — two men and one woman.

She picked up a photo and looked more closely.

It was before the barbed-wire neck tattoo and he looked about thirty pounds lighter, but she was sure one of the "Jacks" was Nick. She knew Nick had been in a punk band that had recorded a CD or two and sold concert tickets — granted, they were not the headliners, but still. This must be that band.

She picked up the CD and put it in Petunia's player, then sat back down to examine the jacket. It wasn't Cam's style, but not bad. A woman was on vocals, and she sounded oddly familiar. Cam wondered if she'd gone on to a more mainstream band. Cam took the insert out of the jewel case and looked at it more closely.

The woman in the pictures had the wrong

hair color and entirely wrong style, but paired with her voice, Cam finally identified her. Evangeline had been in Nick's band — that was why she had called him Jack. He might have even gone by Jack back then.

Her heart thumped; she looked more closely at the third person in the band. He was lankier than Nick, but cockier, too, as if it were all a big laugh.

The album credits identified them as Jack, Jack, and Jackie, expanding in parentheses that they were Jonathan Jacobs, Jonathan Nicholas, and Jackie Evans.

Jonathan Jacobs . . . Jean-Jacques. She looked again with the new insight and felt sure that was who the third musician was. Cam had a lot of questions for a lot of people, but the first had to do with how much her sister knew, and for how long.

Petunia didn't look any more relaxed coming out of the shower than she had going in. But Cam's frustration at all the secrets had reached a fever pitch, so she fired away anyway.

"So *this* is your problem with Evangeline?"

Petunia gave her a tired look and went to put a pot of water on the stove for tea.

"And Nick was in a *band* with Jean-Jacques?"

"I didn't know that until after that first party, when Nick told me. Neither of us knew he'd be there. Nick thought he'd never see him again. The name Jean-Jacques didn't ring any bells."

"But you knew Nick's connection to Evangeline?"

"She let him crash with her when he first got out of prison, and that's when I met him, so sure. They were old friends. I don't have to like it."

"You're missing the point. I don't care if you liked it. I care that I asked you your issue with Evangeline and you gave me vague nonsense. I don't like you lying to me."

Petunia rolled her eyes, which annoyed Cam, because she recognized her own eye roll in it and hated evidence she had an annoying gesture.

"So before this week, when was the last time Nick talked to these guys?"

"Evangeline, maybe when we moved in together? Jean-Jacques was before jail. It's not fair they have to ruin his life again!" Petunia, Cam noted, either didn't know about the cosigned loan or was still lying to her.

Petunia broke into tears, and Cam wasn't sure how to respond. She was mad, but she also recognized her sister's distress and was hard-pressed not to respond to that.

" 'Tunia, what is it?"

"That horse's ass got Nick sent to prison in the first place, but that makes Nick look guilty, and he isn't! I swear this is Evangeline finishing the job! Please find proof, Cam. Please!"

"How? I mean . . . what did he do?"

"I don't know. Nick didn't want to talk about it. He's always protecting me."

"I'll find the truth, 'Tunia. I know it wasn't Nick, and I'll figure out who it was."

Cam knew the truth of Nick's protectiveness. She held her sister for a long time, trying to assuage fears that wouldn't go away. Petunia wasn't happy Cam wouldn't commit to pursuing Evangeline. For Cam's part, she agreed at least with part of Petunia's argument. She thought it looked bad for Nick, when Nick wasn't the one who had done anything.

"I'll make sure they don't quit looking, okay?"

Petunia sniffed. "Thank you."

When her dad picked her up to return to the Patricks', Cam was busy brainstorming who might have really done it — sure, Nick's past made him look suspicious, even without the police knowing Jean-Jacques got

Nick sent to prison. But Samantha was a potential suspect, too. She may have been Jean-Jacques's aunt, but clearly there was tension. Evangeline was another possibility, when Cam thought about it. Her presence on that CD with Nick posed several new questions and increased how entangled in this riddle she probably was, even if she hadn't been on Jean-Jacques's call list.

And then Ian was trying to pin everything on Annie. Annie couldn't have done it any more than Nick. Cam kept coming back to the question of why Ian would want to make someone look guilty at all. Maybe Ian was the person with something to hide. Hannah had said he was acting strangely.

Targeting Ian for investigation wasn't necessarily the most logical choice, but it was definitely the most appealing, so Cam decided to devote her afternoon to that option. Ian had been on location, he'd argued with Jean-Jacques, and he was the worst kind of jerk. It would be a pleasure to pin a murder on him.

"You look like you feel better, sunshine."

"Maybe. I think I have a suspect besides Nick."

"Well that would be good. Care to share?"

"Not just yet. I have some questions to

ask, but it seems like a good fit." She ignored the part of her that knew she was trying to trick herself into this.

"Well, that makes me happy, too."

She smiled. Whatever mischief her dad caused was always unintentional. His heart was in the right place.

"We're still on with Annie tonight, right?" she asked.

"Of course we are. If Jane wants a night-cap, she'll just have to wait for me."

"And you're worth waiting for."

"So are you, sunshine. So are you."

Chapter 11

Mr. Harris helped Cam unload the first round of dishes they would need for supper, but then seemed distressed about time, so Cam sent him off to find Jane Duffy. He needed to deliver her to her hotel before he helped Petunia.

The purple sky had again begun depositing large raindrops over everything, but this round was cooler. The summer heat had come early this year, so the cooler air was welcome. She ran into Mr. Patrick as she deposited the last of the warming trays in the kitchen.

"Mr. Patrick, since we're inside tonight, where would be best to set up for supper?"

"Oh, let's do it up in the drawing room. The view of the storm ought to be grand!"

Cam couldn't help smiling. She loved the show of a thunderstorm, too, and an enthusiastic little old man was darned cute. Dragging pans, trays, and food up the stairs would be worth it, though she'd have to figure out a special favor for Rob, who would be stuck helping her. He would be picking up all the food after work, which was no small task.

"Do you know where the magazine crew is?"

"I think they're back at greenhouse three. Joseph said they were there a while ago, and that your friend Annie was upset because they'd neglected to tell her about several things."

"They . . . meaning Ian?"

Mr. Patrick looked uncomfortable. "Joseph might have mentioned her yelling at Ian. She thought he skipped telling her on purpose, or that was what Joseph overheard at lunch — after you left again." His expression tried for baffled disbelief, but he overdid it. Cam thought he wasn't actually surprised.

"Knowing Ian, he did."

"Is he a problem?" Mr. Patrick looked startled — again, not quite believable. Cam could only pretend she believed him, and acted as if he were sincere.

"He seems to resent Annie. We're almost done, though, and the pictures I've seen so far have been amazing."

"Well that's good. Not a total loss."

"Not at all. When the feature comes out, the trouble will be in the past, and all this will be great publicity."

"Oh, I trust you on publicity, Cammi. You're very good at that!"

Cam stopped midcringe and smiled, trying to clear the phoniness out of it. "Thank you, Mr. Patrick."

There was only an hour left before the photography work for the day would be officially done, and another hour after that before supper would arrive and it would be time for Cam to take over, so for now she decided to find the crew.

She asked Giselle for an umbrella and was shown to a large supply of them. Since she'd be in the same clothes all evening, she chose one that seemed excessive — a golf umbrella, if she put a name on it. It was in the maroon and orange of Virginia Tech, and it kept all but her ankles dry as she made her way to greenhouse three, "Summer."

Once the door was closed behind her, shutting out the elements, she could hear the fussing. She also started sweating, as the building was kept at about eighty-four degrees and a sprinkler system misted everything four times a day, a detail she'd just pulled into her press packets. Between the rain and the greenhouse, everything felt unpleasantly moist.

She set the umbrella against the wall, breathed deeply, and then made her way toward the shouting.

"Are you two still at it?" she asked once within earshot of the crew.

Annie turned and shook her head, conveying a "not my fault" message Cam was familiar with. Unfortunately, it was a gesture that often went with an action that actually was Annie's fault. Annie's issues with rules meant she had often challenged them, so what she *really* meant by "not my fault" was "only did it because it had to be done." Cam suspected somehow, similar rules applied here.

She nodded and moved on. "I wondered if I could borrow Hannah for a little bit."

"Are you sure Ian wouldn't be more helpful?" Annie said, eyebrows raised, a phony smile pasted.

Cam found it hard not to laugh but was sure it was even harder for Annie not to laugh at her response.

"Positive." She nodded again, this time with her straightest possible face.

Hannah looked to Tom, who nodded, then Annie and Tom got back to work while Ian scowled and criticized in the periphery.

Cam headed back out, sharing her large umbrella with Hannah as they braved their way back to the house.

The current downpour was intense enough that Hannah didn't talk, but when they were under cover of the porch she asked, "So what are we doing?"

Cam tried to think of a good cover story, but failing that, decided to take the straightforward route. "I have some questions. I thought maybe if you helped me set up for supper, I could ask them."

"You're questioning me?"

"Not exactly . . . okay, sort of . . . but only because I think, of your group, you are the observant, reliable one."

Hannah nodded. "I suppose that's true. I mean . . . Tom's reliable, but he doesn't notice much, other than visual stuff — then he notices a lot." Hannah looked uncomfortable at first, as if she'd betrayed Tom, but then appeared content with the assessment. Cam remembered her own twenty-two-year-old self and thought Hannah was proud at being thought reliable but nervous about what it might mean.

"So what did the police ask, since it wasn't about the body?" Hannah's confused expression caused Cam to elaborate. "When they were investigating the murder."

"Where we were?"

In spite of the questioning tone, Cam smiled and went on. "And y'all were sleeping?"

"Of course we were."

"Which is hard to prove."

"Well . . ."

"What?"

"Not for Tom and me. We were . . ." She blushed deeply.

"Together? Hannah, no shame in that. I can tell the two of you care about each other."

"You can?"

"Of course I can." It was more obvious from Hannah than Tom, but there was no reason to get technical.

Hannah seemed to relax. "So anyway, I know he didn't leave, and he knows I didn't."

"But neither of you knows about Ian?"

"Well . . . not specifically. He wasn't with us, of course. But we didn't hear anything."

"And would you say you were . . . real tired or sleeping lightly?"

Hannah fidgeted a moment, as if struggling for the right answer. Finally she said,

"I suppose by nearly morning, totally zonked."

"Okay." Cam pretended that settled it,

though she marked it in her mind as evidence of innocence for two, but not the third — not by any means, especially if the two had been up most of the night in extracurricular activities. They were probably down for the count. "And this morning . . . what did you mean about Ian acting strange?"

"I didn't . . . I mean . . . I think it's because of Annie. He's just really jumpy."

Ian made both Annie and her irritable, so it was fair they returned the favor; still, she hoped his jumpy behavior was evidence of guilt and that she'd find more of it. She went on to ask a little about each of the *Garden Delights* team.

Hannah had worked with Tom from the start, about nine months, but she hadn't known Ian for long, and had never traveled with him, so she couldn't say whether his current behavior was normal for him.

"It's not very professional. He wouldn't have a respected position at a prestigious magazine if he flew off the handle so easily all the time."

Cam internally agreed, though she was not above thinking Ian might just be a jerk who normally hid it better. "That first night at the party — when Jean-Jacques and Ian argued — do you have any idea what that might have been about?"

"Just a clash of egos as far as anything we saw. Tom asked Ian later and he claimed he'd never met the guy before, so it wasn't some old argument."

Rob came through the house then, dripping slightly.

"Cam, how do you want me to get the food in without drowning it?"

"I'll ask Mr. Patrick if maybe you can pull into the garage."

He gave a thumbs-up and left, assuming it would be handled, so Cam pointed out to Hannah which tables would need to be cleared for the food, then excused herself to find one of the Patricks.

She found Evangeline first, and Evangeline happily opened the middle bay of the garage. It was a newer addition tastefully added to the side of the house, so it didn't draw from the historic ambiance. All the bays held cars, but the middle car was a sports car, small enough that it allowed Rob to back most of the way in behind it, though the nose of the Jeep was still being pummeled by rain.

Cam and Rob unloaded the takeout onto a cart Evangeline had parked just inside the house. Cam decided it was time to brave her theory.

"You've heard Ian is saying Annie did this?"

Rob looked grim. "Jake is barking up that tree, too, at the moment."

"You're kidding! Just because he's a two-timing —"

"He's not — it was his sister and nephew who Annie saw him with, and Annie's reaction was pretty darned bizarre . . . dumping garbage at his house?"

"One bag," Cam said defensively, though she knew he was right. It was a strange thing to do.

Sister. That made sense, actually. And it also made Annie look pretty bad, even if the damage wasn't permanent. She clearly hadn't let Jake explain.

"You're sure?"

"That it's his sister? He showed me a picture from when they were kids. I believe him."

"But now he thinks Annie —"

"Is a nut. Look, I won't let him go that route for long, because I know Annie. She went off half-cocked — a temporary nut, not a permanent nut. I get it. So he wants to think about it for a while. Seems fair, but I'll pull him back."

She loved him for that. An earlier boyfriend had been jealous of all her friends, but Rob really liked Annie. His loyalty was important.

"Why didn't you major in psychology?"

"I minored in it, in case you forgot."

"Right."

She had forgotten his minor, and almost forgotten her point, but as they finally moved the loaded cart inside, she remembered.

"Anyway, I think Ian is trying so hard to make it look like Annie did it, because it's really him. He's been acting suspicious." It was an exaggeration, but she felt it was warranted.

"Hey, I've got something else." Rob got closer and dropped his voice to a whisper. "You might like this, too — not as well as Ian as killer, but at least it isn't Nick or Annie."

Cam raised an eyebrow. This sounded like it might be a good news, bad news thing. "What?"

"Jake got a copy of Jean-Jacques's financial stuff — he was supposed to inherit a bunch of money — hadn't come yet, but listen, the executor on the money is Samantha."

"Samantha already has a bunch of money — she wouldn't kill him over money."

"Cam, having money isn't an indication somebody doesn't want more — or maybe she just felt he didn't deserve it."

"Samantha isn't like that — she's not judgmental like that."

"Think about Jean-Jacques."

"He was her family! She wouldn't kill her family for something petty like that."

"Fine, we're back to Nick then."

"We are not back to Nick!" Cam felt her face grow hot. Part of her regretted asking Rob to come.

"Do you two need any help?" The interruption startled Cam, and she nearly ran into a wall with the cart. She hadn't noticed until now how much their voices had risen.

Joseph stood in front of them expectantly. She hoped he hadn't heard the specifics of their conversation; she did not care so much if he'd heard her accusations about Ian, but the whispers against Samantha were another story. That would be bad. Samantha would learn of it, and Cam hated that thought.

"Oh, no thank you — we have it," she said.

"Rob, would you like a drink when you're done? Neil asked me to host the early arrivals, as he's still getting ready."

"I'd love a beer, if it's no trouble."

"A beer it is. I will bring it up to the drawing room."

Rob looked at Cam, wide-eyed. She shrugged, trying to convince herself it didn't matter, and at the moment, she was more annoyed at Rob than worried about what Joseph might have overheard. Besides, there was no helping it now — hopefully he wouldn't tell anyone, but if he did, he did.

"I didn't see the brownies," Cam pointed out as Joseph left them in the corridor.

"Brownies! They're in the passenger seat."

"Conveniently in reach of the driver's seat?"

He ignored her teasing, probably because her tone was a bit cold after his Nick comments. "I'll come back down for them."

As Cam and Rob struggled to get the cart up the steps, Cam cursed herself for not accepting Joseph's offer of help, but it was all done in five minutes, and there were no mishaps.

She and Hannah got the food loaded into the warming trays, and then Cam went back downstairs to go over details of the evening with Evangeline. Evangeline had written an agenda because the evening seemed so filled with potential land mines. As they were going over the schedule, Annie entered the lower-level door dripping from the rain. She looked at Cam apologetically.

"The others have gone to the guesthouse — we're done with all but the people shots, but . . ."

"Oh dear, come here."

Evangeline took pity on Annie and rushed over, wrapped a large beach towel around her, and then pulled her up the stairs, suggesting a hot shower. She urged Cam to follow. "Let's find her something dry to wear," she said.

"I need my equipment, too," Annie said as Evangeline pushed her toward the bathroom.

"Oh, honey, you don't need to go back out there. I'll send Giselle over with a covered cart. She gets to go home soon, anyway, so she won't mind."

"You're a lifesaver."

Cam wasn't sure what the statuesque Evangeline would have to fit Annie, who was at least seven inches shorter. She gave Evangeline a few hints at Annie's style, then headed back to greet guests, hoping Evangeline and Annie could work it out. As she stood and waited, she decided to call Jake with her theory about Ian as Jean-Jacques's murderer.

"That's pretty far-fetched, Cam," he responded once she'd finished giving all the details.

"Maybe, but Ian and Jean-Jacques argued from the first time they ever set eyes on each other, according to their claims. Why would that be?"

"They're lying about knowing each other. But Ian and Annie argued, too. They might also know each other and Annie's lying about it."

"Annie wouldn't lie to me like that."

Jake paused, having trouble being patient. "I'm just saying, by your definition it sounds like Annie and Ian actually have a connection, too, even though they haven't met before. If you believe that, I mean."

"And what connection could they have? He's got her confused with another girl." She ignored the information about Paul, hoping she could will it not to be true.

"This is a murder investigation. I can't tell you that. Ask Annie if you're so curious. You leave the investigation to the professionals, though, okay?"

Cam fumed. She hated being patronized more than anything, but a close second was being told what to do. The two together made her blood boil. She hung up on Jake with a growl.

"Sounds bad. What happened?"

Evangeline had just come out of the kitchen with a bottle of wine and a tray of evenly filled glasses. She held up the tray in offering, and Cam nodded gratefully. She took one of the glasses and followed Evangeline down the hall.

"I've got some ideas about the murder and Jake won't listen, but I can't know if they mean anything unless . . . look, can I ask you some questions? I mean . . . I don't want to offend you . . ."

Evangeline set the tray on a table in the entryway and helped herself to a glass of wine, too.

"Peach. Should go well with the barbeque," she said. After she'd taken a sip, she looked at Cam again. "Fire away. My life is mostly an open book anyway."

"They're trying to pin this murder on Nick."

"Nick? You mean Jack? Your brother-in-law?" She looked and sounded disgusted, which was encouraging.

"I noticed that."

"Okay, that's a good starting place. Why do you call him Jack?"

"Because when I knew him, we were all Jack." She sighed heavily and sat on a bench, sipping her wine again. "It was me being too clever, I suppose. I am Evangeline Jacqueline. Jean-Jacques was Jonathan Jacobs, and Nick was Jonathan Nicholas. We had 'Jack' in common. It was brilliant marketing, especially with the eye patches

— we might have made it if we were just a little better."

"So that *was* you in the punk band?"

Evangeline took a large drink and went on. "I grew up in pageants — every step watched, every word recorded — always proper. I went to an Ivy League college, still watched, and even more paranoid, as it was a lot more blue bloods, so I worried I didn't quite fit in. Daddy was new money and not a ton of it at that. When I finished college, I went a little nuts — dye job, alias, an old friend who knew how to live rough . . ."

"Old friend?"

"Jack the first — Jean-Jacques — or Johnnie, as I knew him. My parents lived around the corner from Samantha, and he and his sister used to stay summers with her. I think Samantha hoped I'd be a good influence, but instead he was the bad one."

"So you knew him for . . . years? Did you tell the police?"

"Of course I did."

"And then what about Nick?"

"Fluke, really. We were still up north. Johnnie and I wanted to start a band. I sang, he played drums. We needed a guitarist. We searched clubs in Jersey listening for what we wanted. We heard Nick at a club, outclassing his bandmates by a long shot, and invited him to join us. He was ready for a change of scene, so he did."

Giselle came through with the cart. "Where to with this, ma'am?" A tarp had clearly been removed from the equipment, but Giselle still dripped on the sandstone.

Cam reluctantly rose to help move Annie's equipment. It was part of her job. "I'll help you get it up on the landing where Annie has access to all of it," she said. "Evangeline, I'll be right back, okay?"

Unfortunately, she was still moving things when guests began to arrive, and Cam and Evangeline took it in shifts to lead them upstairs. Rob had done his best talking to Joseph, as he could tell Cam and Evangeline were busy, but with the influx of guests he couldn't keep it up. To say Joseph was no help with the crowd was an understatement, so after a handful of people had arrived, Cam joined Rob in the drawing room to help get the guests situated.

Annie came down from the third floor, stunning in a royal blue dress of Evangeline's that was probably very short on their hostess, but came to midthigh on Annie and looked fabulous. Annie's blue eyes popped more than normal, which was saying something.

"You look pretty hot," Cam said, ignoring Annie's glare. "I hate to suggest this, when you've worked for forty-eight hours straight, but this might be the best time to get people shots. Your stuff is all on the landing."

"Ack! All of it? Can you help me put some of it where nobody will be tempted to play with it? Happy, though, to shoot these people. Photographing them is definitely preferable to talking to them," Annie mumbled. "Besides," she said more loudly, "I am all over anything that makes tomorrow less work."

Cam helped her stow the extra supplies in the den below, which was not being used. It was true Annie looked much more at home with a camera in her hand, and Cam breathed a sigh of relief as the party began in earnest. Everyone seemed to be having fun — everyone other than Ian, anyway.

CHAPTER 12

Ian's expression was more sour than ever when he arrived with Hannah and Tom.

"Smile," Annie said, shooting their picture, then letting out a quiet cackle that only Cam heard.

Cam raised an eyebrow at Annie, but humor was a better way to handle this than some of the other options Annie had probably considered, so she left it alone after that.

They only socialized briefly before Cam and Evangeline encouraged everyone to fill their plates. They had bibs for everyone, so some laughter ensued about bibs complementing semiformal clothing. Annie caught a lot of laughter on film, which had been the primary goal when Cam and Evangeline had debated the messy, traditional Southern options.

It was all going better than Cam had expected up until shouting called everyone's attention to one corner of the room.

Tom and Hannah looked posed for a photo, leaning together, faces touching, but their expressions were frozen in clownish horror. Their smiles stuck, as if trying to call the moment back. Ian had stood and encroached on Annie's space — something Annie didn't tolerate from bullies, so she held her flash up and began a slow strobe in Ian's face.

"Back off!" Her voice was low but unmistakable.

"Geez! Will you stop it?"

"Not until you back off! I am just doing my job, and I don't need you in my face!"

"You don't need shots of these two."

"The magazine may not. But maybe Cam does to publicize this lovely event." She smiled her most saccharine smile. Cam cringed.

"You're a psychopath — a woman who bashes in windshields with crowbars, and I'm convinced you killed Jean-Jacques because he rejected you! You thought it was time to up the ante!"

Cam had made her way over, but Jane Duffy beat her to it; her low growl didn't carry, but it still had the authority of a mama bear.

"You go cool off! If you can't be professional, I'll have you sent home first thing tomorrow!"

Ian yanked an elbow out of her reach and left via the balcony, instantly blown about in the storm. Joseph, who was closest to the door, stood flustered as the curtain flapped in the wind, then finally reached out to slide the door closed. Ian had not taken his eyes from Annie as he stomped out and toward the stairs that led to the garden. Annie turned back toward the crowd, trying unsuccessfully to blend as she snapped a few more pictures. She worked her way to Cam.

"Is your laptop here? My memory card is full," she said after looking closely at her camera.

"Sure."

Cam led Annie downstairs to the study where they'd stowed her spare equipment earlier. Annie sat to download pictures. Cam thought Annie probably had backup memory cards and that would have been faster, but she suspected this was also an effort on Annie's part to get people to forget the scene.

Cam returned to the party, wanting to check in with Mr. Patrick, but she couldn't find him.

"Neil went to get some bourbon. He thought it might set everybody back at

ease," Samantha said.
"Where's Evangeline?"
"Tumblers. She said something about tumblers." Samantha winked this time, a conspiratorial gesture, so Cam smiled back.
She supposed a little extra oblivion couldn't hurt, but after five minutes she wasn't the only one who had begun to wonder what the delay was. On the upside, by the time Annie returned, people had all but forgotten the row that had set all this in motion, though Cam still let out a breath when Evangeline finally reentered the room.
"Nowhere! Isn't Neil back?" Evangeline's hair was mussed, and Cam thought she might have dug through every cupboard in her kitchen looking for the tumblers.
Cam shook her head, but Evangeline spotted something else.
"There!" She stooped in front of a side table and pulled out a crystal tumbler. "Samantha, would you like to pull out enough of these for everyone, or go check on Neil? It shouldn't take this long. The bourbon he likes best is on a top shelf, and I'm worried he may have fallen."
"Evangeline, I can get Mr. Patrick," Cam offered.
"Don't be silly, honey. This house has a maze for a basement," Samantha said, "but

I know right where he is." She ducked out.

"You can help me wash these out, Cam. They're pretty dusty — haven't served bourbon for twenty in quite some time." She laughed as she stood to look for a tray to put the glasses on.

They passed Mr. Patrick without seeing Samantha as they took the tray to wash glasses, and then all had a great laugh when guests, bourbon, and tumblers finally converged in the same room. Everybody toasted "to bourbon worth the wait."

Annie, Cam noted, had caught much of this on film and was glad something positive had come from her spat with Ian.

When everyone finished eating, Samantha brought in the brownies. People began to rave about them the moment they took their first bites. The night seemed to be salvaged, and was punctuated by the arrival of a spectacular lightning show for ten whole minutes before Cam heard retching behind her.

"Great," she mumbled. She turned and saw Barney, the terrier, choking, before he projectile vomited on the corner of a Persian rug.

"Evangeline! I don't know how it happened, but it looks like Barney got hold of a brownie!"

Evangeline leaped from a love seat where she'd been talking to Madeline Leclerc, rushed over, and then shouted for a servant to clean up the mess. She picked up Barney carefully.

"What happened, big fella? You get something that make your tum tum . . ." Cam imagined a lot of people spoke baby talk to their pets, but that didn't make it any easier to listen to.

"I'm going to be sick!" Before Cam could clear her mind of the impression that this announcement resulted from the baby talk to the pooch, Joseph rushed toward the balcony, handkerchief to his mouth.

Cam nearly cricked her neck as she caught Joseph sprinting outside, only to be pummeled with rain. Mr. Patrick looked at Joseph's plate in concern. Joseph had left only crumbs of his brownie.

"I think the brownies have been poisoned!" Mr. Patrick shouted. People around him began to gasp, staring at their dessert plates.

"Nonsense, Neil. I feel fine, and I've eaten one," Samantha said. Cam thought maybe she'd actually had two or three, but that wasn't her business, and it didn't make the point any less valid. If anything, it made Samantha more right.

"Maybe only some of them were poisoned!" he persisted.

Cam couldn't hold in an annoyed sigh before turning toward Annie, who looked stunned. Annoyed sigh or not, worry knotted Cam's belly. She knew the implications of such an accusation, even one that had no merit. She stepped forward.

"That doesn't even make any sense. I helped bake these. They're fine," Cam said to deaf ears.

"He's going into convulsions!" Evangeline shrieked. At first Cam thought she meant Joseph, but Joseph must have still been outside. Then she saw the dog.

Neil Patrick rushed his wife and the sick dog out toward the car. People muttered uncomfortably for some minutes after their hosts left, and then Joseph stumbled back in from the balcony. Cam thought he'd gone down the balcony steps to the covered porch below and then come in from through the lower level. He was soaked and looked very ill.

"You!" Joseph accused Annie. "You made me sick!"

"No, Joseph, wait!" Cam stepped between the two. "I think Ian has been trying to frame Annie from the beginning."

Joseph blanched. "Ian?"

Everyone turned and stared. Cam hadn't meant to blurt it, but she couldn't stand another person blaming Annie for yet another thing she didn't do.

"Maybe he put something on them once the brownies got here so she'd look guilty."

"How would he know she made them?" Joseph didn't like to be contradicted and it showed.

"Tom and Hannah were there when I asked her to make them. Is it possible you mentioned it?" she looked at them hopefully.

Tom shook his head, but Hannah answered, "Maybe," which was enough to create doubt. Cam smiled at her gratefully.

"Maybe we should talk to Ian," Samantha suggested.

"Or maybe we should call Officer Moreno. We can let the police sort this out," Joseph suggested. "I'm going to call."

He left again, cell phone in hand.

Annie had made a noise when Joseph spoke, but Cam pinched her. Protesting about the police would look bad. No one other than she and Rob knew about the romantic debacle between Annie and Jake. Cam only now remembered Annie didn't know what she'd learned from Rob. She edged closer to Annie.

"She's his sister," she said to her friend.
"Who's whose sister?"
"The woman. Jake's sister."
"What?"
"The woman and boy you saw with Jake. Sister. Nephew. Should I spell that?"
"But . . ."
"N-E-P-H . . ."
"But Cam!"
"I know. You dumped garbage on his porch. He'll get over it."
Annie still looked distraught, and then Cam was brought back to their other reality — poisoned brownies — by an exclamation from Madeline Leclerc.
"I wonder if maybe she caught who did it on film."
It took a minute for Cam to realize Madeline meant the pictures Annie had taken.
"Madeline, you're a lifesaver! But . . . the brownies were in the kitchen."
"We could at least see who left and when." She looked pleased with herself, but then her face fell and she seemed to change her mind. "No . . . I'm sure everyone was gone at some point."
"That's true. You know, though . . . Ian left," Cam said, grasping at straws.
"He did!" Madeline said.
"While I agree about Ian leaving and pos-

sibly having a motive to do this, this was hardly premeditated. What kind of lunatic carries poison around?" Samantha asked.

Cam frowned. She wished more people would buy into the solution that was best for all of them.

"It's a good idea, though. Annie, let's look at pictures," Samantha said.

Annie ran down the stairs to get her camera from the study where she'd left it earlier, and returned moments later, a stunned expression on her face. "It's gone!"

"What?" Cam asked.

"The camera I was using! Gone!"

"Well, it can't have gone too far!"

"Unless the poisoner took it!" Annie said.

"You just had it, didn't you?"

"I traded! The digital one I used earlier was downstairs!" Annie's voice squeaked in frustration.

Cam wondered why there was no sound of a siren yet, or at least a knock downstairs. She stepped out onto the second-floor landing to call Jake and tell him that in addition to the alleged poisoning, Annie's camera had gone missing.

"What alleged poisoning?" Jake asked when she called.

"Didn't Joseph call you?"

"Maybe. I'm not at the station. I'm on my

way over."

That made sense; she'd called his cell number, because she happened to have it, but the station was the first number on his card and was therefore the one Joseph must have called, though she did think the police dispatcher might have sent another car, one that could have arrived a bit more quickly.

As they waited, Cam and a servant cleared plates. Cam worried the treasurer would fuss over paying Annie for the brownies, in spite of the fact Cam *knew* the brownies had arrived *sans* poison. She couldn't grasp, though, who would have messed with them besides Ian. It was a puzzle.

Annie continued to search frantically for her camera, but Cam suspected the guilty party had hidden it well, and without the Patricks at home, they could hardly begin turning the house inside out — though the idea that the camera had been squirreled away within the Patricks' sprawling mansion suggested the culprit was someone familiar with the house. Unfortunately, that included all the Garden Society board and household staff, as well as the Patricks themselves. At least, it eliminated Annie. Unfortunately, it also probably eliminated Ian, unless he'd come back in through the downstairs door and took it with him.

When Jake arrived, he began to organize people for questioning about the poisoning and the missing camera, but he'd barely gotten started when Hannah and Tom ran into the drawing room, Hannah crying. She gasped for breath and sputtered rain out of her face, trying to speak and mostly failing. They dripped all over the Persian rug, which didn't help.

"Ian. Dead." Tom didn't appear to be breathing much easier than Hannah. Cam suspected Hannah was more used to exercise, but at least he wasn't sobbing, so he could get his point across.

"Show me," Jake said. When others started to follow, he held out a hand to stop them. "Just me."

Cam sat, dumbfounded, and then looked at Annie, whose brows were knit together in confusion or annoyance.

"Now we really need evidence of who left," Annie muttered.

Cam nodded, but it was reflex.

"Otherwise these buzzards will pin it on me."

"What?" That startled Cam out of her haze.

"When I downloaded the memory card — I was gone about ten minutes. Somebody will have noticed."

Cam sighed, knowing Annie was right. How could they prove where Annie really was?

"You *did* download the memory card?"

"Yes."

"So we show them what you were doing. The computer has a time stamp."

Annie looked around. "I think it's better — in the long run — if nobody knows those pictures got saved."

"But —"

"Cam, someone stole my camera, probably to get rid of evidence. Those pictures might have it, and your laptop has a short life if we go public."

Cam's first selfish thought was of all the work she had saved on her laptop.

"What about just the police?" Cam suggested.

"Oh, yeah, because Jake is now my biggest advocate."

Cam frowned at Annie's sarcasm. "He's honest, at least."

"Says his sister."

"It *is* his sister!"

"Look — share tomorrow if you have to. But back it up tonight. A little paranoia never hurt anybody!"

Cam snorted but saw the sense in Annie's

proposal. "Deal."

Sirens approached as the Garden Society sat growing more depressed. They knew the routine this time. Nobody got to leave until they were excused. For a while Cam tried to act cheerful, but Annie told her soundly to just shut up or not only would she lose her eyebrows, but she'd also be sporting a Mohawk. It was a relief, actually, as nobody had believed her cheerful tone or words, anyway.

About ten minutes after the arrival of his siren-blaring backup, Jake returned to the house.

"Nobody left?"

Everyone just stared blankly in response.

"No. We've done this dance before," Cam said.

At the word "dance," Annie and Jake glared at each other, and Cam regretted her word choice.

"I'll need to interview all of you. I wish I hadn't left you alone, but it was urgent. Any minute now, though, a sergeant will join me and we can get started."

He was a lot less friendly this time around. Cam felt guilty for some reason, as if they'd shattered Jake's innocence. It was ridiculous, of course, as a cop could hardly be all that innocent, and the Garden Society as a whole hadn't done anything wrong, but she felt it anyway. Then she remembered the other place she was supposed to be.

"Shoot!"

"What?" Annie asked.

"My dad was meeting us at my place."

"Us? Like you and me?" Annie asked.

"Yes, us. He thinks of you like his third daughter, you know."

Annie looked uncomfortable. "I've asked too much of him."

Cam was caught off guard. "Like what?"

Annie shook her head. "I'll tell you later. It's not a good time. But it's his fault — for being the cool dad and all."

Annie's eyes were glassy. Cam wondered if Annie was on the verge of revealing the big secret her dad had hinted at — the one Ian had so badly misrepresented. Or had he? Cam studied Annie more closely and realized how devastated she looked. Was it possible she had killed Ian? She knew Annie wouldn't poison everyone to get one person, but . . .

She bit the inside of her cheek to stop this train of thought. The wine and stress were combining badly. The last thing she needed was to question her friends that way, especially her best friend. Annie wouldn't harm anyone.

But then Ian had provoked her badly.

"Yoo-hoo! Cam? Where are you?"

Cam jerked herself to attention. Annie's face was inches from hers.

"Maybe we should put some coffee on?" Annie suggested.

Cam looked over at where the majority of the Garden Society sat, still drinking wine, some of them to poor effect. It definitely seemed like a bad idea to keep the alcohol flowing at this point.

"Right. Good idea. Be right back."

"Oh, no you don't. I'm not going to be left alone with those nuts! One of them's a murderer!"

Annie's melodrama made Cam snicker, so she grabbed Annie's hand to pull her downstairs to the kitchen. Rob eyed them longingly, but Cam had avoided him since their argument earlier. She wasn't going to start talking now.

"You're terrible!" she admonished Annie.

"Me? It's true!" Annie feigned innocence, and Cam hugged her.

"We'll be okay," Cam said.

Annie sniffed, but Cam ignored it because when they pulled apart, Annie turned away, embarrassed.

The kitchen was empty, but the coffeemaker was on the counter and there was coffee in the freezer. While it brewed, Cam found thermoses and Annie found cream and sugar containers. They filled everything and put it on a tray with mugs.

"Better?" Cam asked when they were ready to return.

"Well, I'd rather keep drinking, but it's probably not such a hot idea."

"No sign of your camera yet?"

"I wish! Man, I hope I don't have to replace that. It's insured, but I have a two-hundred-and-fifty-dollar deductible."

They had just reentered the drawing room, coffee service in hand, when Cam heard a whistle behind her. It was Rob.

"Are we talking?" she snapped as she set down the laden tray she was carrying. "I don't think we're talking."

"Why aren't you talking?" Annie asked.

"He insists on clinging to Nick as the suspect. He won't listen to me."

"Listen? What else have you said? You won't let anybody be a suspect!" Rob said.

Cam remembered that the suspect she'd tried to sell to Rob and Jake was now dead, so unlikely to be the guilty party.

"Shoot!" Cam looked at Rob. "I *know* Nick is innocent. But the person I thought had done it is dead."

Rob started to choke, and only then did Cam recognize he'd taken a bite of one of the brownies.

Joseph rushed over. "Those are poisoned!"

Rob snatched the glass Cam had been clearing back from her hand and took a drink of his merlot. After a large sip, he ate the rest of the brownie in one bite.

"No," Rob said confidently. "They've been sitting out for an hour, so a dry crumb got caught in my throat. I helped make these, and I had two earlier. They're fine."

"But," sputtered Joseph, "because of those brownies, Ian's dead! And the dog got rushed to the vet!"

"Ian died of a brownie overdose? Was he even still here when dessert was brought out?" Rob asked, his eyebrow raised.

"Well . . . we assumed . . ."

"For your information, dogs are allergic to chocolate, so it wouldn't be a surprise for a dog to be poisoned if some moron gave him a brownie. But brownies aren't poisonous to people." He grabbed the last brownie from a nearby tray and took a large bite, grinning with chocolate crumbs in his teeth.

Cam stared, wide-eyed, unsure whether to cringe or cheer, though she did feel her annoyance dissipating. Just then, the Patricks returned.

"It was just a reaction to the chocolate. Dogs shouldn't eat it," Evangeline announced cheerfully, cuddling Barney, who was wrapped in a baby blanket and licking her face. When Evangeline saw the room of dejected guests, she handed Barney off to her husband.

The people in the room looked at her but offered no information, so she asked, "Well . . . what happened?"

"Ian's dead," Cam said.

Evangeline fainted, and Rob had to help Cam catch her. Joseph stared at the dog Neil thrust in his arms. He tried to pass it back, but Neil was too concerned about his wife. Finally, Joseph convinced Samantha to take Barney. Cam sank into a chair and put her head in her hands. She was beginning to think the photo shoot was jinxed.

CHAPTER 13

It was the longest night in history, as Cam perceived it, but finally, around three in the morning, the police at the scene told them they could go home.

Cam told Annie and the magazine staff they could wait until ten to show up for work the next morning, but begged Rob, in spite of still lingering annoyance, to take her to the Patricks' at eight. There was too much unknown for her comfort.

When she arrived, she began by assaulting Giselle with questions.

"I know you left last night before all the guests arrived, but some things went missing. I was hoping you could keep an eye out."

"Of course."

"Primarily, a good digital camera, though there was some film from a thirty-five-millimeter camera, too."

"Camera. Film. Very well. And you're here

all day?"

"In and out, yes."

"You know you must avoid the servant's house?"

"Of course. It's where the murder was."

"And the break-in. Somebody broke in this morning and turned it over looking for something."

"The police weren't guarding it?"

"I don't know. Maybe just one in front. It looked like whoever broke in went in a window. Coffee?"

"Please!" She gave Giselle a thankful smile, and Giselle winked and crooked her finger for Cam to follow. Cam was rewarded with an extralarge mug.

"Thank you. I need this."

"I heard you were all here very late. The Patricks asked not to be woken until nine." Cam noted the French accent was back.

"Then I'll be extra quiet. Say, Giselle . . ." A question had just formed in Cam's mind, sparked by Giselle's comment on the Patricks' plan to sleep in. "The morning Jean-Jacques died, Annie picked up a pan. Do you remember?"

"Yes." She frowned slightly.

"She thought you looked happy it was her. Is that true?"

"I suppose. I was relieved it wasn't Jean-

Jacques back again, upsetting everyone. At the time I didn't know he actually *did* come back again — just not to the door."

"He came here . . . to the door?"

"Well, yes. He asked to speak to Mrs. Patrick, claimed he was expected. Mr. Patrick heard that and flew into a rage. He yelled something about not borrowing money from his wife and that he should feel lucky he had the job after the way he'd behaved. Mr. Patrick asked him to leave, and I saw him drive off."

"Wow. That's some morning. Do the police know all that?"

"Well, yes, or most of it. I answered all their questions."

Cam tried to look sympathetic, then thanked Giselle for watching out for the camera.

Cam began in the parlor, searching more carefully now that all the party guests were gone. She wondered how she'd not heard about Mr. Patrick's angry encounter with Jean-Jacques before now.

For the time being, however, she had moved on to Ian's murder. What she really wanted to know, though she suspected she wouldn't find out until she talked to Jake, was Ian's cause of death. She didn't think brownies had anything to do with it, since the Patricks had announced that Barney's reaction was nothing more than chocolate's natural toxicity to dogs.

When she was confident the parlor held nothing interesting, she decided to check with the police officer who was still assessing the murder scene in the servant's house, in hopes she could convince him to share something.

"Miss? You shouldn't be here," he said as she approached.

"Sorry. I was here last night. I just wondered."

"You'll need to stay out."

She tried a few more times to just talk to him, but it was useless. So much for that, she thought, glaring at the unfriendly officer.

"Fine. Where did Tom and Hannah go?"

"A hotel, maybe? At least until all our evidence is collected."

Cam nodded, irritated that none of her leads was panning out, but reluctantly admitting to herself that if any evidence had been in the little house, it had probably been taken anyway.

After the previous day's rain, the morning air felt thick, even though the temperature wasn't too warm. It was perfect flower weather, primed to bring about happy blooms.

She yawned and began to pace the garden, hoping for a little peace, since she obviously wasn't going to get any answers just yet.

She wandered for about ten minutes before she found Henry Larsson. He was replacing a rosebush that had only a single leaf with blight.

He looked up and saw her frowning, then looked back to his rosebush with pride.

"Spreads like wildfire if you let it."

Normally, Henry was too reserved to invite conversation, so Cam was surprised when he spoke. In fact, this was only Cam's second direct conversation with him, but she welcomed it.

"Oh, I know — worst thing for a rose garden ever. I'm just impressed, in this huge garden, you caught it so fast."

He chuckled. "I suppose that's what they pay me for."

"Roses were my mother's specialty. Do you remember my mother?" It was a hunch, but Roanoke was only so big. Her mother had been a gardening enthusiast, too, before the Garden Society existed.

He nodded, smiling. "Lovely woman. She shared one of her specially bred plants with me. It's a hybrid-tea variety, similar to the

Voodoo, but with more defined veins of coral through the yellow — it's lovely. She called it a Campet. Now I've got four of them at home. Another pair and I may share with Neil, but don't get his hopes up. I'm awfully attached."

Cam knew the breed — her mother had actually helped a botanist create it. She'd called it Campet for Camellia and Petunia — it was gorgeous, and her mother had been very proud of her success. Cam smiled at the memory.

She hoped this earned her a little insider credit, but then she had a disturbing thought. "You don't know about what happened here last night, do you?"

"I know there's something going on. I saw the police car up at the guesthouse. I make it my business not to snoop, though."

"A man was killed last night."

"Another one?" He looked thoroughly startled.

Cam nodded. "And last time . . . You remember when I asked you about the jasmine? Well, I found the victim's cell phone in the bushes. Would you mind just keeping an extra watch? And anything you find — that looks off, could you just let the police know?"

"Well of course. Was that the mangled jasmine bush?"

She nodded. "The first guy, the photographer, must have died in it — the girl who identified him said he smelled of it — that's why I asked you about it."

Henry nodded, then went back to trimming, and Cam figured he preferred to be left alone.

Cam wandered a bit longer but finally turned in the direction of the house. The camera crew would be arriving soon. They'd agreed there were only two or three hours left to finish the project, so they should plow ahead in spite of everything. The weather looked as though it might cooperate for an hour or two in the event they had any outside shots left to take.

As she neared the house, she saw a familiar face.

"Jake!" She couldn't tell if she was glad to see him or just shocked, but decided to go with glad, as it would be more productive.

He looked uncomfortable. "Um . . . Hi, Cam."

"So, can you tell me anything?"

"Not really. It's still under investigation." He scuffled his feet and wouldn't meet her eye, but she attributed his demeanor to the situation with Annie.

"Look, Annie's heard that was your sister."

"Listen, Cam, we're swamped. I'll talk to you later, okay?"

"I'm going to hold you to that," she said. She was annoyed that he'd blown her off, but more than that, she could tell there was something he didn't want to tell her. She doubted that was good news.

Then Cam spotted something. One part of her mission had just walked out of the servant's house in the hands of a woman in a protective suit, or rather, it was carried out in a large ziplock bag.

Annie's camera had been found at the scene of the crime. And if Cam wasn't mistaken — though she hoped she was — it appeared to have dried blood on it.

Cam closed her eyes and tried not to think about it as she went inside the main house. She sank onto a sofa, hands over her face.

Finally the staff for the shoot began to arrive, Jane Duffy first, delivered by Cam's father, then the photo crew from *Garden Delights,* then a few members of the Garden Society, and finally Annie, cutting it close, but making the official start time.

Unfortunately, as soon as Annie appeared, Jake descended upon her and began reading her her rights. Cam started to hyperventilate; she couldn't believe Annie was being arrested. She could barely concentrate but managed to hold it together, designating alternate tasks to get the *Garden Delights* crew out of the way.

Cam felt torn in a thousand directions. She argued with anyone who would listen. Annie could not have done this. What she understood from the responses she got, though it was clear there was a lot she wasn't grasping or being told, was that Ian had been bludgeoned with Annie's camera.

She sank back into the chair and absorbed very little else for a while.

"Miss?"

Giselle brought Cam out of her daze. "Yes?"

"You said something about a lost camera and film. I think you meant a good camera, but Miss Hannah, the gal who was staying in the servant's house, said she found a camera in a corner of greenhouse one."

" 'Winter'?"

"Yes, ma'am. I just thought to ask her when I saw her this morning, and she gave it to me. She said she found it yesterday and put it in her duffel and forgot."

Giselle held the strap of a small point-and-shoot — a lower-end digital camera. Cam stared, wide-eyed for a moment, then thanked Giselle and took a bit of the strap. She didn't have a ziplock bag like the cops used, but she did have a plastic grocery bag she carried for those odd occasions a person needed a receptacle for their garbage, so she dropped the camera in. Giselle scurried away. Cam was sure it wasn't Annie's, but it might be useful in any case.

The policemen with Jake had taken Annie around front to the police cars, where Annie now sat as they made their reports and calls. Jake was still at the servant's house, looking at what Cam imagined was evidence with his forensics team. Cam approached, holding the bag by just the tips of her fingers.

"Jake?"

He turned, surprised. "Hi, Cam." Not exactly enthusiastic, but he sounded at least a little warmer than he had earlier. She supposed now that Annie's arrest was behind him, there were no more avalanches to set off, so he was less afraid to talk to her.

"Giselle found a camera. She was looking for Annie's camera, and this obviously isn't it, but I thought it might be important."

"Annie's camera isn't lost. It was used to bash in the head of Ian Ellsworth."

"Fine. You'll excuse me if I don't believe that means Annie did it. Do you want this or not?"

"Yeah. Give it to Doug. He's the guy —"

"I can figure out who to give it to. I just thought maybe you gave a damn." She stomped away without letting him respond.

Cam was annoyed, and not in the mood to cooperate if nobody was going to listen. She walked around front to where Annie waited in the police car.

"Annie, you want me to make sure your stuff gets to your house?"

"Please, the cameras especially. I don't want them all lying around."

"It's all evidence, ma'am," said the officer guarding Annie.

"No, it's not," Cam argued. "For starters, Annie didn't do this, but besides that, only the one camera was involved."

"And the poisoning."

"There was no poisoning. Take a brownie sample if you want proof, but just for the record, nobody got sick except the dog, who was reacting to the chocolate, not poison, and Joseph, who may have come last night with a bug already. If it was poison, all of us would have gotten sick."

The officer looked uncomfortable.

"Cam. It's okay. My purse is in the den with the photography stuff. Why don't you bring it out for the officer?"

Annie communicated without words. Cam was to take what she needed and bring the rest.

What Cam *needed,* at least if she was going to make any progress investigating what really happened, was a car.

So Cam retrieved Annie's purse, making sure there was nothing too embarrassing in it, and extracted the keys. Then she brought the camera equipment in three trips, carefully documenting each scratch and ding out loud as she set things down and noting them on a pad of paper, so the officer would be worried about damaging the state-of-the-art equipment.

The officer finally left with Annie, shooting a nervous look behind him. Cam followed only a minute later, toting the camera from the greenhouse. She'd changed her mind about turning it over right away, as police competence seemed to be low. She headed for home in Annie's Bug.

She got as far as her kitchen table, retrieved a pair of disposable gloves she'd swiped from Jake two days before, and began to look at the pictures.

She gasped.

Almost all of the shots were of Evangeline, wearing not very much.

She shoved the camera back into the plastic bag and then rushed back to La Fontaine. She'd changed her mind — Doug was definitely the best person to take the camera into custody — she wanted nothing to do with it. She was just glad she'd known enough to wear the surgical gloves she'd lifted from Jake.

The hardest part was sneaking back in the house with it, but she managed.

"There you are, sunshine! They said you were here, but I couldn't find you!" Nelson Harris greeted Cam warmly, his eyes reflecting his concern. She'd found him chatting amicably with Henry Larsson.

"Daddy!" Cam hugged her father, and he held her close. Henry excused himself with a nod.

"What's all this nonsense about Annie?" he asked after a moment.

"They think she's the murderer!"

"Annie? Our Annie?"

"They arrested her. Look — can we go? Just . . . go?"

"Of course we can. Let's go to your place. We can have some coffee and talk."

Cam nodded and told Samantha they were leaving; her father told Jane Duffy the same.

On her way back out with her father, she turned over the bag with the camera to Officer Doug, telling him everything as it had happened, except, of course, her detour to see what the pictures were of, then they left, her father in his car, Cam in Annie's.

Cam didn't say anything as she made coffee and got out bagels. Her father arrived ten minutes later with a bag of Krispy Kremes and pushed the bagels aside, opting instead for a fruit-filled delicacy that coated his lips with powdered sugar.

"So how do you think this happened?" he asked as she set his coffee next to him.

"Someone hit Ian with Annie's camera, but I think the idea that Annie's the murderer was planted by Ian himself — this crowbar accusation."

Recognition crossed her father's face, and Cam felt momentarily stung.

"This crowbar accusation. It's real, isn't it?"

"I said it was Annie's secret to tell, and it is, but it sounds like she meant to tell you — and as she's not here . . ." He breathed deeply a few times, took a sip of coffee and a bite of doughnut, then scooped cherry filling out with his finger and licked it. Finally, he looked Cam in the eye. "When you were in Chicago, Annie thought she was in love. Probably she was in love. Do you remember?"

"Paul, right?"

"Paul. Paul lived in Lynchburg, but that isn't so far, not like a really long-distance romance. They only could see each other weekends, but that was fine, too. She was working at that art gallery, the one that made her realize she wanted to *make* art, not manage art."

Cam smiled. She remembered that much.

"He always came here, which Annie took for chivalry . . . It was all going pretty well. She thought he was getting serious and she was happy — and I was happy for her. She and I used to have supper every Thursday back then — that was Mother's auxiliary night, remember?"

Cam nodded — her mother had had dozens of commitments.

"I think Annie was keeping an eye on me." He looked at Cam knowingly.

Cam smiled. She loved that her friend would do that, and knew that had been the reason, though Cam hadn't had to ask. Annie had always gotten along with Cam's dad better than her own.

"Anyway, one weekend she decided to surprise him. She'd taken a timed picture of the two of them and blown it up — very artistic. She spent quite a bit of money having it framed. She decided to deliver it. She'd gotten his address from his driver's license, which she had snuck out of his wallet just for the surprise, and she drove up there. When she arrived, he was putting a toddler in a car seat and getting into the car with a woman. He didn't see Annie, and Annie followed them, wondering what the explanation was. They spent a day at the zoo, I think."

"Ouch. Things are falling into place."

Her dad ignored her. "She waited all day — probably in a bar or pub, and then after dark, went back to Paul's house and used a tire iron to smash the windshield of his car, yelling and screaming the whole time she did it. That made for a number of witnesses — neighbors who later reported she seemed quite insane and said they feared for their safety.

"Paul came out and there was a heated argument, during which Paul's wife called the police. Annie was arrested."

"And she called you?"

"I was glad she felt she could. I was outraged for her."

Tears stung and Cam felt glad, too. "So what happened with it?"

"Paul agreed to drop charges if Annie agreed never to contact him or his wife again. It looks like he must have told his family she was a former, rather than a current, girlfriend."

"Geez. Poor Annie! And Ian is Paul's brother?"

"Seems that way."

"But Annie didn't kill him. Ian, I mean."

"No. I wouldn't think so. My Annie wouldn't kill anyone."

"Then who did?"

"I wish I could help you, sunshine, but I don't have that answer."

Chapter 14

Talking to her dad had helped answer a number of questions about Annie, but it had also multiplied Cam's desperation. She felt stronger than ever that she needed to help find the real killer, as the police seemed stubbornly determined to pin it on Nick or Annie, or at the moment, Nick *and* Annie.

Fortunately, based on the pictures she'd just had a peek at, she believed she had a new suspect. Evangeline Patrick had clearly been a victim of somebody's perversion, and if that somebody was Jean-Jacques Georges, then there was an adequate motive for murder, by either Evangeline or somebody who felt protective of her. Cam almost wished she'd looked at the photos more carefully. She'd seen Evangeline climbing into the hot tub in one, standing at a window in a negligee in another. These had obviously been taken from the grounds, but she had no idea if Evangeline had actually posed for any of the shots or if the subsequent photos were even more risqué, as she'd been afraid to look further. Her guess was that Evangeline had been unaware they were being taken, but she couldn't be sure.

The photos didn't explain Ian's murder. She doubted he'd been the one to take them. But they gave her enough to go on for the moment.

Cam intended to milk this situation, exploring it as if Evangeline were the murderer, after lunch. The conversation they'd begun the day prior was plenty of reason to keep going, but now Cam was armed.

Her father left to get back to his afternoon's commitments, which included helping Petunia, and Cam wiped the table and cleaned the coffeepot. She then spent ten minutes pinching off the sticky buds of a rhododendron that was about half done for the year. She loved the bush; its coral-colored flower clusters cheered her, but the sticky task of deadheading had to be done in small doses or she'd saw it off at the base in frustration. Still, the mindless task did put her back in the right frame of mind, and she washed up and headed back to La Fontaine.

"Cam! I'm surprised to see you!" Evangeline said by way of greeting. "You know . . . everything has pretty much ceased here — no photographer and all." Cam tried to convince herself Evangeline was hiding something, but she couldn't quite buy it.

"I know." Cam looked at Evangeline sadly, hoping to gain some sympathy. "I was hoping for maybe . . . an ear. Annie's been arrested. Petunia's a wreck."

"Oh, honey, come on in. Giselle! Could we get a pot of tea in the drawing room?"

Evangeline took Cam's hand to lead her up the stairs to the room where the party had been. The move made Cam feel like a creep, given she was hoping to prove Evangeline had committed murder. She decided to start with the topic where they'd left off the day before.

"I hope I'm not too forward," Cam began.

"Oh, honey, I'll just tell you if I don't want to answer. Marrying one of the wealthiest men in a smaller town, when I'm almost thirty years his junior — I've been asked pretty much everything."

"I just want to protect my sister, and you seem to be the only one who knows anything about Nick besides her." Cam felt queasy lying to someone who'd been so nice — and worse, *about* someone she loved — but it couldn't be helped.

Evangeline leaned forward and grasped Cam's hand, again surprising her with the affection.

"I don't think your sister has anything to worry about. Jack . . . Nick's a prince — one of the good guys."

"But we got interrupted before I could find anything out. Just to reassure me? So he was in a band with you and Jean-Jacques . . ."

"The One-Eyed-Jacks. We played up and down the East Coast for a little over a year — opened for a couple mediocre bands, but mostly played bars. It was fun, until I learned Johnnie was sticking his hand in the till when he could. He bragged about it after a gig in Memphis. I told him he had to stop, and I thought he did. I thought it had only been for kicks and I'd set him straight. Then after a gig in Arlington we were finally busted. They searched our stuff and found the missing money, plus some vintage music paraphernalia, in Nick's things. Johnnie was always smooth, and he'd been my friend for ten years by then. He convinced me Jack really did it — that Johnnie had stopped when I told him to, but he must not have been the only thief. I feel terrible for believing him."

Cam started from a sort of daze when she

heard Evangeline sniff. The emotion was clearly real.

"So Nick went down," Evangeline continued.

"Did you tell the police that? Now, I mean?"

Evangeline hunched her shoulders and cringed, a guilty look, Cam thought. "I guess I thought it looked like a motive for murder, so no."

"And you really know Nick never did it?"

"Johnnie and I were having drinks a year or two later — he was Jean-Jacques by then — Samantha had bought him a fancy camera. He bragged about what he'd done to Jack, as if it were all a big laugh! He acted like we'd framed him together. I was furious!"

"What did you do?"

"I wrote a letter — said I had new evidence, but it was hearsay — not admissible. When Nick got out, though, I felt like I had amends to make. He crashed at my place for a while, until he got a job. I was back in Roanoke by then. Jean-Jacques got a couple impressive gigs, and he even sent me money he said was for Jack — that Jack wouldn't take it directly from him, so could I get him to. Jack wouldn't, of course, but I felt like Jean-Jacques had turned around. Now I think he was just manipulating me; I fell for it. Again." She cursed then, and stood to pour something stronger in her tea.

"Anyway, then I met Neil — seems unlikely, I know. He was a friend of my father's, so it was more a reacquaintance, but we got along so well. And I was so tired of boys my age and the stupid things they did. I didn't see much of Jack after that, but he seemed to land on his feet. Johnnie, though," Evangeline growled. "I think he never did change."

"What do you mean?"

"Oh, it's nothing. A leopard just never changes its spots."

Cam could tell that conversation thread wasn't going anywhere, so she changed subjects. "So you cosigned on the Spoons loan."

"You know about that?"

"It's part of what the police are looking at."

"Heavens! It is? I mean in reality, it's not such a big deal. I trusted Nick — I felt guilty, honestly, and I was in a position to do it. I knew he wouldn't run out on it, loving Petunia like he does. And with all his cooking skill, I was betting they'd make it. All I did was sign my name."

"And trust him."

"Yes. I trust him. Is that so bad? He's a trustworthy guy."

Cam didn't feel so keen pursuing Evangeline as a suspect anymore. She couldn't even bring herself to ask why Jean-Jacques had called her the morning of the murder. She liked Nick having a fan who was really just his friend, even if she knew Petunia wouldn't feel so warm and fuzzy about it. There were a couple of questions left, though.

"On the morning Jean-Jacques was killed, why was your screen out? It looked like he'd fallen out the window, but his body really had been moved from the jasmine."

Evangeline scrutinized her, and Cam realized Evangeline hadn't known that piece. Instead of asking about it, however, she answered the question.

"Benny was having such fits. It was still mostly dark outside, and I couldn't make out what he meant. I guess I pushed it out when I was trying to talk to him. That's when I saw the body and called for Giselle to call 9-1-1. I suppose there was a lot of screaming and hysteria involved besides that, but that's what I remember."

Cam had a last question, but had no idea how to bring it up. She fidgeted uncomfortably, sipping her tea as Evangeline babbled, but finally just came out with it.

"When they were looking for Annie's camera, a cheap digital was found in greenhouse one . . . pictures of you . . ."

"Me?"

"They're not . . . Mr. Patrick doesn't take pictures of you . . . in lingerie and your swimsuit and stuff, does he?"

"Neil? He wouldn't need to! He has the real me." The implication then registered. "There are pictures of me? In lingerie?" Her eyes were wide with shock.

"Swimsuit. Workout clothes. A lot of pictures."

Evangeline frowned. Cam believed the surprise was genuine.

"I'd have to see them to know when they were taken, but I haven't knowingly posed like that — I guess maybe twice in Jersey, but I'd have black hair in those; otherwise, not since the swimsuit stuff in the pageant years."

"So somebody took these pictures without your knowing?" That wasn't actually surprising, given the unposed nature of the pictures Cam had seen, but she didn't want to assume too much. "I only got a peek, but I'd guess they were taken here."

Evangeline shivered.

"Maybe you could help the police determine when they were taken. I don't know whether the photos are connected to Jean-Jacques, but they might be. Maybe somebody killed Jean-Jacques for taking them."

Evangeline's face registered disbelief and confusion before it finally settled again. "They would have to have been shot within a certain time frame for Jean-Jacques to have taken them, but I can't think of anyone who would kill someone over pictures."

"Not Mr. Patrick," Cam stated. She didn't think that was even a question.

"Of course not!"

"No one else . . . obsessive? Protective?"

"I mean . . . I still get the occasional weirdo recognizing me, but I can't think of anyone specific."

"Servants? Staff?"

"Well, Benny has a crush on me, but that's sort of sweet."

Now, that *was* curious, Cam thought, but she decided to cruise past that fact for now.

"Anyone in the Garden Society?"

Evangeline frowned again. "I don't think so."

Cam squashed the idea that if Nick was half the fan of Evangeline as Evangeline was of Nick, that reinforced him as a suspect.

Evangeline narrowed her eyes. "Before I call . . . are any of them . . . really humiliating?"

"Everything I saw was PG-13." Cam didn't mention the reason she hadn't looked further was that exact fear. Evangeline nodded, then went on. "I don't want to gossip, but as long as we're getting ideas out there, did you know Jean-Jacques owed Samantha quite a lot of money?"

"A lot?"

"He was trying to get me to front him a portion so he could win back the rest to repay her." That, Cam thought, could easily explain the early morning phone call.

"Which is why he has the gambling debt? I take it you said no?"

"I did say no. Winning didn't sound very sure to me, even if I trusted him enough to lend him money, which I didn't. I don't know anything about the gambling debt, though."

"What I know is Samantha used his debt to her to get him here for the shoot, and that he owes a bookie here in town."

"Quite a bit to know." Evangeline eyed her. "Should you know all that?"

"It's nothing supersecret. Rob is covering the case, and my brother-in-law was the first one accused, so I've taken an interest."

"Oh, I can understand why. It can't help to have your best friend be the second accused."

"No." Cam sat quietly with that idea, but Evangeline gave an oddly helpful suggestion.

"What if someone just wanted it to look like Annie did it?"

"I had the same idea, only I thought it was Ian who was trying to set Annie up for the first murder. Obviously, that's not the case. Do you think someone else is trying to frame Annie for Ian's death?"

"I don't know — the killer might just hate out-of-towners. But what if the second murder only happened to throw suspicion off of the killer for the first?"

Cam's eyes went wide. "What a wonderful, horrible, rotten idea!"

Evangeline laughed. "I love the Grinch."

The idea that Ian's murder was just a diversion from the first opened a whole new angle, because honestly, unless Tom and Hannah were freaky serial killers, Cam couldn't see how the same person would have it in for both Jean-Jacques and Ian — well, unless somebody had decided to murder all the world's arrogant jerks. But if she looked at the second murder in this new light, several more suspects came to mind.

The list would continue to include Nick, though Nick couldn't have killed Ian, so if

Nick *had* killed Jean-Jacques, and Ian's murder was just a cover-up for the first, that meant Nick had an accomplice. She quietly quashed the idea that this theory made Petunia a suspect for murder number two. She knew *that* wasn't possible — even more impossible than Nick's being a murderer, which was already impossible. The idea also made Samantha seem a more likely candidate, and ironically, Evangeline, as well as all the people who might want to protect those two women — Joseph, Neil, possibly Benny — as Jean-Jacques seemed to be harassing both.

Cam wondered who knew about the harassment. The killer would have had to know about it before the first murder.

She decided it was time to visit Samantha again. There were surely enough Garden Society issues to merit a meeting between the group president and the public relations specialist.

On impulse Cam drove Annie's Bug to Samantha's, rather than calling ahead. Joseph's car was in the driveway, which she suspected was true a lot of the time. Cam hoped she wasn't breaking up anything romantic, though she remembered Samantha saying Joseph was quite old-fashioned.

She rang the doorbell and a woman answered. It triggered Cam's memory.

"Are you Francine?"

"Yes, miss."

She introduced herself. "I wondered . . . a couple days ago . . . the day Jean-Jacques was killed . . ."

A frightened expression clouded the woman's face.

"I hadn't seen him since the day before!"

"No! I know! I didn't think so. I just wondered about the trouble waking Samantha."

"Oh, yes. Well, usually she's having tea when I arrive."

"What time do you arrive?"

Francine looked away and seemed to be shaking.

"It's okay. I just need to know what time you tried to wake Samantha."

The woman glanced around, still avoiding eye contact. Finally, she said,

"You see, miss . . . it's just . . . I didn't know how important it was, and I told a little white lie. My sitter had some trouble, so I didn't get here until nine, but I told Samantha eight. I'd even left a message on her machine at six thirty or so, knowing I'd be late, but it hadn't been checked when I got here, so I thought I'd dodged getting my pay docked. I didn't know how important it would be. I erased my message."

Cam nodded. "I won't say anything unless for some reason the police investigation needs that information."

The woman nodded gratefully and then led Cam into a small, pretty parlor she hadn't seen the last time. Samantha looked up from a desk where she was writing in a ledger.

"Camellia! Lovely to see you!" Samantha rose and kissed both her cheeks. Joseph stood from a chair on one side of the room and briefly grasped her hand in both of his.

"Samantha, I should let you go. I've got things to attend to."

"Nonsense, Joseph. Stay and visit."

"No, really!" He ducked out without another word.

"Sorry to chase him off," Cam said.

"Oh, honey. He needs to man up a little. He's just so shy!"

"But I don't want to scare him away."

"He needs to be scared away now and again to prove there is nothing to be scared of. The poor man is afraid of his own shadow!"

"If you're sure."

"Of course, I'm sure. Honestly, I love him to pieces, but he's very needy. I'd like to see him expand his network a little."

"But does my scaring him off help that? Or hurt it?"

"I think it helps. Okay, strike that. I *hope* it helps — teaches him he can't solely count on me, and I *know* it helps me. It's a burden to have a person so dependent on you."

Cam smiled, encouraged.

"I hope you won't change your mind. I have . . . some curiosities . . ."

"Oh! Speaking of curiosity, you know I was thinking. That sleeping pill? I bet Johnnie did that."

"Johnnie?"

"Well, yes. He was obviously up to something, sneaking off in the wee hours of the morning, showing up at the Patricks' like that. It makes sense he wouldn't want me to interfere."

"That does make sense, I guess."

"Okay, so what were you curious about?"

"I'm concerned for my sister." The lie, she noticed, was getting easier.

Samantha nodded, her brow slightly wrinkled.

"And I've just learned from Evangeline that Nick — Petunia's husband — was in a band with Evangeline . . . and Jean-Jacques . . ."

"Nick's the one who stole the money," Samantha said. Her voice had dropped, and she looked away from Cam.

"According to Evangeline — she didn't know until Nick was in jail, but Jean-Jacques stole it, then saw he was going to be caught and framed Nick."

Samantha bit her lip. "Oh dear. I was afraid that might be the real story." She looked truly sorry but then frowned again. "So Nick didn't kill him to get even, did he?"

"No! Nick didn't kill him at all! I'm just trying to . . . understand Jean-Jacques, I guess."

"Why do you think Nick wouldn't kill him for that? It seems like a pretty good motive to me."

"Because I know Nick . . . He wouldn't kill anybody for any reason. And there was a second death while Nick was in jail, so if Nick did kill Jean-Jacques, then we have two killers. But it doesn't matter. Nick is gentle — well, other than normal posturing. Given the chance, he might have punched Jean-Jacques, I suppose — he might think he deserved a crooked nose for the rest of his life. But he'd never quietly kill somebody. If he had to — or thought he did — there would be honor involved. It would be public."

Samantha's mouth stood open. She clearly hadn't considered that angle.

"And what does all that have to do with me?" Samantha asked.

"He was your nephew. You knew him."

"Oh, I don't think I knew him. I always wished he wanted more of a relationship. His sister, Margo, and I are quite close, but *my* sister, his mother, is pretty self-absorbed. An actress — second-rate at best. I think he never got proper attention or discipline, and he and I never bonded like I did with Margo."

Cam wasn't interested in Jean-Jacques's childhood deficits, but a little history might help.

"He came here summers?"

"Both of them did. Six weeks a summer from when Johnnie was thirteen. My sister did a summer Shakespeare festival somewhere — maybe New Hampshire. Anyway, she was divorced and needed a place for her kids." Samantha's body language was a little stiff, and Cam wondered why.

Cam went on to ask about the friendship with Evangeline and their activities, not really sure what she was looking for, trying to avoid a shutdown from Samantha.

"Evangeline seemed pretty mad about Jean-Jacques framing Nick."

"Well, she didn't mention that to me, but I know she was mad about him trying to borrow money again."

"Money?" Cam had had a hint of this but wondered what Samantha would volunteer.

"Oh, it never amounted to anything — Evangeline learned how to tell him no years ago, but she grumbled about it recently." Samantha sat back, finally relaxing a little. "I wish he'd been more like his sister. Margo and I had a great time — days at the country club by the pool — shopping. Johnnie always acted entitled, as if the rest of us should pay for his company, but then he wouldn't behave so anybody else might have a nice time. Evangeline lived around the corner and she caught his eye."

Samantha was rambling, but Cam found it fascinating.

"Their family wasn't quite as privileged, but I found if I also invited Evangeline, then Johnnie would behave to impress her. It worked beautifully for about two summers. Then both of them got it in their heads they'd rather do their own thing, and honestly, I was just glad to have him out of my hair. I pretended it worked for several more summers, until I saw he didn't seem serious about college or a job. The camera seemed productive. At least he was somewhat dedicated. I wanted to see him succeed — be self-supporting. But that's not a cheap business to start up."

"So you loaned him the money, which he didn't pay back," Cam said, surmising the remaining details. "And after a while, you figured you'd never get it, so instead you used the debt to pressure him to come here."

"That's the short version." Samantha looked guilty.

"And when did he get here?"

Samantha shrugged.

The gesture reminded her oddly of Joseph, who, Cam now remembered, had been the one who told her Jean-Jacques was staying at Samantha's house.

She wasn't sure what this shared gesture meant, but concluded that Samantha and Joseph must spend a lot of time together. It was a commonality like those she and Annie had.

Joseph burst in then, reminding Samantha of some lunch they had to get to, and it looked like Samantha's concentration and attention evaporated.

"Cam, I've enjoyed this. I'd love to chat more later. I know you need a friend."

Cam grasped Samantha's hand and asked when would be good, ignoring the fact Samantha might only have said that to be polite.

"Any time after two."

Joseph smiled, though Cam figured it was only for appearances. She could see he liked to keep Samantha to himself as much as possible. Cam decided what she needed was a little quality time in her garden. Pulling out the weeds that didn't deserve to make their homes in her beautiful beds required a certain frame of mind, but she had just entered that zone. A little selective herbicide was exactly what she was in the mood to do.

CHAPTER 15

Talking with Evangeline and Samantha had helped, but she needed a sounding board — Annie would have been ideal, but she was in jail. Pulling out a long strand of nightshade that had crept around the fence from her neighbor's yard was a little satisfying, but when the dirt under her nails started to bug her, she was ready to talk to someone.

She called Rob, hoping the news of Annie's arrest would help her convince him that police leads could be misleading.

"Are you talking to me again?" he asked when he heard her voice.

"Will you stop it? We settled this last night. I don't want to fight. Just don't tell me Nick did it, because he didn't."

"Neither did Annie."

"Well, I agree with you there. I hoped you had some time to talk through some other ideas I had."

The pause was too long, but because she got the answer she wanted, she decided to ignore the time lag.

"Where are you? I'll pick you up."

"Can you swing by for some takeout and come to my place in an hour? I have a couple things I need to get done first," she said.

He agreed and she hung up, then went to bring her gardening things inside. Just as she opened her back door, her phone rang again. She glanced at the caller ID display and rolled her eyes. Madeline Leclerc undoubtedly had some imaginary crisis, and Cam wasn't in the mood for it.

"Cam, I really need to talk to you about some things. Do you have time?"

"A little."

Madeline sighed but requested Cam come to La Fontaine.

"I'll be out there in ten minutes."

Cam would have asked to have their discussion by phone, but La Fontaine had to have some of the elusive answers she was looking for, so maybe she'd just poke around a little with Madeline as an excuse.

She drove to La Fontaine, psyching herself up for whatever Madeline had in mind. Cam found her just inside the front door, pacing as she waited. It looked as though

Mr. Patrick and Evangeline had abandoned her for other obligations.

"I just wanted to see how the investigation was going from your perspective, Cam."

"My perspective? I'm hardly a detective." She was annoyed that this was the emergency, though careful not to show it, as Madeline was her boss.

"I hear you've been asking a lot of questions."

"A few, I suppose." She grabbed onto the only detail she felt Madeline would really approve of. "I tried to convince the police that Ian was the murderer, but unfortunately, somebody killed him."

While Cam had thought Ian was a legitimate suspect, and had willingly, though fruitlessly, pointed the police in his direction, she hated feeling that her boss would prefer she say anything, even lie, to ensure the Garden Society members remained off the investigators' radar.

"And what are you up to now?" Madeline asked. "Surely the murderer is one of the two they have."

"I know it's not," Cam said sternly. "I'm trying to figure out who would want to hurt the Garden Society so badly, but I really need to check some things in back." She headed outside, hoping Madeline believed the fib and wasn't offended with her escape. Cam wasn't in the mood to lie more than that to her boss, and she didn't think her boss was really within her rights to suggest Cam investigate a murder. Especially the part where she was supposed to implicate her loved ones.

She walked along the jagged path that wove through the lily leaves of the giant mosaic. The rain had knocked many buds from several flowering bushes onto the ground, and the buds emitted sweet scents in protest. Every few steps Cam breathed deeply. She almost bumped into Hannah, who was doing the same thing.

"Oh! Hi! I thought you were at a hotel," Cam said.

"We came back for our stuff; they wouldn't let us take it last night in case there was . . ."

"Evidence?"

Hannah looked down, half a nod of agreement. "They don't want us to leave town until the weekend, in case there are more questions, but we'll go back to the hotel."

"That's understandable. Ian was murdered in the servant's house. I certainly wouldn't want to stay there."

"Yeah, a policeman is checking everything before it gets packed. He said it would take a while with Tom, so I could go until it was my turn."

The whole idea was gruesome to Cam, but still fascinating.

"What do they think they'll find?"

"I think they hope the memory card from the camera will show up. I guess it wasn't in the camera when they found it, so they're scouring in case it just fell out."

"I'll bet whoever killed Ian took it. You heard about the break-in last night?"

"Break-in? I didn't hear about that," Hannah said. "But it's also possible they were looking for this." She held out what looked like a cigar box. She covered her fingers with the tips of her sleeves to open it — it was full of cash.

"Hannah!"

"Ian asked me to hide it in my bag — I had it at the party. He said it was a surprise. I thought maybe it was a present for Tom or something. I didn't open it until we got to the hotel last night."

"Holy cow! Did you count it?"

"No. I didn't want to touch it. I'm going to turn it in when it's my turn."

Money was a huge alarm bell, and she was glad to know that both Hannah and Tom were honest enough to turn it over. Cam wondered what the heck it was about. The talk of the memory card, though, reminded her of something else from the night before: the pictures downloaded onto her own laptop. She couldn't believe she'd forgotten in the chaos of the arrest that she'd been meant to copy them and then share them with the police.

She made her excuses and sprinted around the house to Annie's car. She sped away fast enough to make Annie proud.

At home she opened her laptop and pulled up the pictures. They looked like normal party shots — some people hamming for the camera, others trying to escape it. She was surprised, in fact, to see adults behaving so much like her friends had in high school.

She decided to go through the pictures one at a time, enlarged enough to fill her screen, as viewing them in the smaller format hadn't revealed any real detail. There had certainly been no people obviously sneaking in or out. Besides, she thought Madeline was right: everybody had left the party at some point, and pictures couldn't really give an accurate view of who was gone for an extended time — long enough to get to the servant's house and back.

The first time through the enlarged photos, she looked at food shots, wondering if some of the brownies had actually been poisoned — or some other food, for that matter. The trouble was, it was impossible to prove poisoning based on a photo, short of catching the actual act, which she doubted she would.

Cam refocused her attention on the faces in the photos. In a number of shots taken well before dessert, Joseph looked a little sickly. In fact, Cam noticed, he was flushed before the arrival of guests. Perspiration was visible on his forehead in a photo of he and Samantha taken just a bit later; Annie had captured them in the midst of an argument. Cam almost wondered if someone had put something in Joseph's drink, though she was sure Joseph would have claimed it was Annie.

Then Cam spotted something even odder. It was a shot of the Roanoke Garden Society Board, taken about twenty minutes after the argument, according to the time stamp. Samantha was flanked by Neil Patrick on one side and Joseph on the other. It was a close-up, and they filled the foreground, Joseph still sweating slightly but looking a little happier. Cam wished she could remember what time the brownie incident had happened. She was sure this was prior, as Neil Patrick still had on his bib. Behind the trio the photograph was meant to capture, Benny, whom Cam couldn't remember seeing at the party at all, had his head close to Ian's, as if they were sharing some secret. She wondered what could have brought Benny to such an event. His father wasn't even present.

Cam frowned and enlarged that corner. Annie's camera was good enough that the image's background details were readily visible once magnified. Ian was handing Benny something that looked an awful lot like money.

She remembered Jean-Jacques and Benny owing money to the same bookie and wondered if maybe the three of them, Ian included, were entangled with the same criminals. Maybe the money Ian had asked Hannah to hang on to was more proof of that. It would sure save a lot of grief if that were the case. But what kind of crime? Pornography came to mind, given the pictures of Evangeline, though for pornography, the shots were pretty mild. Whatever the case, money connected Benny to both of the dead men. It seemed ominous.

She burned all the pictures onto a disc and decided to take them to Jake after she had lunch with Rob.

■ ■ ■ ■

Cam called Jake to see if he would be around that afternoon for her to bring in the new find. Jake acted singularly uninterested.

"How do I know you haven't tampered with the photos?" he asked smugly.

"I don't have the skill to tamper with them, and if I were going to frame somebody, I'd go with Evangeline at the moment, over those pictures of her and . . . well that's who I'd go with. She had plenty of reason to kill Jean-Jacques!"

Jake didn't respond. She wondered if he'd even seen the photos from the camera she'd given to Officer Doug earlier. Probably not, or he would have lectured her for looking.

Jake's recent evasiveness was wearing on her. She realized, though, he'd paused too long. "What?" she asked.

"It wasn't Jean-Jacques's camera."

"Whose, then?"

"Look, Cam, this is not your investigation, and you have a vested interest in us not convicting either of the top suspects. I need to go."

"I'm pretty darned sure the prints didn't belong to Nick or Annie!"

"Good-bye, Cam."

"Okay, if Annie's the killer, why do you still have Nick?"

"Because Nick didn't have the money to meet bail, and they still have evidence implicating him in the first murder."

"But they couldn't both do it!" She knew there was a better legal argument than that and cursed herself for not doing a little research so she had it at the tip of her tongue.

"There are two bodies and a money trail."

"So you claim Nick killed Jean-Jacques and Annie killed Ian? Un-freaking-believable!" She clicked her phone shut, totally annoyed it wasn't a landline she could slam down.

"You look ticked. Not at me, I hope?" Rob handed her a bag from Subway as if it were a peace offering.

Cam growled and then apologized. "No, not at the moment. I found some good evidence for a different suspect and Jake won't even look at it!"

She led him through her apartment and out the back door, where a blanket had been laid under a blooming crab apple.

"It's not you; he's annoyed the evidence is leading him on a wild-goose chase."

"So he's not interested in new information? Seriously?"

Rob described Jake ranting about Annie's record and feeling guilty about not taking Ian's accusations seriously.

"I mean, the guy wound up dead. Jake feels like he killed him by not listening."

"But Annie didn't do it. I can't believe he even looked her up over dumping a stupid garbage bag! Seems like an abuse of his position to me."

"I agree, but . . . there was a threatening note at the servant's house. It sounded like Annie wrote it . . . something like, 'Lay off or you'll be sorry.' "

She turned and stared. "So someone really is trying to frame Annie?"

Rob nodded grimly. She was glad to see he was on her side this time.

"It was done on computer, not handwritten. If we could find the printer it was printed on . . . Jake said it was a dot matrix. You don't see those too often anymore."

"Certainly not hooked to Annie's computer; her stuff is high-end," Cam mumbled. "You know . . . Evangeline suggested I look for who might want to frame Annie. Sounds pretty smart to me. Especially with this note thing."

"With the stuff you found, it sounds like

maybe Evangeline would have a reason to frame her."

"Why, then, would she suggest something that would implicate herself? Still, it is a more likely scenario than Nick framing Annie from jail."

Rob frowned. "I guess you have a point there, but what if the two murders aren't related? Jake thinks Nick was hired."

"By whom?" This was the first Cam had heard as to what a money trail meant.

"I don't know, but that's why they're holding him as long as they can. I think they hope he will give up the person who hired him."

Cam thought it sounded like a lot of excuses. "Rob, do you want to hear my new evidence or not?"

His eyes popped open as if he'd forgotten all about the point that had started their conversation.

"Of course I do. Shoot."

"Well first, I learned from Giselle this morning that Jean-Jacques came to the door and rang the bell the morning he died."

Rob nodded.

"You knew that?"

"Yeah, then he drove away, but only far enough to park and walk back."

"Why didn't you tell me?"

"I'm sorry — it sort of got dropped when they found all the connections to Nick. There was an address in the car, too."

"Address?"

"Little house somewhere in the Blue Mountains — Patricks own it."

Cam growled. She couldn't believe she'd been so desperate for non-Nick evidence and Rob had withheld this. "So there maybe was an affair or something?" she shouted.

"No, Cam — it didn't pan out. The caretaker up there says nobody has been there for years. Jake thinks Mr. Patrick might have been helping Samantha out by offering Jean-Jacques a place to stay that was free, but out of her hair."

"But nobody's asked them? After Mr. Patrick was so mad?"

"Look, you're right — especially after the murder last night — Nick isn't the killer, so they should look into it again. I'll remind Jake."

"I thought this was your investigation, too." Cam felt a little better after reading Rob the riot act. She then explained about the money exchange between Ian and Benny that she'd seen in Annie's photos as well as about the box of cash Hannah had showed her, and began describing all the angles that had blossomed as a result.

Rob interrupted, which annoyed her, until she realized his input was useful.

"What is money ever exchanged over? Porn is one, but you're right, those pictures don't sound much like porn — tabloid stuff maybe, but there's not much money in that unless the person is a big celebrity or cheating on their spouse. Then there's drugs, gambling, crime . . ."

"So if we can connect Benny to one, that might be it. And there's that camera from the greenhouse . . ."

"With his fingerprints."

"His? Are you sure?"

Rob looked guilty. "I think that was secret."

"I'm not doing a press release. I just wish Jake would get over himself."

"I know, but they don't want anyone to know because they hope someone might trip up."

"I won't tell! You could trust me a little bit — that would help, too." She felt her neck heat up and knew her face would soon be red. Not her most attractive look. She had to make an effort to calm herself, because it wasn't really Rob she was mad at anymore.

"Do you have anyone you could talk to? About Benny, I mean . . ." Rob asked.

"You forgot love."

"What?"

"As a motive."

Rob rolled his eyes. "Didn't sound to me like Ian loved anyone but himself. And how could paying Benny be about love?"

"That's true. Maybe Benny was selling something. Ian sure had a lot of cash, though — he had to be planning something bigger. Maybe that money to Benny was a down payment for something."

"Like?" Rob said.

"I'm going back to talk to Samantha again after I drop off this disc to Jake. I've already talked to Evangeline enough today, but Samantha had to cut me short. Plus, there were a few pictures I wanted to ask her about. Samantha and Evangeline are the only ones I feel comfortable with — picking their brains and all."

Cam half expected Rob to make a zombie gesture. Brain picking usually got that — a grunt and a grab, stiff-armed and monster-mouthed. Rob hated the term. In fact, he hated most slang and mocked it where possible, but he stayed serious, concerned, even.

"Two women who might be suspects, and there's something fishy about that tea with sleeping pills. Be careful."

"Fishy? Like what?"

"I don't know yet. Jake just said forensics wanted to do a bunch more tests."

Cam pondered that, but she didn't want Rob to worry. "I'm always careful. I know how to talk to Samantha and Evangeline, trust me. Besides, I don't think Evangeline is really a suspect."

"Why not?"

Cam couldn't answer. She hadn't revealed even a third of what she'd learned about Nick from Evangeline. She didn't want Jake hearing it if it wasn't necessary and wasn't sure if Rob might spill it in trade if she told him. Besides, Rob would take it the wrong way — as evidence of Nick's guilt. And truthfully, Evangeline's support of Nick had earned her a lot of slack in Cam's estimation, even if there was evidence giving Evangeline a pretty strong motive.

Rob eyed her sternly. "Because she's nice? It's an old trick, Cam. Just be careful."

She rolled her eyes and opened the door for him, not wanting to admit to the possibility she would need caution.

"Meet me for supper, okay? So I know you're fine? Six?"

Cam agreed and then went inside to examine the pictures again. She searched the Internet for information on azalea symbolism while she was at it — "fragile passion" seemed the only potentially relevant meaning she found, but at least she was fully armed before handing the disc and summary over to Jake.

Cam drove toward downtown, not feeling overly optimistic about Jake after their morning conversation. His disinterest in the pictures of Evangeline had been discouraging, so she felt a lot of weight resting on the exchanged money angle.

When she got to the station, she was irritated but not surprised to find Jake had found some other priority, so she wrote him a note and left the CD with pictures and her azalea summary for him. The poor deputy she scowled at looked afraid, but she knew that wouldn't get her anywhere with Jake.

At Samantha's house, Cam rang the bell, but nobody answered. There had been plenty of time for Samantha to return from her lunch. It was past three. Cam knew, however, Samantha spent a lot of time in her yard, so she walked around the side of the house.

Instead of Samantha, she found Joseph, glove-clad and pruning.

"Hi, Joseph! Where's Samantha? I would have thought you'd be with her."

"She went back into town to buy some line. One of her climbing roses needs some therapy after that storm. I let her know at lunch." That seemed odd, as Samantha was the one who had invited her to come back, and Cam wondered if Samantha had been disingenuous, but she decided to accept it as just a timing flaw.

"So you're helping her get it sorted again?"

"Trying. It's a big yard for just Samantha."

"Henry and Benny help, don't they?"

"Oh, they do, but I like to help, too."

"Do you ever work with them? Henry and Benny, I mean."

"On occasion, mostly during planting season. Why?"

"Ever see Benny . . . acting funny?"

"Oh, Cam, I find almost everything young people do funny, and I don't mean amusing." He paused awkwardly. "Not you, of course, but . . ."

Cam tried to smile reassuringly. She knew what he meant because she knew how he was. He was prim and old-fashioned. She needed to get to her point.

"I mean . . . suspicious?"

He stared at her for a moment, as if trying to read her intent. "I guess, maybe. I usually see him lurking near greenhouse one at the Patricks'."

"Lurking?"

"Lurking might be wrong. He is just there a lot. I thought maybe he fancied the winter plants — a little dark and morose? Isn't that what young people like?"

Gears turned in Cam's mind. The camera had been found in the "Winter" greenhouse. And Benny's prints were on the camera. Perhaps the greenhouse had a view of the hot tub or something. "I suppose some young people might. I've always liked spring myself. Did you ever see him in there with a camera?"

"Benny? Why would Benny be photographing . . . wait . . . camera?" Joseph turned and stared at Cam, shocked at the idea.

"Is there something else strange about a camera? Are you thinking of Jean-Jacques, maybe?" Cam tried to draw out what Joseph had found so odd.

"Well, that's who I'd have expected to be connected to any questions about cameras."

"Was Jean-Jacques taking pictures *here?*"

"Hardly! Not a one! In spite of my showing off Samantha's gorgeous garden. I even asked him, and he said gardens didn't interest him. It's unfathomable, really, what with her *Chionodoxa gigantea* and the way she's coaxed it to keep blooming into April . . . in zone seven!"

Cam thought Joseph had entirely missed her point about the strange pictures at the Patricks'. She needed to get him back on topic.

"Do you think . . . um . . . Jean-Jacques was inappropriate with Evangeline?"

Joseph looked confused by the question. "I can't say I noticed one way or the other. I suppose they seemed friendly."

"You don't feel a little protective of Evangeline, too?"

"Oh, Evangeline has Neil! She doesn't need me."

Cam tried to assimilate what she'd just learned from Joseph. He seemed very protective of Samantha. Had he been angry at the way Jean-Jacques had taken advantage of her financially? Maybe, although Cam had a very hard time picturing Joseph having enough initiative to commit murder. The protective-admirer angle also gave an additional motive for Benny, whose crush on Evangeline might have led him to act out over Jean-Jacques's attentions to her. And after what Cam had learned recently about

Mr. Patrick's outrage at Jean-Jacques the morning of the murder, perhaps he'd had a protection motive as well.

It was a tragedy, really, if Benny had done this. Cam felt sure if he had, he wasn't really able to understand right from wrong . . . Then again, maybe Benny's crush on Evangeline hadn't been the motive after all. Maybe Benny had seen Ian kill Jean-Jacques and then tried to blackmail Ian. That would explain the money changing hands!

"Cam?" Joseph's voice startled her out of her musings.

"Sorry, Joseph. I haven't had enough sleep lately. I'm just daydreaming."

She didn't want Joseph to think she was losing it. She went on to her next loose end.

"You wouldn't know who might have something against Annie, would you?"

"Well, *I am* the one who got poisoned!" Joseph sputtered.

"Annie didn't do that. I'm hoping some of the pictures might show who did, if anybody. You know, Barney's reaction to the brownies had nothing to do with poison; chocolate is toxic to dogs." She held her tongue that she was sure he'd been unwell before the brownies were served. There was no need to be confrontational.

"Pictures?"

Cam stared. She'd been sure he'd be more interested in the poison.

"Annie took pictures at the party all night," she replied.

"Oh, yes. I hope they help."

"I'm sure the police will tell us."

"Let's hope so." He smiled. "I hear Samantha now!"

He seemed awfully excited, considering his next suggestion was that Cam go in and talk to Samantha on her own. He wanted to keep pruning. She knew social interactions were a strain on him, and he was probably just tired of being so social, but he could be terribly abrupt.

She left him to his bushes.

CHAPTER 16

"Cam! What a nice surprise!"

"Hi, Samantha." Cam frowned. She was under the impression she'd been expected. As she climbed the stairs from the lower level, however, she smiled, truly happy to see Samantha again, largely because she felt ready to burst.

Samantha wasn't at all like Cam's mother, but she seemed to care in a maternal way, and at the moment, that was just what Cam needed, along with a little sanity.

"It's almost five. Gin and tonic?" No, nothing like her mother at all.

"I'd love one. Weak, though. I have Annie's car." She glanced at her watch. Ten after four really wasn't almost five, but who was counting?

Samantha's version of a weak gin and tonic was on the medium-strong side to Cam, but she thought one wouldn't hurt.

Samantha excused herself then, to double-check that Joseph's feathers weren't ruffled and take him the twine she'd just bought.

Cam picked up her drink and wandered, looking at Samantha's art and souvenirs from her travels. There were a few tasteful masks and drums, along with paintings and baskets, all of which Cam thought were probably from Africa. She lifted the lid of what she thought was an Egyptian jar, if the hieroglyphs were any indication. Inside she found a memory card. She frowned, but the chance of it being *the* missing memory card was very slim.

Samantha returned with some water crackers, a wedge of Brie, and a small dish of roe.

"Caviar!"

"I know. We should drink vodka, which I am embarrassingly low on. Joseph won't eat caviar with me, though, and I can't afford to feed a big party, so indulge me."

Cam thought Samantha could afford it, but it would be pretentious for a large affair, so she didn't argue. She was too curious not to try it, at any rate. She put some on a corner of cracker and took a bite, then squealed.

"It's so salty!"

Samantha's smile grew. "You've never had it before?"

Cam shook her head as she'd filled her mouth with gin and tonic to balance the flavor.

"Oh, I adore it . . . about three times a year. It's too much for a frequent snack, but I'm just so delighted Joseph didn't scare you off this morning. I was worried he had."

"Why?" The gin, almost gone from her glass far more quickly than she'd intended, had made her blurt the thought she normally would have filtered.

Samantha seemed to misunderstand her question. "It reminds me a little of when Evangeline used to come by . . ." She trailed off, then seemed to skip ahead. "She's married now and does it so seldom anymore. I guess I like having a" — Cam prepared to hear the word "daughter" or "protégée" but instead got — "younger sister of sorts. My own sister hasn't talked to me in a long time, even with her ex-husband's recent passing."

Cam thought Samantha must have had wine for lunch. She normally wasn't quite so forthcoming.

"Were they Jean-Jacques's parents?"

Samantha nodded sadly. "Margo, Johnnie's sister, was quite distraught — she was closer to her dad than I knew — and that falling out at the end." Samantha's face looked distant for a moment. "My sister and I fell out over Johnnie's discipline. Margaret, my sister, was a bit of a con artist, and he picked up the trait. In college Johnnie tried to convince me to pay his tuition — cash. His father, I learned recently, was willing to pay for all of it, though only directly to the university. I thought he was out of the picture, but he didn't want to be. I'm convinced to this day Johnnie and Margaret were just trying to get money from me."

"But . . . I thought Jean-Jacques owed you a lot." After she'd said it, she hoped it wasn't offensive, but Samantha took it in stride.

"He did. I paid directly to the school for a one-year photography course, not a cheap one! And I bought his equipment, very *good* equipment. I wanted him to have a vocation."

"He did well with it."

Samantha took a rather large drink and savored it in her mouth a moment before continuing.

"I suspect the field is conducive to the con. Tell some tall tales to get in somewhere impressive, then suddenly you actually get some impressive shots. Pretend you are an event photographer, suddenly you've met the important people. I know he had real talent — that was obvious — but his talent with the con helped him as much as his photography skill."

"That makes sense, actually." Cam remembered Annie's comments about him. They suddenly seemed insightful, rather than snarky. Annie would never stoop to a con job. In fact, she hid her connections when they might actually open doors, embarrassed about any unearned privilege. "He really did take great pictures, though."

"That's the thing about a con. It can go on only as long as you don't get caught, and if you can't follow through, you will get caught. If I didn't know he was really good, I wouldn't have had him come for our shoot."

As Cam contemplated that, Samantha sniffed and began mumbling about being to blame for Jean-Jacques's death.

"Samantha, it's not your fault. He made a lot of people mad, and that wasn't on you. They don't have the right person yet, though. I'm sure they don't. I was wondering if I could run some ideas by you."

"You mean you think I'm trustworthy?" She poured herself another drink and turned to look at Cam, a strange expression on her face.

"Of course I do. You obviously wanted the best for Jean-Jacques, even if he screwed up a lot."

"That's true. I loved him in spite of everything. Why don't you think . . ." Samantha paused, then her eyes widened.

"What?"

Samantha looked momentarily mortified, then went on.

"Joseph's so sure it's Annie . . . with Ian's accusations . . . and then poisoning the brownies . . . She was there that morning, you know. And with Alden for a father — that couldn't help."

Cam frowned. She thought Samantha had changed subjects, but the new one was interesting, too. Alden was Annie's dad. Cam hadn't known there was any controversy surrounding Senator Schulz, much less that Samantha was on a first-name basis with him. She took a breath for patience.

"Okay, I helped bake the brownies, and they were fine. Chocolate is toxic to dogs, and Joseph looked sick all night — there is photographic proof, though I'd prefer you didn't mention it to him; I just think it might offend him. And . . . I would think judging people based on their families would be something people would know better than to do." Cam worried she'd just been rude again and considered gin might not be her wisest drink choice.

Samantha blushed. "Oh, I do. Please don't misunderstand, but with what Ian said . . . then Ian ending up dead . . ."

"I am one hundred percent convinced Ian is dead because he planted the idea that Annie killed Jean-Jacques and the killer thought that was a smart way to go — to frame the person who'd been accused, so the police would stop searching elsewhere."

Samantha looked momentarily shocked, then recovered with a swig of gin. "Okay — so if not Annie, who do you think the killer is? And how do you think I can help you solve this?"

"You remember, this morning we talked a little about Jean-Jacques, Evangeline . . . and Nick? But I'm also interested in what Evangeline and Jean-Jacques's friendship was like — back when they were young."

"You don't think . . . Evangeline?" She seemed deliciously scandalized.

"No! I mean . . . I don't think so. I'm just trying to get my bearings."

"Oh, I see. I think she thought of him like . . . her naughty friend — the one she could get in trouble with and not get caught. Of course, I didn't know that at the time, but it's true. I wouldn't have told her parents. In fact, between you and me, I encouraged her to do the pageants so she'd be more careful about . . . keeping out of trouble. I knew she did some bad things, and I could see she enjoyed it more than was a good idea. But I also knew the lesson would stick better if it was her decision. Not a lecture."

"Really?" Cam would have been shocked had Evangeline not already mentioned her need to go a little wild after college, but it did raise the question of whether Evangeline was completely reformed.

"I really liked her! Still do. I was thankful, too, since Johnnie was so unmanageable without her. I worried about his influence, though. I didn't want her sneaking off to get high and getting arrested or worse . . . pregnant! She's smart and so pretty! I guess I was trying to ensure her future."

"And it worked."

Samantha nodded sadly. "But it gave me false confidence in how much I could control. First I helped Margo — and I think I really did — she ended up with a full scholarship because of the opportunities I gave her. Then I helped Evangeline, at least . . . well, I thought I did. I thought I could help Johnnie, too."

"Do you think Benny's in love with Evangeline?" Cam blurted, staring at the bottom of her gin and tonic glass.

"Oh, I'd say so!" Samantha laughed, not recognizing, or maybe just relieved, that Cam had changed the conversational track; Cam thanked the gin.

"For how long?"

"I'm sure since she moved in. She's very good with the help. Makes a game of the work but still treats them with dignity."

"Do you think Jean-Jacques had the same kind of crush?"

"Same kind? No. I think he wished or hoped, but he wouldn't have been devoted that way. Evangeline would have known that. I could swear they were never . . . what do kids say . . . friends with benefits? He was a ladies' man with a lot of other attention and knew where he stood, so he didn't pine. Just hoped."

"I think Benny might be our guy."

"Heavens! Why? I mean why *think* that? Isn't he . . ."

"Not the sharpest tool in the shed, that's true. But that might lead him to certain faulty thinking." Cam explained the pictures, though she left out her broader enlightenment on the misguided protective instincts of love-struck admirers. It wouldn't do to have Samantha confronting Joseph.

"It sounds plausible when you put it that way!"

"I hope I can find some evidence."

"So do I, honey. So do I, though . . . poor Benny . . . poor Henry." Samantha looked as if the idea appealed to her, though.

Samantha refilled Cam's glass as she said it. Cam was unprepared for another, even stronger drink, but it *was* sort of nice.

Samantha turned the tables on her then, asking her if there was any other evidence and for whom. Other than discounting facts pointing at Nick or Annie, however, Cam didn't have much to share. She wasn't fool enough to offer her speculations about Samantha or Joseph.

She finally tried to take back control of the conversation. "Can you think of anybody who has anything against Annie? Or . . . maybe her dad?"

"Camellia, Annie's father signed that commercial use act for that lot west of town that the Garden Society wanted designated as a preserve, remember? The whole Garden Society despises him. But we're all adults, and his daughter is clearly not him."

Cam nodded, unhappy there was a large group of people who might see Annie as a revenge target. Samantha had also just been inconsistent — earlier she'd cited Alden as a reason to suspect Annie, and at the Patricks', Samantha had defended Annie to Ian because she was the senator's daughter. It seemed what she was saying now, under the influence of gin, might be the truest of the three reads.

Cam began eating in earnest as she pondered. She wanted to be sure she could still drive. Besides, it wasn't even supper time, and she also wanted a clearer head to expand her suspect options with Rob. She planned to go over all the clues with him at dinner. Maybe together they could figure something out.

Cam drove to Annie's shop, where Annie's car had an all-day permit. She then walked the couple of blocks to meet Rob for Italian food at their agreed-upon destination.

He looked at her suspiciously when she arrived, a half-eaten basket of bread and an almost empty glass of red wine in front of him.

"Sorry. But . . . I've been productive."

"I hope so. The waiter has been shooting me voodoo eyes."

"Ooh! Effective!" Cam teased, feigning horror at Rob's face. When he touched his face in automatic response, she laughed, then poked his ribs and kissed him. "We'll tip him well. This is worth it."

The waiter came over, and Cam passed on wine for the time being. She was on a mission and needed to keep her wits about her.

"So, my new BFF and big sister, Samantha, is a lovely hostess. I've been consuming gin and tonics and caviar," she began.

Rob raised an eyebrow. She wished it was in response to the big sister comment, but she knew Rob well enough to know he was reacting to the chat slang.

"Annie is your *BFF*," he countered with exaggerated slowness on the initials and looking at her like a child.

"Okay, you're ruining my story."

"The one fortified with alcohol?"

"My big sister was only looking out for me! That's what big sisters do."

"Have you ever poured liquor down Petunia's throat?"

Cam narrowed her eyes. "Do you know Petunia? She hardly needs encouraging."

"Exactly my point. Wild little sister. Big sister's job is to *keep them in line.*"

"Oh, don't be stuffy!"

Rob lectured her about driving when she was tipsy, though she insisted half of her behavior was just that she was excited. He began force-feeding Cam ravioli as soon as it arrived. He was eager to get some food into her so she would be more coherent and display fewer of Annie's qualities — something she seemed to pick up when tipsy.

Finally she pushed his hands away and said, "Done! I'm done! But I do feel more sober, so thank you. Now do you want to hear what I learned or not?"

"Of course I do."

"Okay, you're the one who told me about the fingerprints on that camera from the Patricks', right?" Cam explained that Evangeline had confirmed Benny had a crush on her. She then told him about the meetings with Samantha and reminded him about Annie's pictures from the party.

"Okay, you're babbling." He sounded irritated, and Cam hoped the quality of information would ease that.

"But you weren't writing it down. I'm reviewing. Plus, I learned more. Just listen."

He listened, pulling out a notebook, but he didn't seem to find her as clever as she'd found herself, so he interrupted.

"So you think these guys — Jean-Jacques and Ian — were connected before they came to town for this magazine spread?"

"Maybe not, but maybe because of the shoot, they connected another way. It may have been true for Benny, too. Remember,

Jean-Jacques and Benny owed the same bookie money."

"Okay, we need to get this all straight." He made a grid on his notebook and pushed his linguine with clam sauce to the side. "Our suspects so far are . . . Nick and Annie . . ."

"Who didn't do it . . ."

"Right, but we still need to have them on the list to keep track of clues."

Cam rolled her eyes.

"Samantha, Evangeline . . . now Benny . . ."

"Maybe Joseph — same reason as Benny, but for Samantha instead of Evangeline. And then Mr. Patrick — that argument and the address."

"Okay." Rob wrote it down. "Anybody else?"

"Not with Ian dead."

"Right. So let's go over our clues."

"Benny found the body and had apparently been taking peep photos of Evangeline."

"Which is related to the murders how?" Rob asked.

"Money maybe. He owes the same bookie as Jean-Jacques and was seen taking money from Ian — so money connects him to both dead guys. Or he could also have been trying to protect Evangeline — he is around a lot and may have heard Jean-Jacques harassing her."

"Okay, Nick?"

"Didn't do it."

"Fine. Go to Evangeline. There's overlap."

"Evangeline got a call from Jean-Jacques that morning, and Jean-Jacques pulled her into framing Nick."

"And framing Nick is a pretty powerful motive," Rob said.

Cam scowled as Rob wrote down the details next to both Evangeline and Nick, but went on. "Evangeline and Jean-Jacques were friends as kids. They knew each other for years. And we just learned he never stopped pressing her for money. Say, what if he knew something embarrassing about her?"

"He probably did, but think about what she had on him. She could have kept him quiet that way — he would have lost all his big clients if she went public with the fact that he'd framed someone for a crime he committed."

"I thought you liked Evangeline as a suspect."

"She's okay. I like her enough that I want *you* to be careful around her, but she's not my favorite."

"Who's your favorite?" She regretted it as soon as the words were out. Nick would be the favorite for the first murder — Rob had not forgiven Nick for keeping his prison history a secret.

"Samantha, maybe." He surprised her. "What do we have on her?"

Cam grinned. She'd much rather come up with clues that pointed to Samantha than to Nick. Still, she felt compelled to defend Samantha a little. "She was drugged while it happened."

Rob's eyes glittered. "Ah, but was she?"

"What do you know?" Her cheek twitched. This might be good news . . . in a bad way.

"The tea was drugged, but none of that drug residue was on the side of the cup with the lipstick. The drug might have been added later."

"Did Jake tell you that?"

"No, actually. He's been a bit tight-lipped, so I found a source in the crime lab. He told me about the fingerprint, too."

"Why would Samantha do that?"

He raised an eyebrow. "For an alibi?"

"What?"

"Look, this isn't sure, but it looks like maybe she wanted it to appear she'd been drugged."

"Shoot!" Cam knew she'd given Samantha that idea, if it was the case. She didn't say that to Rob, though.

"So what else on Samantha?"

Cam came at it with a vengeance now that she was feeling like a fool. "She didn't show up that first morning — claimed to have slept, possibly because of the drug in her tea, but there are no witnesses."

"I thought —"

"The maid was late for work. She lied about it so she wouldn't be docked pay — she never knew it would matter. She didn't actually get there until nine." At Rob's confused stare she added, "I just found out today," and went on. "And then we already knew Jean-Jacques owed Samantha money — that was how she got him here. And then there was that fight we saw."

"Mr. Patrick?"

"Husband-boyfriend angle, but confirmed with the reaming Giselle saw and that address, maybe. Mr. Patrick seemed to want Jean-Jacques farther away from his wife, at least."

"And you said Joseph?"

"His crush on Samantha is weird — hovering. And he seems awfully eager to pin this on someone."

"Namely Annie."

"Yes, but he sounded eager to cast doubt

on Evangeline or Benny, too."

"When you were asking him for ideas, basically begging for dirt on people?"

She frowned. She didn't think she'd been that bad.

"So you like Benny for now?"

Cam nodded.

"You ever buy drugs?" Rob asked.

"No." She frowned. She had no clue where he was going with this.

"I was just thinking, if I were growing . . . maybe pot . . . those greenhouses might be a convenient place to do it year-round."

Cam pondered that, disturbed at the idea. "That's true, but wouldn't Henry notice? Or Mr. Patrick or Evangeline?"

"I'm not saying it happened. Just . . . if it was . . . that would explain a lot. Maybe Evangeline knows."

"I doubt that. She got into . . . wait a minute . . ." Cam almost argued about the pageants requiring good behavior, but Samantha had said she pointed Evangeline toward the pageants hoping to keep her out of trouble, and Evangeline admitted to rebelling the first chance she got after that. "I guess we check greenhouse number one, right?" Cam asked.

"Why one?"

"That's the one where Joseph said Benny

spent time, and it's where the camera with the Evangeline photos was found. So that's where I'd check."

"Where *I'd* check, you mean. Nobody in the house could fire *me,* and I could probably convince the paper it was necessary for the story, even if I got in legal trouble."

"But Benny is an employee, right? He could lose his job if we *do* find out he's growing pot."

"Yeah, but isn't his dad like . . . the best? What if he quit? They might let Benny stay to avoid that . . ."

". . . but only if there were no police." Cam sat concentrating for quite a while. Finally it occurred to her that if she and Rob were caught snooping in the greenhouse, she could pretend to be looking for something of hers. It would be trespassing, but she doubted the Patricks would be angry if she used that excuse. She explained the plan to Rob. Thankfully, he seemed to think it made sense.

Cam thought Rob was a little curious and a lot protective, but that was okay. She planned on having a triumphant glass of wine before they left the restaurant, and after her afternoon gin and tonics, it would probably be best if somebody else drove.

Over wine and a subsequent cup of coffee, they discussed Annie's best defense, though Cam could tell Rob was humoring her by offering up alternative killers. He rattled through each Garden Society member in turn, with Cam alternately defending or laughing at the suggestions. None, however, rang true. She realized she'd convinced herself Benny was the one.

"Can you think of one reason someone might frame Annie?" she asked.

Rob frowned.

"A very small number of people might have some personal reason, though I doubt Ian committed suicide to frame her."

"Wouldn't put it past him," Cam muttered, but Rob ignored her.

"Other than that, her dad is the only reason I can think of, but I see endless possibilities where he's concerned."

"But she's not her dad! She's never even voted for him."

Rob's eyes went wide in amazement. "Seriously?"

"Seriously. She disagrees with him politically."

"But family is family."

"I didn't say they weren't speaking, or that she didn't buy him Christmas presents. She just doesn't want his political party to be in power."

Rob shrugged, not grasping how a family could compartmentalize in that way. "Still, a murder charge for his daughter would hurt him. If *that* was one of the killer's goals, it could work."

Cam hadn't thought about it from that angle and hated admitting it had some merit. "So finding out who might want to damage him politically would help. Unfortunately, he killed a big land preservation bill last year, so that's pretty much the whole Garden Society."

"Seriously?"

Cam nodded, disappointed there wasn't something more to go on, but slightly encouraged at the peripheral idea that at the very least Annie might be able to cast doubt on herself as a suspect and offer a motive for someone framing her. Cam hoped this never came down to a trial, though.

By the time they had eaten, drunk, and tipped, Cam figured they'd made it to only two hours too early to break into the greenhouse.

"So what do you want to do?" Rob asked.

"Show you the pictures," Cam said. She spotted Rob's frustration only after the fact. She'd had too much to drink to realize he wanted a romantic encounter beforehand, but she wasn't in the mood, so it was easier to feign ignorance. What she currently craved was focus.

When she entered her apartment, she found it.

"Annie!"

Annie grinned. "I hoped you wouldn't mind I was here."

"Not at all!" Cam rushed over and hugged Annie tightly several times in her tipsy exuberance. "Why didn't you call?"

"They still have my phone at the station, though they haven't formally charged it with anything." She snorted at her own joke. It was just like Annie to make light of the situation. "And I don't know your number anymore because you're on speed dial. Your dad bailed me out, but I didn't think to ask him for your number. Besides, I knew you were swamped. I also knew at some point you'd come home."

"That's true, but I'm your best friend."

"Who I'm counting on to solve this thing! Jake's no help."

"Rob is." Cam smiled.

Annie winked at Rob. "I *knew* Rob would be. I never doubted that. But I didn't want to interrupt you."

"Well . . . I guess we've got some stuff . . ."

"Like what?"

"Well . . . something we're looking into in a little bit. But there's also the pictures from the party for you to look at. I took copies to the police, and I saw some helpful bits of information in those shots. Maybe while we're gone you can go through them more closely. You have a better eye."

"Sounds good. There are a lot of things I'm not supposed to do, but looking at pictures I took isn't on that list. Still . . . what are you two up to?"

Cam looked at Rob, who nodded, so Cam explained their theory on the greenhouse.

"Greenhouse one? Isn't that 'Winter'?"

"Yeah. It's the one where the camera was found."

"Well, sure . . . for pictures it might be ideal. If it's got the most direct view of the hot tub and all that. But if Rob is right and this is about pot, I'd check 'Summer.' That's where year-round growth would occur."

Cam realized she hadn't taken the drug idea very seriously until this point. She certainly hadn't thought about the plant properties of pot, but if it really was a possibility, Annie was right. "Okay . . . so we have two greenhouses to check . . ."

"And I will cover the pictures," Annie said, reaching for Cam's computer expectantly.

Cam grinned. "Excellent!" She pulled her computer out and pointed out the file. "We might be a while, but I know you've got plenty to do."

"Including sleep — cupcake shop isn't covered tomorrow. This will help me unwind, though — far better to do something and sleep later, than to try to sleep with a head full of crime riddles."

Cam hugged Annie again.

"I'm just glad they set bail. I worried a bit they wouldn't."

"You're not the only one. The judge was one of those guys my dad used to eat for lunch when he was a trial lawyer. Fortunately, it was *your* dad there for me instead." Annie picked up Cam's laptop and headed upstairs.

CHAPTER 17

Cam didn't pull her rebel boots on very often. Part of her was giddy with excitement, and part of her was terrified. She had no experience at all at being busted. She wasn't sure she could handle it. She delayed for at least ten minutes, stowing flashlights, drawing maps, and suggesting the order they'd look. Finally, when she suggested a secret code, Rob drew the line. They left for La Fontaine, intent on breaking into at least greenhouse one, possibly one and three. Cam's stomach fluttered and her brain complained this wasn't very well thought out.

"Cam, if we get caught, we get caught. Your rationale for being there is good."

Cam had brought her day planner. The minute they entered the greenhouse, she'd stash it, so there was really something to "find."

Rob parked the equivalent of a block

away, though out of town like they were, the actual streets were sporadically placed, rather than an evenly spaced grid. They climbed out and for the first part of their journey held hands as they walked. The evening breeze and the passage of time since her last cocktail had finally left Cam feeling relatively sober.

The driveway was well lit, but after passing quickly through the gate, they rushed easily to the side, into the myriad bushes and trees, and out of view.

As they walked around the side of La Fontaine, Cam noted the servant's house was dark. The magazine crew was at their hotel, and nobody had taken over — the crime-scene tape still hung across the door. The fountain was lit. Cam thought it might be on a light sensor.

Three steps into the back garden they were met by an obstacle Cam had forgotten. The yapping hysterics of Barney, as the little dog rushed at them, were startling in the silence. There was a dog flap on the back door, but Cam worried he would wake someone, so she acted instinctively, scanning the patio for playthings. Finally she found a squeaky bone. She threw it, and Barney set out to chase it. She was impressed she'd remembered the trick. When he carried the toy back, he was willing to let Cam pick him up, with only the minor squeaks of bone chewing now breaking the white noise from the fountain.

She whispered to him, and Barney wagged his tail and wiggled. She dropped him. He dropped the bone toy and bounced a few times, as she'd only ever seen Jack Russells do, and then he growled.

Cam's second, "Hey, sweet boy, com' 'ere!" followed by a scooping up of the bone, however, calmed him, and he leaped into Cam's arms again and began licking her face.

She scratched him, ruffled his fur, and carried him as she and Rob made their way deeper into the garden. They chose the darkest of the paths that headed toward greenhouse one. After a bit she put Barney down again and tossed his squeaky bone. He seemed content to walk along with them after that, stub of a tail wagging, plastic bone in his jaws.

They entered greenhouse one quietly, Cam stashing her planner on a side table. They then made their way slowly through the rows of bushes and shrubs that dominated "Winter." While it took twenty minutes to walk all the rows, they found nothing interesting at all in the plants. Cam was disappointed but not surprised. Annie's suggestion that "Summer" would be the place to grow pot sounded logical. Then Cam spotted scaffolding. She ran the flashlight up, and Rob approached it.

"Down here, Cam. Help me see."

"I don't think you should . . ."

"Come on. We need to check."

"It's just for the sprinkler system."

"Cam."

She slouched, but finally aimed the flashlight so he could climb. At the top, he fiddled with something Cam couldn't see, and then said, "Bingo!"

"What?"

"View of the hot tub, indeed. I bet this is where Benny does his peeping."

"So, on to three?"

Rob grunted ascent as he climbed down. The main door to three was locked, but Cam had considered this likelihood. In fact, she'd been surprised greenhouse one had been so easy to access. Many high-end greenhouses had sides that, like garage doors, could be rolled up in the event of too much heat. Cam figured the Patricks would have the best, so they went around to the side farthest from the house. It didn't take long to find a door that would roll up.

Rob shivered.

"What?"

"There's just enough light from the moon that these plants look menacing. I'm pretty sure one is going to grab us."

"Oh, stop!" She wanted to laugh, but a shiver ran up her spine instead.

"Might help if we fooled around a little."

"Will you stop? That's the last thing we need to get caught at when we're already trespassing."

Rob acted annoyed, suggesting Evangeline seemed like an understanding woman, but Cam knew he was teasing.

"Back just a little farther and we can use our flashlights," Rob said.

They started at the back and worked their way forward The place was creepy in the dark. But that didn't worry Cam as much as the fear of knocking over something valuable. The plants were almost all native, but a few of them were nearly extinct, and very pricey.

As they took a few more steps forward, a loud scrape broke the silence. They were not alone in the building; someone had run into something. Cam killed the flashlight and followed Rob into a crevice between plants.

The person who'd entered wasn't nearly so careful about bumping into things as they had been. There were noises with relative frequency, and once, a crash. There was, however, no light, which indicated to Cam that the other person had also snuck in.

Cam turned to Rob, holding a finger over her mouth in a "keep quiet" gesture and pulling him back even farther. She half hoped she'd spot the intruder and a piece of the murder puzzle would slide into place, though that would also indicate a greater danger than just being caught trespassing.

Rob hung back obediently, massaging her neck but doing nothing noisy or flamboyant until he suddenly leaped past her.

"Annie?"

"Rob!"

Cam tried to grab Rob, tried to take back the noise, but realized Rob was right. The person crashing around behind them was Annie.

"Shut up. You want us to get caught?" Annie said.

Cam snorted, then had a hard time not bursting into loud laughter. "After all the noise you just made? If anyone was here to hear, they heard. Why are you here?"

"I figured if you two squares couldn't even work out that 'Summer' was the better place to grow it, you certainly weren't going to be able to identify it. I bet neither of you even knows what pot looks like."

"We know!" Cam and Rob said together.

Annie nodded, eyebrows raised. "Right."

Cam knew it was true, though it irritated her, that Annie was much more likely than she or Rob to have had a friend over the years who "grew his own."

Annie ignored them and went on. "I think I got stung by a plant, though. My calf is getting numb, and it hurts like hell."

Cam frowned at Annie's face but then knelt with the flashlight to examine Annie's calf.

"That's not a plant sting. You got a spider bite."

"Great. So how long does my leg have? Long enough to identify the pot plant for you, or am I going to die immediately?"

Rob knelt as if Annie's question was serious, and looked at the bite.

"Looks like a wolf spider to me."

"A what?"

"Wolf spider. You have at least twenty-four hours, but we don't need you."

Cam elbowed Rob. "It will get worse for half an hour or so, then reverse." Cam hated spiders, but she'd had a variety of spider bites with all the gardening she did, and was at a theoretical truce with them. At least they ate many of the bugs that destroyed gardens.

"You need me and you know it," Annie said. Cam could tell she wouldn't be so sassy if she hadn't heard Cam, but she was addressing Rob.

"Fine! Wait . . . how'd you get here? I still have your keys and your car is at the cupcake shop," Cam said.

"Yeah, I noticed." Cam could almost hear the eye roll. "I hid in the back of the Jeep while you two took forever getting ready."

Rob looked disturbed.

"I was under a blanket," Annie added. Cam thought she was probably smirking, though it was too dark to see well.

She started scanning again with the flashlight, Rob and Annie checking to either side as Cam moved forward.

It took Cam a few minutes to realize Barney was still contentedly scuffling between them. He hadn't let out so much as a growl when Annie joined them.

"Some watchdog," Cam accused.

"I fed him," Annie confessed.

Barney growled toward Cam, as if he understood her words. She tried to scoop him up again, but he went to Annie.

"I'm sorry, smart fella. Annie tricked you. She does that."

"You're not winning him back. Food

trumps fun in the dog world. There!" Annie stepped forward as Cam tried to convince Barney to approach her again, but he jumped into Annie's arms. Annie scratched him but then dropped him and moved two plants to the side.

"What?" Rob asked. "There's nothing there . . . empty table."

Barney finally leaped back into Cam's arms.

"And when you look around this overloaded greenhouse, how likely do you think it is that almost a whole table would be sitting empty when the rest is so crowded?"

Rob went forward to check the spot more closely.

"It does look pretty odd, Cam. There is some dirt, and some rings back here, like a bunch of containers were moved."

"I wish we could tell when. They could have been moved at any time," Cam said, disappointed.

"I think we're screwed if we were hoping to find evidence in here," Annie commented.

"Yeah," Rob said. "Something *not* here is no proof of anything, at least not officially."

There was a creak, and Barney shot out of Cam's arms, running toward the front of the greenhouse, barking.

"We should go," Cam whispered as a flashlight beam began scanning the greenhouse.

They edged their way back toward the open sliding door but were caught midway.

"Stop! Right there. I could shoot, but I don't want to. Who's there?"

It was Jake. Barney's jaws were clenched to his pant leg, and the dog growled menacingly.

"Shoot!" Cam said a little too loudly. She was trying to shoo Annie out, but Annie wouldn't budge. She elbowed Cam.

"Nice word choice, moron," Annie said. "You know if you don't just learn to swear, you could get us all killed."

"Jake! It's Rob and Cam!" Rob shouted.

"I count three."

"Damn moonlight," Annie muttered.

"And Annie, but I made her come," Cam lied.

"Annie is out on bail," Jake said. "This is a really bad place for Annie to be."

"I needed to find my planner, and she had it last." Cam saw Jake frown.

"And you didn't tell the Patricks you'd be trespassing?"

"I thought I did. I'm sorry."

"You're trespassing. And it's dark. How are you doing this in the dark?"

"I have implicit permission!" Cam shouted, scrambling. She ignored the darkness comment.

"Is that a legal term?" Jake asked. Cam was sure his eyebrows were raised.

"No! Just . . . I mean if you asked Mr. Patrick, he'd say it was okay!"

Rob whispered something about the missing pot plants in her ear, but she stepped on his foot. Telling Jake they were investigating the murders would not help their situation.

Cam worried Jake had overheard Rob, but he seemed to be focused on Annie. Cam couldn't stand it, so she broke the awkwardness.

"Ah! Yes. Jake! Crowbar incident: the guy leads Annie on; they dated for months. How many months, Annie, ten?"

Cam continued without waiting for an answer.

"She thought he was going to propose. She finds out he's actually already married. The jerk had been lying that whole time. Annie got a little carried away *on the car.* Not the guy who deserved it, but *his car!*"

Jake frowned. Annie elbowed Cam.

"How'd you hear that?"

"My father, under duress, and only after you'd been carted off to jail. He thought you were planning on telling me or he wouldn't have."

Annie sank on the spot, putting her face in her hands.

"A married guy tricked you?" Jake asked.

"Look," Cam interrupted, "can't we . . . forget all this for now?"

"I need to make sure the Patricks don't object."

"The Patricks don't object."

Cam gasped. Evangeline stood behind Jake, lacy nightie flowing, Barney cuddled in her arms.

"Cam is forward thinking, and we appreciate it. Sorry to inconvenience you, Officer. I just misunderstood the timing."

Cam let out a long, relieved breath.

"They have permission to be here?" Jake asked.

"Yes, but I forgot to cut off the alarm. I thought they would be calling when they were on their way, but we did discuss this." Evangeline was a smooth liar.

"Yeah, sorry I forgot to call, Evangeline," Cam said. She was glad it was dark because she knew her whole face was bright red.

"Did you get what you needed?" Evangeline asked.

Cam and Rob nodded. Annie stood to join them, still looking very upset.

"Y'all need a nightcap after being scared out of your wits?" Evangeline asked.

Rob started to say no, but Cam stepped on his foot again. After she'd saved them, it seemed rude to say no.

"That would be nice."

As they went to the house, Jake left, casting a lingering look at Annie, who wouldn't look at anyone.

Evangeline turned on a patio light and pressed a code into a panel, opening a minibar. She offered beer or bottled cocktails to everyone, and then sat in a chair with a mojito.

"So what was this really about?" Evangeline gazed at Cam as she sat.

"I had a few hints today that gave me the idea Benny might be growing marijuana here . . . greenhouse three seemed most logical."

"Benny? Marijuana? Nonsense!"

"We have a picture that shows Ian giving him money, but that's not the only thing."

Evangeline suddenly seemed nervous, and Cam knew she was thinking of the photos.

"Then what?"

"Benny and Jean-Jacques had debts with the same bookie. Benny wouldn't need money if he wasn't in some kind of trouble."

"Somebody using him, maybe," Evangeline said.

"That may be, and if it's true, we certainly want to find that out."

"Using him for pictures of me?"

"That's what I thought at first, too — we did find a spot in greenhouse one where most of the photos I saw must have been taken. But what if someone also had suggested easy money for raising a few plants? Don't you think he might fall for it?" Cam said.

Evangeline's face shifted. "Well now, that makes sense if he'd met the wrong sort of people, and gambling people might indeed suggest something like that if they knew about the greenhouses. Did you find anything, illegal plants, I mean?"

"A table that had been cleared. We think someone might have tipped him off — got wind we might be looking."

"Who would do that?"

Cam shrugged and shook her head. She really had no idea. Now there was no evidence left except a spot from which pots had been removed.

"Evangeline, thank you for not ratting us out to Jake."

"I trust you, Cam. From our conversation earlier, you seem to be earnest, and I'd love you to solve this."

"Good. I do have a few questions, if you don't mind."

"Sure. Anything."

"How come you stayed quiet about the loan?"

Evangeline sighed. "Neil knows. Of course. We are approached often — even by friends. But there are a lot of . . . old acquaintances of mine who ask — Jean-Jacques even — I'm sure you know. We just have to be careful and quiet. So it's become a habit."

"And when are Benny and Henry here?"

"Normally four mornings a week, though I'm afraid we've monopolized more of Benny's time since the *Garden Delights* people arrived. He's perfectly capable of all the basics, which we couldn't let fall behind when we had a camera crew here."

"Are they here tomorrow?"

"I expect so, yes."

"Thank you," Cam said as she stood, indicating to the others it was time to go. "We should let you get to bed. Thank you, Evangeline."

"Was that weird, or what?" Annie asked when they were finally on their way.

"Pretty strange. Any chance of you and

Jake ever seeing eye to eye again?" Cam asked.

"I doubt it. I only ever look at his Adam's apple."

Cam rolled her eyes at the literal interpretation based on Annie's vertical challenges.

"I saw understanding." Rob ignored the joking, as usual.

"Not enough understanding that he could stay and have a conversation."

"Did you ask him about the woman?" Rob replied.

Annie didn't answer. Cam could tell by her silence she wore a pouting expression in the backseat. Annie hated to be wrong almost as much as Cam did.

"So maybe tomorrow y'all can work it out?" Cam said.

Her question was met with more silence; the backseat pout continued.

"Speaking of understandings with Jake." Cam turned to Rob. "What was that near confession?"

"He's been pretty good to me — shared information. I felt obliged there for a minute."

"Except we could have been arrested."

"Yeah. There's that. Thanks for the reminder."

Cam nodded, then changed subjects.

"So how do we catch Benny?" she asked, trying to avoid the awkwardness that now went two directions.

"I'd say I need to follow him," Rob said.

"You? Why you?"

"I'm the reporter? I have a legitimate reason?"

"And you have the subtlety of a sledgehammer. I need to do it," Cam said.

"Neither of you stands a chance of getting information. You're way too obvious," Annie said.

"And you can do subtle better?" Cam asked.

"You bet I can! Unfortunately . . . I can't. I have to work."

"I can do it," Cam said emphatically, glad Annie was too busy to help so she would have the chance to prove herself.

"Right," Annie answered.

"I didn't hear where I came in," Rob said.

"You didn't," Cam and Annie said together.

Chapter 18

They swung by and picked up Annie's Bug on the way home. Their adrenaline was still rushing when they reached Cam's place. Annie insisted she needed to crash, as five in the morning was already too near, and she left, though Cam thought she looked a little disappointed.

Cam and Rob sat on Cam's sofa.

"So you think Benny would kill someone over a couple of pot plants?" Rob asked.

"It doesn't make much sense," Cam admitted. "I mean, it looks like there would have been a pretty steady cash flow set up, so why would he? Especially when we know Ian gave him money — talk about looking a gift horse in the mouth."

"Do you think maybe Jean-Jacques was edging in on his territory?"

"Rob, Benny has a learning disability. He does not have the mentality required to be a drug overlord."

"Then who was Benny working for?"

"You think he was working for someone?" That idea surprised her.

"Sure. How would he get the idea otherwise? I think anybody doing that who isn't very bright, and who hasn't been caught, must be following orders from somebody smarter."

Cam nodded. "And that somebody might be a murderer. I still think he might have been protecting Evangeline, though."

"By selling pictures of her?"

"There's no evidence he sold them. Try to think like Benny for a minute. I know it's hard with that big brain of yours, but try."

"Mocking just might get you handcuffed."

"Jake lend you some?" she asked hopefully.

Rob stared at her. "That appeals to you?"

"I didn't say that."

"You didn't need to. I'm just . . . surprised."

"What? I can be naughty."

"Since when?"

"Try me."

He raised his eyebrows, then shook his head as if he were trying to wake up. "Cam! Drugs? Pornography? Benny?"

"Right." She was actually shocked he hadn't taken her up on her offer. She was feeling like a little diversion at the moment, though she wasn't very serious about the handcuffs. Annie just put ideas in her head sometimes. "I think he worshiped Evangeline from afar, wanted to worship . . . erm . . . more of her, and got protective when Jean-Jacques started harassing her. You ask *me?* That's our motive. Drugs are coincidental."

"Who's to say Nick didn't get protective? It sounds like he and Evangeline were close."

"Friends. They were friends! *Are* friends." The romantic feelings that had sparked with the handcuff conversation were figuratively doused in cold water as Rob brought up the sore subject again.

"Friends that lend each other a lot of money?"

"Not lend. Cosign. It just means she thinks he's trustworthy to pay it back. And who killed Ian, then, smarty-pants?"

Rob sighed. "I should go. You want me to come with you in the morning?"

"No, you have work. I'll figure it out." She didn't want him on her mission, reporter skills or not. She had something to prove.

"You can't investigate without a car."

"Watch me." Annie had to do cupcakes all morning. Cam would borrow the Bug, but

Rob didn't need to be in on the secret. She was too annoyed to share at the moment.

Cam went in her room and shut the door, leaving Rob to show himself out.

Annie woke up Cam at six.

"What?" Cam buried her face in her pillow.

"Well, I was thinking since I have to work today, you could have my car."

Cam rolled over and grinned, though she kept her eyes closed for a moment.

"You're my fairy god-Annie!"

She loved it when the best friend mind-meld happened. And it was the only way she'd get to do this investigating alone, something she felt was crucial to a good outcome for this press event, but she needed a car. Rob certainly wouldn't lend her his for her to go off alone. She struggled to pull herself out of bed, but Annie handed her a cup of coffee. It smelled like it had hazelnut cream in it.

"Why are you spoiling me?" Cam asked.

"I need you to solve this puppy. I wish I could help you."

Cam yawned. "I'll cope. But on our way, I want to bounce something off you."

Annie nodded.

Cam headed into the bathroom for a

quick shower, after which she forced in her contacts, wincing, and ran a brush through her hair, deciding the day called for a headband. As soon as she was dressed, she and Annie went to Annie's car. Cam grabbed an energy bar for each of them on the way out.

As they drove, she abused Rob for a while on his insistence that Nick was still a suspect.

"He was in jail when murder number two happened," Annie commented.

"Thank you! Exactly what I said."

"Sheesh, almost sounds like Rob thinks Petunia did the second murder to take Nick off the suspect list."

Cam didn't respond, mostly because she'd had that same thought before, and she wanted the idea to go away. "But his point about somebody else protecting Evangeline . . ."

"Why just Evangeline?"

"There just aren't many other options." Though opening the field appealed to Cam.

"You think Mr. Patrick could bludgeon someone with a camera?" Annie asked.

"Ew. Though . . . well . . . there was that witnessed argument between him and Jean-Jacques, but I still don't think so."

She sighed. She really didn't want to expand her list. She wanted a magic suspect who had nothing to do with any of them to appear with the proverbial smoking gun, but the shears and camera were in custody, so she knew better than to hope for that.

"Yeah, well, here's something else to consider," Annie said, cutting into her thoughts. "Imagine if it was your eight-hundred-dollar camera that will cost at least twelve hundred to replace — used for murder, then rotting in jail!"

"Oh, geez, Annie. I didn't think about that," Cam said.

"Never mind. It's insured, except the first two fifty, and that will be on my bill."

Cam rolled her eyes but felt true sympathy.

"Anyway, getting back to the suspects list, I think it could have been someone protecting Samantha, or . . . I don't know . . . someone else," Annie said.

"I guess. I'll brainstorm with Rob again. It will give me an excuse to stay ahead of him."

Annie shook her head at Cam. "There is no need to be so competitive with your boyfriend."

"I'm not."

Annie pulled up behind her cupcake shop and climbed out, staring at Cam in disbelief.

"Right. And I'm not the hottest woman in

three counties."

Cam snorted, scooted over to the driver's seat, and pulled away. She had a stakeout to get under way or the last several days of work would be for nothing.

Cam had a two-part plan for the morning. First, she hoped to find Henry Larsson. She thought the parent of a son with some learning issues might keep a close eye, even if the son was now an adult.

She was in luck. When she got to La Fontaine, Giselle knew Henry was planting annuals on the eastern edge of the huge garden, so Cam was able to find him easily.

"Well, hello, Camellia. What brings you out this morning?" He kept digging and putting in plants.

"I hoped you might . . . have you noticed any . . . suspicious friends of Benny?"

He stopped and looked at her. "Suspicious how?"

"The kind who might ask him to do things maybe he shouldn't?"

"I don't know what you're suggesting!" He sounded angry.

Cam decided to brave it anyway. "Like growing pot plants."

"No! I watch out for my son! He's not involved in anything like that!"

Cam thought he was protesting too much, but she made her excuses about just needing to check and retreated to Annie's car to regroup and formulate a different approach.

A stakeout was far more boring than it sounded. Cam could certainly see why police officers turned to doughnuts and coffee. She left La Fontaine, driving around the corner and parking under a tree with low hanging boughs. Then she walked back, crouching down to watch from the bushes. She watched for a long time, all the while craving an old-fashioned doughnut for the first time since age twelve. Her father's gift of Krispy Kremes yesterday had surely seeded today's craving. It had been the childhood Saturday morning "let Mom sleep" trick — her dad taking her and Petunia for doughnuts.

Refocusing on the matter at hand, Cam could see Henry, still on the eastern border, and Benny, who didn't seem to be up to anything suspicious. He dead headed, trimmed, and swept debris from the pavement slowly but steadily. After a while, though, he went to greenhouse three and when he came out, he looked around, scratching his head. It seemed to confirm the pot plants, or whatever mystery plants they'd been, were his. But it looked as though Benny thought Henry had gotten rid of them. She watched as Benny found and confronted his father, and Henry's annoyed, angry response to Benny's shouting did nothing to lessen the idea. She was too far away to hear why Benny had jumped to his conclusion, though she was annoyed Henry seemed to have lied to her. Henry clearly knew more than he was telling.

Benny left in a hurry, and Cam had to sprint to get back to Annie's car in time to follow him. She didn't know what kind of vehicle to watch for, but she was sure Benny was leaving the premises and there was only one logical way to go, so she started Annie's car and waited.

A few minutes later a small, dark-colored pickup truck that had been in the Patricks' driveway rounded the corner, going at least ten miles an hour over the speed limit. Cam thought it was one of Henry's work trucks. She waited briefly, then followed.

Following at a reasonable distance was hard, even outside of town. Cam feared for what would happen when Benny got into the city where they would be at the mercy of stoplights, but fortunately, he veered north, bypassing most of town.

He headed into a poor suburb of clapboard houses and duplexes, many with broken-down vehicles in the yards. He wove through narrow streets. Cam avoided getting too close but then remembered that given his learning issues, Benny was unlikely to realize he was being followed so long as she stayed back at least a little. Besides, she doubted he'd recognize Annie's car, and even if he did, he had even less reason to suspect Annie would follow him than Cam.

When he finally pulled over, she drove past and continued three-quarters of the way around the block. She parked on a side street that led to the one Benny had parked on, and thought she could see through backyards to the pair of houses he'd parked in front of. She was glad the nearer one was yellow. It stood out among the tans, whites, and grays.

She got out of Annie's car and debated walking on the sidewalk versus hiding in the bushes. Initially, she took the sidewalk, thinking it was less conspicuous, so she strolled slowly up the block, trying to take in every observation she could.

The last house on the block looked empty, so Cam walked up the front walk as if she planned to ring the doorbell, then ducked behind a shrub and went around to the back of the house. She stood in the deserted expanse of backyards and evaluated the terrain. It wasn't a neighborhood with formidable fences, though there were a couple she'd have to climb.

The biggest obstacle would be the Rottweiler currently sleeping two yards away; his nose periodically twitched, obvious even from this distance. She wondered how much of a watchdog he was and how well contained he was in his yard. His fence clearly wasn't the type that was meant to hold in an animal that large. She would have gone around, but the yard behind the one the dog was in had a six-foot chain-link fence with plastic slats woven through to block prying eyes. It seemed like a sign of no tolerance where trespassing was concerned.

She guessed the house Benny had gone into was the fifth or sixth away from her.

She eased across the first yard and into the second. As she stepped over the short fence, a stick popped up and snapped, giving her an idea. She picked it up and crossed the yard toward the dog.

He heard her, twitching at first, then emitting a low growl.

"Hey, boy. Do you like to fetch?"

His ears pricked and his tail stub twitched, though the growl continued and he didn't lift his head.

"You wanna get the stick? You like a stick?"

She ran toward the fence, stopping back from it a good five feet so the dog didn't feel threatened. She didn't think the fence stood a chance if that dog was determined. She threw the stick over the fence, and he shot after it.

She spotted the chain tethering him, a good sign. He retrieved the stick and brought it back toward her as far as the chain would reach. He dropped the stick and whined, cocking his head.

"Good boy! Aren't you smart?"

He whined again, panting with what looked like a dopey smile, so she climbed over the fence and retrieved the stick, throwing it again.

He fetched it and brought it back before she was across the yard, so she threw it once more in the other direction. He chased after it, and she climbed the fence on the far side of the yard.

When he brought the stick as far toward her as he could and saw that she was out of reach, he whined three or four times. She didn't return, so he began to bark. Once the barking began, there was no mistake that a neighborhood dog was distressed about something, so she threw herself under a half-withered rhododendron and waited.

A sliding glass door whirred open.

"Cujo! Shush!"

Cujo barked three more times.

"You stop that! Do I need to make you come in?"

Cujo whined and sat, still looking in Cam's direction, but done barking. The woman who'd yelled had accomplished what she wanted. The door whirred again and she was gone.

Cam was glad she hadn't known earlier that the dog was named Cujo. She liked him and wasn't sure she could have if she'd known the name. She waited awhile longer, until the dog went back to the patio and laid down.

When she finally moved on, she felt as though she hadn't breathed for ages. Cujo continued to whine until she was too far to hear, and Cam felt guilty.

A healthy stand of raspberries, not yet bearing fruit but full of thorns, was the only other obstacle she had to skirt before arriving at the pair of small houses. She could see Benny's pickup in front, resting right on the property line. She held back to watch, but from this distance, she couldn't tell which house Benny had gone into. Both houses had closed shades or drawn curtains on the main floor. She decided to creep into the bushes between the houses and try to listen to both, hoping she would hear where Benny was.

She managed to not be spotted, and found her way to the shrubs on the side of one of the houses. She leaned her ear against the wall, then a window, but heard nothing coming from inside. A wait of ten minutes brought no change, so she darted across to the other house, though the cover wasn't as good. She was standing in a mass of day-lilies that hadn't bloomed yet and only reached her thigh.

She carefully moved farther toward the front of the house to see if she could see anybody coming or going, and was shocked as she peeked around the corner to have her arm grabbed by a balding man with graying stubble on his chin.

"What the hell are you doing?"

Cam tried to smile, but knew it looked bad. There was no mistaking that she was trespassing and sneaking around.

"I'm sorry. I followed a friend of mine. Someone told me it was his birthday, and I wanted to . . . you know . . . wish him happy birthday. But I wanted it to be a surprise."

"What's this friend named?" He smiled now, as if he were being friendly, but he was a bad actor. He was definitely suspicious, and possibly evil, Cam thought.

Her split-second, panicked logic told her it was better to give a real name than a false one. She hoped it wouldn't get Benny in trouble for allowing her to follow him.

"Benny Larsson."

"Benny?" He sneered, and didn't sound like he believed her overly much. Then he let out an ugly laugh. "Chick like you wants to wish *Benny* a happy birthday?"

Cam nodded, trying to don an innocent face.

"When his birthday is the end of December?"

Her heart sank. The man's incredulous expression frightened Cam.

"I thought . . ." She was scrambling for the right words but kept coming up empty. She fought her face, knowing it was trying to give too much away.

He laughed again. "I'm kidding, princess! I have no clue when the kid's birthday is. He's more of a ladies' man than I thought if a pretty lady like you is looking for him. I don't think it's his birthday, though. Had a party last winter."

"But . . ."

"Should I set him straight? About lying to pretty ladies, I mean?"

"Not if it means hurting him!"

"So, you like him?"

"Of course I do! He's a nice boy!"

To Cam's surprise, the man broke into real laughter, not the mocking kind of a moment ago. "Feel protective, then?"

"Any decent person would."

He laughed even harder. "Okay, princess. Well, how about this? I promise not to hurt Benny. Would that help?" His chuckling had grown annoying, but Cam continued to play dumb.

"A lot. You really promise?" She didn't believe him, and Benny's safety hadn't been her original concern, but acting protective seemed to be working, having been caught and all, and in case this man was sincere, it couldn't hurt. At the moment, she wanted to get out of there in one piece. "Should I just go, then? Since I have your word, I mean?"

The man laughed again, but he was back to the menacing demeanor of a few minutes earlier.

"I can tell you're harmless. I can also tell you are very naïve. But I don't have that authority, so you'll just have to wait a bit."

Cam sighed and allowed herself be led by the arm into the small, poorly made, even more poorly kept, house. Half a dozen people alternately stared at and ignored her;

a few more were milling about less attentively. It seemed a lot of activity for a house of that size. The bald man led her to an upstairs bedroom, and for a minute she panicked, but he just pushed her in.

"Hey! Watch this one, will you?"

A chiseled silhouette of a man looked in, eyebrows raised, and nodded before shutting the door.

When she finally calmed down, she thought the room had been picked as "easy to guard." There was only one window, which was above the patio in the backyard, so an attempt to jump meant certain injury, and the only door led back to the hallway, where the rather-too-handsome thug had been instructed not to let her leave. Cam pretended for all of twenty seconds that he was permitted to come enjoy her company, but in her vulnerable circumstances, it made her feel way too exposed. All future fantasies of captivity abandoned her forever.

She paced, going over her options. She thought about lowering herself out the window, but there were no sheets on the bed — in fact, it was only a mattress on the floor, topped by a sleeping bag. Unless she was kept here for days, which she doubted was the intention, it was not worth the risk, any more so than trying to break a hole in the walls or fight the muscular man in the hall. It was only in her fantasy that she was the type of girl who could break out of imprisonment anyway. She didn't have any illusions that she was actually that tough. Annie was tougher, and she was five-two. Cam's best skill had always been negotiation. She would have to talk her way out. That option, though, held promise.

She hoped appearing worried about Benny would continue to work, though she would have to be careful not to accuse anybody of anything dastardly. And clearly what she'd said so far hadn't been considered cause for concern, or somebody would have tried to talk to her already. Then it occurred to her that the pictures of Evangeline, or rather, the existence of them — not the real pictures — would serve as the best motive for her chasing down the "boy" and expressing her "worry" as to what he had gotten himself into. She tried to keep her thoughts in terms of "boy" as it was the only way to make the transgression sound both innocent and undesirable. She approached the door and shouted.

"Please! Can I just talk to Benny?"

"You're just supposed to sit tight," the thug said. His voice was handsome, too, deep and melodic, Cam noted with irritation.

"Pretty please." She hoped acting girly might help. "I just want to make sure he doesn't publish those pictures!"

To her surprise the man guarding the door opened it. Bright blue eyes flashed at her from an olive-toned face. He looked at her, rather intrigued, and gave a shout.

"Benny? Have you been a bad boy?" He sounded terribly amused. Cam panicked as she realized it sounded like the pictures were of her.

Benny arrived a few minutes later, looking unsure.

"Ms. Harris, I don't know what you want."

"She wants to make sure those girlie pictures of her don't go public!" The man chuckled, delightedly. His teeth were straight, too! Drat!

Cam glared at him, and Benny just looked confused. Then in a strategic moment, Cam decided to go with it. She figured she'd never see this man again, and it made for a more coherent case.

"Just to make sure none of those pictures you took are released to the public!"

"What?"

"You!" Cam pointed at the handsome thug. "What's your name?"

"That's Dylan," Benny said.

"Dylan, can Benny and I have a minute?"

Dylan shrugged, still laughing, but he wouldn't go, so Cam went on.

"We found the camera — you know the one I'm talking about — it had your fingerprints on it."

Dylan frowned at that, and Cam cursed herself. Fingerprinting was a police activity. Benny, of course, didn't seem to catch the implication, but she thought Dylan had. Benny did realize, though, he had trouble. He stepped into the room and shut the door on Dylan. He looked stricken.

"I'd never release those! Those . . ." But he trailed off.

"But might you protect her? If someone else had pictures like that to release?"

"Nobody would do that. Nobody who knows Evangeline, anyway."

"Nobody?"

"Look. Mr. Patrick is okay. He's nice enough. I wasn't unhappy before they got married. It's a job, ya know? But Evangeline has . . . well, he's more generous now with bonuses, and thinks of all of us more . . . as people. All the help likes her."

Something seemed off, but she couldn't put her finger on it at the moment.

"Why would you take those pictures if you

like her so much?"

Benny looked down, embarrassed.

"She's beautiful. I guess . . . I maybe fantasized she was mine. I didn't mean anything."

Cam gave a scolding look. "I guess I'll go, then."

"You followed me here about that?"

"I didn't want to talk to you about it at the Patricks'. I was worried Mr. Patrick would overhear."

"I guess that's all right, then. But it's not very smart to follow me. I know some . . . rough people." He looked at the door. Cam didn't want to think of Dylan as rough — rogue, maybe, not rough. She looked back at Benny.

She almost blurted a question about the bookie, but decided it was stupid, given where she was and that she'd already gotten caught.

"Okay. I'm glad you won't do anything with the pictures. You know the police have them, though?" she whispered.

He shrugged. She wasn't sure whether he didn't care or was just acting tough.

Cam followed Benny back down the stairs, and they had nearly reached the front door when someone started yelling at Benny.

"Larsson, you idiot! What's this supposed to be?"

"I'll be there in a minute!" Benny shouted, trying to shoo Cam out the door, but Cam was acting stupid, moving at a snail's pace. She wanted to hear what this was about.

"This is only a quarter what you promised!"

"I ran into some trouble. I'll get the rest!"

Benny pulled the door open and practically shoved Cam out, but with the open windows at the front of the house, she still heard.

"I have enough for the races this afternoon, and I'll fix the problem tonight."

"You better!"

The missing product was no mystery. The pot plants. And races. That probably meant stock cars, as Benny didn't really seem a horse-racing sort. Roanoke's track was north of town. Roanoke's love for stock cars had a relatively long history, and the Roanoke home of Curtis Turner, a local racing legend, had been turned into a museum dedicated to the early days of the sport. It shouldn't be too difficult to track down times for the afternoon's races. As all this registered, though, the one thing that seemed off finally slid into place: Benny

Larsson didn't seem nearly as dim as he had let everybody believe.

CHAPTER 19

When Cam arrived back at her car, she called Rob. She felt sheepish about having followed Benny, but more so about having gotten caught. That was nothing, though, compared to her heart pounding in fright, so she confessed. Rob wasn't at all happy, but as his voice calmed her, the feeling of triumph at having new information soon trumped any negativity. She gloated a little about how smooth she'd been in making it out of there.

"Fine. You were fabulous. So now you need to give me a chance to do something." She heard his sarcasm, but ignored it. "You can't show me up like that and not give me a chance to catch up!"

Cam snorted. "Fine, macho man. What's your plan?"

"To go to the Patricks', talk to the help. See if anybody else knows anything about those plants, maybe look for a printer? I won't tell anyone anything — I can be vague, but anyone who knows will get what I'm asking about. Then I'm on racetrack duty."

"But that gives you two things."

"One has an excuse — as a reporter. The other — those people already caught you once today. They won't be nice to you if they catch you again!"

"Okay, fine." Cam sighed and pretended to pout. He was right on both counts, though she was largely agreeing to avoid an argument.

"Listen. How about some other interesting news?"

"Okay."

"That money from Hannah caused a search though the bank accounts of all the suspects. We should know if the money came from any of them this afternoon."

"Well, that's something."

After she hung up, she thought more about what Rob was doing; she realized the killer was the one most likely to understand Rob's questions and know what they were up to. She tried to call him back, but he'd turned off his phone. She cursed herself for letting him get ahead of her.

Cam went to Spoons to help Petunia with

lunches again. Petunia was on a cloud. Apparently whoever had posted bail for Annie had also posted it for Nick, and they'd been told the charges would likely be dropped due to lack of evidence. Cam knew it was her dad who had paid the bail, but Petunia seemed to prefer to think of this as a matter of karmic rightness, so Cam wasn't going to burst her bubble, at least not while it was so freshly inflated.

She helped with lunch anyway, hoping to give the couple a break in the afternoon to share a little alone time. They seemed appreciative. Nick, in particular, kept shooting her sheepish looks that said, "You're the best."

Cam viewed Nick a little differently now, knowing his history. He'd never been a guy without a past, but the punk band seemed more tangible now, and Evangeline's involvement made it all the more colorful. Jean-Jacques's betrayal had, in Cam's mind at least, transformed Nick into a tragic antihero, though Cam had to hold her tongue, as Petunia wouldn't find any of this amusing.

Nick knew his wife, so seemed to grasp the need to not talk openly about it, but Cam was less secretive when she explained

Benny Larsson was her current favorite suspect.

"I think he has a huge crush on Evangeline and thought it was a way to protect her. He has some learning issues, so he may not even have known it was wrong." Though as Cam said it, she realized she didn't think this was true anymore. If Benny had committed the crime, he'd known full well what he was doing.

Petunia scowled. "That woman could get any man to act against his own common sense!" She glared at her husband but wouldn't say any more.

"Sorry. I thought she'd be pleased that there's another suspect," Cam whispered when she and Nick were alone for a minute.

"She's never really understood my friendship with Vange. Any guy who claimed to be Petunia's friend tried to sleep with her — and who could blame them, really?"

"TMI, Nick." Not only TMI, but confusing. Petunia was all bony limbs as far as Cam could see. Evangeline was shapely and gorgeous.

"Sorry, I just mean I never felt tempted with Vange. She was always more like a sister or something — like you, Cam. But Petunia doesn't believe me."

Cam started to pat his arm, but Petunia

came back, so she made an odd gesture instead.

"Last lunch! What are you waiting for?" Petunia bellowed.

"Sorry! Just dropped something, and I had to make sure it was okay, but it is. You packed it well." Cam lied.

Petunia and Nick thanked Cam profusely when they were done, and Cam drove Annie's car back to the cupcake shop just in time for the afternoon lull.

Cam sank to the floor against the wall opposite where Annie was frosting cupcakes behind the counter.

"What? You don't want to play with frosting?" Annie asked.

"I might. First I need a computer."

"You know where it is."

Cam rose. She was too curious about the details not to look up the races. She logged on and typed in "Caution Flag stock car races."

"Shoot!"

"Bang!" Annie said. A normal response to Cam's non-swearing.

"There's nothing there!"

"Where?"

"Caution Flag — the place stock cars are usually raced in Roanoke. There's nothing listed, but Benny said there were races this afternoon."

"Call them."

Cam frowned but obeyed, then clicked her phone shut. "Crap!"

Annie raised an eyebrow.

"They're now!"

"What are now?"

"Stock car races — only it's not races. It's time trials — preliminary stuff. I bet Rob doesn't even know. He would have looked online and decided I misunderstood. We have to get out there!"

Annie shrugged, wiped her hands, and said, "I'm in. I couldn't go this morning, but you need backup. I can finish frosting when I get back — buttercream stays nice for hours."

They raced out to the Bug and dove in, Cam reading directions from Annie's laptop, which she held in a death grip. Annie's driving had her normal urgency.

Cam relayed her morning adventures, and Annie called her "idiot" in all the right places, reiterating Cam's need for supervision, then she proceeded to call Rob an idiot, which was a little more gratifying. She was intrigued, though, that this drug avenue might prove promising.

"Who knew we hung out with hoodlums?"

Cam's leg vibrated. She fished her cell

phone out of her pocket and answered it.

"Rob? What's up?"

"Got some interesting stuff. Henry admitted having moved the plants, but catch this — orchids. Benny was mad because they're a special project of his, and he thought it was too early in the year to have them outside."

"What? Do you believe him?"

"I'm not sure. Maybe. And then I talked to Giselle, who didn't have anything new, really, but she did let me use the office. It has an old dot matrix printer. I'm not even sure where they find ink for that dinosaur. That note had to be printed here. There was a document on it, but Giselle didn't want me to touch it in case it was something of the Patricks, and she was sort of hovering, so I cooperated."

"Good work on the printer! Did you see anybody . . . suspectwise?"

"Not other than Evangeline, but I was talking to people most of the time and could only be in one place at a time."

"I'm helping Annie right now." She wasn't sure why she was lying, except that he would try to stop her if he knew where she was headed. "We'll head for her darkroom afterward, so just call, okay?"

"You got it! Love you!"

"Love you, too."

Cam had been thrown off by the orchid stuff. She shared it with Annie but then pushed it to the back of her mind with all the other tidbits she'd gathered, because when she looked up, they were at the track.

She wasn't sure what she'd expected from stock car races, but this was about six tiers down. She'd imagined an arena full of excited people drinking beer and cheering. This arena was big all right. There were stands on either side topped by VIP boxes, but there were only maybe three dozen people watching. If Cam were guessing, she would bet all the people present had some connection with one of the drivers. So qualifiers must not be that big of a deal.

It wasn't hard to spot Benny. He stood on the first landing in the stands talking to four others, including Dylan, who elbowed Benny when he spotted Cam.

"Why does that guy know who you are?" Annie asked.

"Room guard," Cam said.

"Then why the heck would you ever leave? He can guard my room any time!"

Cam gave Annie her mock evil eye as Benny walked toward them. He was laughing, but his tone was annoyed.

"Miss Harris, have you fallen in love with me?"

Cam was trying hard not to look at his face, knowing it would only make her own grow embarrassingly red. Her forced restraint meant she noticed the stack of papers in his hands.

"What are those?"

"You gonna report me?"

"Why would I report you?"

Annie sighed. "Because betting is illegal, my naïve friend. Tell me, Benny, did you have trouble with your supplier for these?"

"Yeah, his machine's down. How'd you know?"

"Cam, I think we've misinterpreted. A lot."

"This is the supply you were short on, the one the guy at the house yelled at you about?" Cam asked.

"Yeah?"

"And what did you used to have growing in greenhouse three that got moved?"

His disbelief couldn't quite hide his embarrassment.

"None of your business."

"Not pot?"

"At the Patricks'? With my dad everywhere? Are you kidding me?"

"Orchids?"

"Well, if you knew already, why are you asking?"

"Why are you embarrassed about growing orchids? You're a gardener."

He sputtered a bit but then finally confessed, "Because I did it to impress Evangeline, okay? Everybody thinks I'm an idiot, and 'Oh, isn't that sweet?' But her birthday is in July and I wanted blooming orchids to show her."

"And did Jean-Jacques have anything to do with those?" She gestured at the betting forms.

"Not that I know. Not these, anyway."

"Does your bookie cover other gambling?"

"Of course he does. Sports betting mostly, but sometimes there's some high-stakes card game or something."

"And why did Ian give you money?"

"He didn't." Benny shifted uncomfortably. He was a bad liar.

"Benny, I have it on film."

Benny's eyes opened wide. "Geez! What, have you been following me?"

"No — you were just behind the people the pictures were supposed to be of. Now answer straight or I take all this to the cops."

"Okay, sheesh. The morning Jean-Jacques died, I was doing my thing and just before I found him, I saw Ian standing on the porch of the servant's house, staring toward the big house. It looked like he'd been there awhile — like he was almost in a trance or something. Then, when I found the body, he was gone."

"So Ian did do it!"

"No. I don't think so. I went and found him later and asked him if he did it. He swore he didn't. But he said he saw something, and was getting a lot of money to keep quiet, and if I'd just keep quiet about him, he'd cut me in."

"You don't know who really did it?"

"Don't want to! What if . . . well, whatever. The guy was a jerk. I didn't know who killed him, and the money sounded good." Cam thought maybe he suspected Evangeline, so he was trying to protect her after all, but in a different way than she'd first thought.

"How much?"

"Five grand, which covered my debt, so it solved several problems for me."

"Five grand? To . . . what?"

"Just not mention I saw him. He wanted to stay out of it."

"Yeah, that worked," Annie said.

Cam elbowed her but kept looking at Benny. "Okay, I guess that's all."

Dylan had approached. "Your princess can't stay away?"

"Miss Harris just had a mistaken impression and is leaving," Benny said.

"Miss Harris? I see." He approached Cam and took her hand. "Well, if at any time Benny here is unable to satisfy you, you just let me know."

Cam thought the innuendo and grin were sheer evil in how appealing they were.

"Thank you, Dylan. I'll keep that in mind." Her face had grown very hot and was probably also very red. She avoided Annie's gaze, as she was sure it would just make things worse.

Instead of kissing her hand, he flipped it over and ran the tip of his tongue up the underside of her wrist and then kissed the center of her palm. She tingled from somewhere near her tailbone but couldn't bring herself to speak.

"We need to go," Annie said, pulling Cam by the arm.

When they got outside the gates, Annie began hugging and hitting Cam from all different angles.

"What are you doing?" Cam asked, waving Annie off.

"You are obviously on fire! Don't you feel it? I'm trying to put you out! I totally would have spontaneously combusted in there. How are you not burning?"

Cam didn't admit she sort of was. She had a boyfriend, after all. And she'd never see Dylan again.

"I can't believe the straightest person I know has a hot gangster after her! It's like *Guys and Dolls!*"

"Annie, I am not interested. Remember Rob?"

"Yeah? Okay, fine! Shoot down my fantasy life, why don't you?"

They drove for a few minutes before Annie looked over at her again.

"Cam?"

"Yeah?"

"Benny's not as slow as they claim, is he?"

"Not so much."

"You knew that before, though, didn't you?"

"I figured it out this morning."

"Are you going to tell anyone?"

"I don't think so."

"Why not?"

"Well . . ." It was hard to articulate, because she wasn't completely sure what was driving her hunch. "I don't think it's related to the murders, and he and his father went to an awful lot of trouble to set it up."

Annie frowned for a minute and then a smirk rose.

"What?" Cam asked.

"You think it might be a useful secret. My nefarious plan to turn you into a deviant is finally working."

They headed toward home, Cam frustrated by the dead ends and wondering what to do next. Rob's ring tone sounded when they were almost to the house.

"Cam! I just left the Patricks'." He sounded breathless. "My brakes won't work! My Jeep won't stop!"

"Where are you?"

"Moving south on Blue Ridge Parkway. I just ran a red light!"

Cam gave a silent prayer of thanks for her years of biking south of town. She relayed a couple things to watch for but knew in not too long, no more stops would be required.

"We'll find you! Keep your phone on!"

She then directed Annie for a few minutes until they were headed the right way.

'They headed south at breakneck speed; for once, Cam was glad of Annie's somewhat reckless driving style for a change. Rob relayed each milestone he passed so they could try to head him off.

"Rob, we're going to try to get in front of you — to slow, then stop you, but if we don't make it, keep heading for Copper

Hill. When you get going steadily uphill you should be able to find a gravel pull-off that will stop you."

"Got it." He sounded too scared to harass her about how she knew such things, which unnerved Cam. Rob didn't normally get flustered.

"We have to save him, Annie!" she whimpered as she lowered the phone. She didn't really think a car, especially a top-heavy Jeep, could make all those curves between where Rob currently was and Copper Hill without flipping over.

"I know we do! I'm on it! Cam?"

"Yeah?"

"Use my phone to call Jake. Whoever did this to Rob is our killer — y'all got too close."

"Right!" Cam fished Annie's phone from her pocket and called Jake, explaining their situation, distress, and need. "He's on Blue Ridge Parkway, heading toward Copper Hill from the Patricks'," she said. "Hurry!" She dropped the phone and directed Annie on the fastest route.

A few minutes later, Annie announced, "Blue Ridge Parkway! We're here! This is where Rob is!" Her excitement wasn't helping.

"Rob, are you looking for landmarks or

mile markers? Where are you?" Cam asked after she retrieved her own phone from between the seats.

"I just passed this gnarled old tree."

"Gramps! Slow down, Annie! He's behind us!"

"Gramps?" Rob asked.

"I'll explain later. Just drive carefully. The road has a couple big bends coming up, and it would be best to slow you down before you get there."

"Got it," Rob said.

Annie obeyed Cam's instructions, too, and they drove more slowly, waiting. Cam turned around and watched. In just a few minutes she saw Rob's Jeep barreling toward them.

"There! Speed up, Annie! You need to be barely slower than the Jeep when he hits, then slow when you're butt to nose."

"Cam Harris, you are either a pervert, or you got a better grade in physics than I thought."

Cam tried to laugh, but she was too scared. The Jeep was coming on fast, but Annie was picking up speed. Her judgment of distance and speed seemed good. The real test was whether the tiny Bug was sturdy enough to take the impact. They could all end up sprawled across the road.

No need to share her negative thinking now, though.

"You're okay, Rob! Don't try to avoid us! We'll be your brakes."

She heard mumbling and realized Jake was still on Annie's phone and getting closer, but he was not going to be able to help at all. She gave him the landmarks as they passed and waited for impact.

"Annie, you have to let him hit us."

"I know." Cam knew Annie's car had been paid off less than six months ago. Her face looked desperately sad. She loved her car. Finally, though, she slowed, and Rob noticed the closing gap.

"I could hurt you both!" he shouted, distressed. He'd obviously spotted the same flaw Cam had.

"Nonsense, we're invincible!" Annie shouted.

"You're a loony," Cam said next to her, giving them their first real laugh. If Monty Python quotes couldn't break through, nothing could.

And then impact jolted them forward; grinding metal hurt Cam's ears. Cam saw Annie's foot instinctively lift, needing to brake, but she stopped herself and gave it a little more gas, in spite of the sparks. The Jeep came down off the back of the Bug.

The scraping as the cars slid apart was, if possible, worse than the first impact, and Annie cringed, but now that she didn't need the gas anymore and she could alternately allow the Bug to be pushed and brake, she was regaining her cool.

"Gravel road ahead. Tell Rob I'm going to slow us enough to turn. The gravel should stop him once he's on it, without requiring the Annie-Bug."

Cam relayed the message and instead of hearing Rob agree, she saw him nod through the back window. He looked like hell, pale, sweaty, and moderately insane, though that was understandable, as he'd barely escaped death.

Annie began to slow with more certainty. There was a lot of bumping and grinding and a fair few sparks as the Bug and the Jeep banged against each other. In the end, Rob's Jeep lost momentum before they reached the gravel road. He drove at about five miles an hour just to get off the main stretch. When both cars stopped Cam told Jake where they were, then she leaped from the Bug and ran to Rob, who couldn't seem to make himself do anything. He lay against his steering wheel as she pulled open his door. She pulled him out. He managed to stand, though not move, and she clung to him.

"Don't worry me like that!"

He wouldn't meet her eye, and she could tell he was shaken, but he tried to redirect the conversation, just as she'd expect.

"Listen to you, Miss 'Captured by Drug Dealers.' " Unfortunately, his voice shook. There was no pretending this wasn't serious. He hugged her, and they stood holding each other far more tightly than usual.

Annie came over and joined their hug, shouting, "Three-love!" She jumped at them. They both extended arms around Annie. Cam laughed but realized she was also crying.

Normally Rob would have rolled his eyes — he had a thousand times before when the three-loves rolled, but he picked Annie up in a tight hug. "You saved my life." He had tears in his eyes, which increased Cam's tears exponentially.

"Now I own you!" Annie joked, then more quietly said, "You would have done the same for me."

"Obviously, but geez! I've never needed my life saved before. So thank you! And you," he said, turning to Cam. "How did you know what to do?"

Cam smiled hugely, tears fully streaming

down her cheeks. "I watch TV." Relief and posttraumatic stress waged war with her emotions. "We have to have all the clues now!"

"What?" Annie and Rob turned as one, which was a bit strange, as usually it was Cam and Annie who reacted in unison. They clearly couldn't believe Cam was back to the mystery.

"What are you so shocked about? Obviously somebody you talked to or saw this morning cut your brakes! Who else would know how deeply involved you were?"

"Or somebody *you* talked to." He sounded more irritable than Cam thought was appropriate.

"I doubt it! Chances of any of those people knowing about our relationship are slim. I'm willing to bet the answer is at the Patricks'. I feel pretty sure of that. It may have been somebody who saw you, though, when you didn't see them."

"Cam, we can't risk getting killed over this. Leave it to Jake!"

"Jake who would pin it on Nick or Annie, then drop it? I don't think so."

"Jake was not dropping it! You know that!" a voice said behind them.

Cam hadn't paid attention to the gravel noises. She'd been too relieved they were all safe, so it surprised her to realize the police car had joined them.

"I know you'd like to make me the bad guy, Cam — I understand, actually, and admire your loyalty. But I never dropped it," Jake said.

Cam and Annie took on identical, incredulous looks, underscoring their years of friendship, as Rob went over to shake Jake's hand.

"So what happened?" Jake asked.

Cam relayed the call and the brake event, but Rob eyed her until she guiltily admitted what she'd done that morning, though she still didn't mention to anyone that Benny didn't seem quite as intellectually challenged as they'd all believed him to be.

"That was so dangerous, Cam. I can't explain strongly enough how badly that could have gone."

"I have some idea," she said quietly, and then found her voice, "and if I'd passed it to you, nothing at all would have happened. At least I got a lead."

Annie elbowed her, and Cam frowned again.

"And then there was the stuff we learned at the track," she added, with a sassy look at Annie.

"What?" Now it was Rob and Jake's turn

to shout in unison.

"Well, Rob was busy checking out the printer!" Annie said defensively.

"So you're all idiots!" Jake looked furious but finally asked for details.

They explained the suspicion of drug dealing, though not that they'd been looking for pot plants the night before. Cam thought Jake was too smart not to eventually put it together, so she left out a number of details and then rushed on about following Benny and overhearing about the short supply. This, she finally wrote off as a misunderstanding, not mentioning the gambling forms.

Jake frowned. Cam thought she'd hear more questions later if everything wasn't resolved.

"But we learned a ton of stuff you never did," Cam said.

"You're probably right." Jake sighed. "But we have procedures we have to follow that don't allow trespassing or invading homes on a hunch — and for good reason, I might add."

Cam rolled her eyes and then decided the best defense was a good offense.

"So how are you going to approach this?"

"First, I will make sure it was foul play. Then we'll take fingerprints and such."

"When you haven't found a single print on anything?"

"Cam, we have no reason to think Rob's car malfunction is related to the murders."

"Give me a break, Jake!" Cam was shocked to hear Rob blow up. "You think there would be some other reason someone would want to kill me?"

Jake looked contrite. "I don't think anyone *did.* A detective with automotive expertise will be here with a tow truck and will look, and then we'll take your Jeep in if foul play was involved." He stopped to check his watch. "Ten, fifteen minutes. Rob, why don't you continue this little tale Cam started, if you think this incident with your Jeep is connected to the . . . investigation you aren't supposed to be doing . . ."

Rob obviously thought they were connected. He explained, but with less enthusiasm for Jake than he'd had in the past. He filled Jake in about the printer he'd been looking at, suggesting it was currently their best lead, but skipped the puzzle solving he and Cam had been doing.

Jake looked at Annie. "And what were you doing?"

Cam felt a gasket blow. "She was at work all morning. I joined her there after my little trip, and she'd obviously been there all day, with dozens of customers and hundreds of cupcakes to back her up. Then, when I realized I had to do this track thing without Rob, because it wasn't official and I didn't think he'd call to find out there was still something there, Annie came with me to make sure I didn't get in trouble, but she didn't do anything! And if you think Annie and I had a plot to kill Rob, it would be pretty stupid of us to bang up her car just to save him!"

Jake looked at the back of the Bug and then at Annie.

"Ouch. Sorry about that. I know how you love your car."

Annie scowled. "I *wish* you knew how much I didn't *kill* people!"

"Okay, I've been a jerk, but I was a jerk because you were a jerk first," Jake admitted.

"I was a jerk because I saw you with . . . with . . ."

"My sister and Hernando?"

"Hernando? That's too cute!" Annie sounded like she didn't want to like the name, but couldn't resist.

"*He's* too cute. He's my first nephew, though my other sister is pregnant, so you might, at some point, see me with her and a baby, too. I understand, though, now that

Cam finally shared the story . . . why your mind might have gone to the wrong place . . . Just . . . ask me next time. I won't lie to you."

Cam leaned into Rob. It was surreal to watch the tension dissolving between Annie and the cop so quickly, and she felt a microscopic betrayal that Annie had forgiven him too easily, as Jake still didn't seem to be taking Cam quite seriously. It was obviously better, though, to all be on the same side again.

The yellow lights of the tow truck appeared, and they all took places expectantly around the nose of the Jeep. They needed to know whether Rob's brakes had been deliberately tampered with, though Cam thought Jake was delusional to think otherwise.

After what seemed an awfully long time examining the brake lines, the detective who'd arrived with the tow truck announced, "Punctured. Not cut. Though it looks like it was done with a cutting tool that couldn't quite sever the line. Scissors wouldn't get this far, but maybe . . ."

"Pruning shears?" Cam offered.

The man frowned. "Yeah, that sounds about right." The detective, introduced as

Jaimison, eyed Cam carefully.

"We think it's the same person who killed Jean-Jacques Georges, and that was done with pruning shears, too," Cam said.

"So you're sure it was foul play?" Jake asked.

"Positive," Jaimison replied.

"Okay. Tow it in for the forensic workup. I'm sure Rob can't be without his car for too long."

The man nodded and began to hook the tail of the Jeep to the tow truck. Jake came over to where Cam, Rob, and Annie stood.

"Okay, so let's say now I might buy your theory. What do you want to do?"

"Drink margaritas," Annie suggested.

Rob and Cam nodded.

Jake shook his head. "That will help?"

"Look at Rob. He's a mess," Annie pointed out helpfully. "He almost died. We saved his life." She blinked, an expression Cam recognized as Annie playing ingénue. She was bad at it, but that was mostly intentional. Annie didn't have goals of innocence.

"I have about an hour of paperwork, but I can meet you at six."

They told Jake they'd be at El Palenque, then Cam crawled into the microscopic backseat of Annie's Bug, so Rob, with his longer legs, could have the front seat. Thankfully, the car started — something that was not a given, since it had taken a real beating.

"I'll reimburse you for the damage to your car," Rob offered.

"Please . . . It gives me street cred," Annie said, flexing her bicep.

Cam snorted.

"Okay, you can help me pay the deductible if we don't nail this bastard and get it from him," Annie conceded.

"Deal!"

Chapter 20

The trio stopped off at Sweet Surprise first, so Annie could properly store the cupcakes and frosting she'd left out earlier. Then they headed to El Palenque. Cam would prefer to be outraged to find that margaritas didn't clarify everything, but she knew it was hardly time to expect a first. At least the salty, sweet, sour tequila treat, along with a few baskets of chips and the spicy house salsa, helped the three of them relax.

Rob kept thanking Annie for saving his life, and Annie kept suggesting outrageous shows of gratitude, streaking up Campbell Avenue being only the most recent. Cam, though, had a nagging feeling the answer to the murders was right under her nose. This was amplified when Rob reminded them of the dot-matrix-printed note that had been found at the La Fontaine servant's house.

Cam slowed her drinking significantly well before Annie or Rob, and was relieved when

Jake arrived and somebody less intent on tequila was there to bounce ideas off of.

Cam whispered to Jake about the dot matrix printer, Annie's printer, and the threat. He scolded her briefly for knowing too much, but then allowed her to express her frustration that Rob and Annie seemed tequila bound. Jake saw how intent Annie and Rob were on getting drunk and sighed.

He sat and took a few sips of the margarita Annie pushed in front of him, but Cam could see his heart wasn't in it.

"We had some news this afternoon about those bank accounts," Jake said.

Rob perked up briefly, and Cam turned with full attention. She hoped for progress. "And?"

"Those guys sure move money around a lot."

"Those guys? Which guys?" she asked.

"Not just guys. The women, too."

"So what can you tell?"

"Well, the first big news is that Ian had deposited forty thousand."

Annie choked, though it might have been on a tortilla chip.

"No way! With the five thousand he had in the cigar box and the five thousand he gave Benny, that's . . . just . . . wow." The assessment felt incompetent, but that was sort of what Cam had to offer at the moment.

"So who did it, then?" Rob asked.

"Don't know."

"I mean who gave him all that money?"

"Don't know," Jake repeated. "There were four other accounts with significant bank activity."

"That significant?"

"Well, in three cases there were large withdrawals, though in the fourth, there was a deposit." Jake looked at Rob meaningfully.

"No."

Jake nodded.

"What?" Cam asked, angry to be out of the loop.

"It's Nick, Cam. Jake's saying Nick was the recipient of a large cash deposit. They knew he got one, but this is the first hint where it came from. That money is why they held him so long."

Cam hit Rob's arm. She was angry he hadn't told her, but figured there'd been some threat to cut off information if he shared.

She felt sick and pushed her margarita away. "It's got to be a mistake."

"The amount is different. He got thirty thousand. We've requested all the paperwork, so we will know where it came from soon."

"Who are the other three?"

"Samantha, the Patricks, and Joseph. All had withdrawals of at least fifty thousand dollars last week, though for Joseph, the money went both in and out, so I'm not sure what that is about."

"So Samantha or one of the Patricks is the killer?"

"Maybe not — that kind of money, maybe they hired somebody."

"I know what you're thinking — somebody like Nick, but it's not true!" Cam shouted.

"Calm down, Cam. We know it's not Nick. We're proving it, right?" Annie patted Cam's leg. Although she was saying the words Cam wanted to hear, Annie was quickly approaching drunk. Rob didn't look far behind.

"We can't stop here," Cam said to Jake.

He winked at her and then turned to the others. "Sadly, I'm not quite done for the day. I have some questions for Cam. We'll be back in an hour. In the meantime, eat something!"

To make sure their friends would obey, they ordered Rob and Annie a large plate of nachos as they left.

"It's not so unusual to need to escape, Cam. Don't be too upset. Though I know why you're intent on figuring out the rest, too. You're like me."

They got to his police car.

"So you trust these people?" Jake turned to Cam and asked. "It sounds like the brake cutting had to have happened at the Patricks' and they're on that money list. But you trust the Patricks?"

"Is that where we're going? The Patricks'?"

Jake nodded. "It's where the brakes were cut, and now we have a second question to get answered."

"And the note — Rob said the printer that printed that note framing Annie is probably the one there. But I do trust the Patricks mostly, or I thought I did. Evangeline is more savvy and intelligent, so she can probably help us more, because she observes more, but Mr. Patrick has my ninety percent trust, as opposed to eighty percent for Evangeline."

"Got it."

They arrived and rang the bell. Giselle answered, and they asked for Mr. Patrick. Giselle showed them into the library and offered coffee while they waited.

"Oh, no thank you," Cam said.

Just then Mr. Patrick came in. Cam let

Jake do the talking.

"Mr. Patrick, I don't mean to alarm you, but another crime seems to have occurred at your residence. A reporter was out here today who had his brakes cut. We think it must have happened while he was here, though we may be mistaken. We don't have any idea if it was staff, a visitor, or even a stranger who had followed him, but I thought . . . well, a lot of these nice houses have sophisticated security. I hoped you might run a camera on your driveway."

"Oho! We do!"

"You do? May we see?"

"Well, of course."

He puttered down the hallway. He seemed to be trying to run, but he wasn't very fast. He led Cam and Jake to a laundry room and opened a closet with a lot of gadgets.

"I don't really know how it all works. Evangeline usually does it."

"Would you mind getting her?" Jake asked.

"Of course." Mr. Patrick shuffled off.

Jake began fiddling.

"I thought we needed Evangeline," Cam said.

"We needed Mr. Patrick to fetch Evangeline to get Mr. Patrick out of the way." Jake pressed a few buttons and watched the feed, then exclaimed,

"Damn!"
"What?"
"It's been written over, which, if I'm reading this right, is against the instructions they've coded. Someone manually recorded over this afternoon."
Evangeline arrived in a swimsuit and robe. Mr. Patrick had clearly retrieved her from the hot tub.
"I'm really sorry to disturb you, Mrs. Patrick, but do you ever record over something on this camera? Intentionally, I mean?"
"Intentionally? I wouldn't have a clue how. I can turn it on and off — every once in a while it's nice to reassure guests there is no security watching. Some people we know are very intent on their privacy. But I don't know how to record over."
"Somebody recorded over this afternoon's footage. Can you tell me who was here this afternoon?"
"Why would they do that?"
"Please, Mrs. Patrick. We can tell you more after you answer."
Cam lost her patience. "Evangeline, somebody cut Rob's brakes!"
Jake glared at Cam, but it kicked Evangeline into action.
"Oh no! Okay, Henry was here all day.

Benny stopped by briefly this morning but hasn't been back. He certainly wasn't here when Rob was. Those kids who stayed in the servant's house dropped by, but I wouldn't tell any of them if I had hiccups. They don't even know we have security, let alone where it is. Regular staff was here, mostly. Joseph, Samantha — here separately. I think we had a kitchen delivery, but those boys are attended the whole time."

Cam wondered if anyone among them had failed somewhere along the way to keep track of visitors. That certainly seemed more likely than a resident or one of the staff having done it, especially since Benny was gone by the time Rob arrived, something to which she could testify.

"Okay. Henry and Benny. Both unlikely but possible. Tom and Hannah — unlikely. How long were they here?" Jake asked.

"Ten or fifteen minutes," Evangeline said. "One of them forgot something, I think."

"Okay, Henry, Benny, Tom, Hannah, all unlikely. Joseph and Samantha. Were any of them here when Rob was?"

"I don't remember — I don't know of anybody here while I talked to him, but he spent more time with Giselle and Henry."

"Do any of those people ever use the computer or printer?" Jake asked.

"Anyone who's here and needs a computer: staff, guests. Cam, haven't you used it?" Evangeline asked.

"I guess I have, though I usually bring my laptop with me. If I need to print something, I plug the cable from your laser printer into it," Cam explained, adding, "I never considered the other printer, because it looked sort of old."

"Do you know if Joseph or Samantha are technically savvy?" Jake asked next, but before Evangeline could answer, his cell phone sounded. He looked at the display.

"Could you excuse me a minute? I should take this." He stepped out the front door and let it close most of the way.

Cam smiled at Evangeline. "We really appreciate you being so nice about this. I'm just trying to figure out —"

"Oh, honey. If Neil had been threatened, I'd do the same thing. I'd certainly do anything I could to put the culprit in jail!"

Cam appreciated that.

Jake came back in and apologized. "Now where were we?"

"How savvy with the tech stuff," Cam reminded him. "Joseph is, at least somewhat. All his historical information is in a complicated computer program. I've used it, and I don't think an amateur would have chosen it."

"They both have security at their homes," Evangeline added. "They would know at least what I do, if not more. In fact, Samantha's system is almost like ours — she advised us when we were updating and recommended the company."

Jake wrote something in his notebook, then looked at Evangeline. "One more, possibly sensitive item. You made a very large withdrawal last week. Can you tell me what that was for?"

"Of course. Neil and I are part of a foundation to lend money to local businesses — in fact, Cam, your brother-in-law got one of the grants we awarded. He said Spoons could make a better profit with an upgraded walk-in refrigerator, and he proved his case well."

Cam looked at Jake with some satisfaction.

"Why didn't you mention this earlier?" Jake asked.

"Nobody asked about our foundation. It didn't occur to me."

Jake nodded. He didn't look like he entirely believed the story. Cam did, though. She felt they'd just narrowed the suspect list and crossed off the person she was most concerned about.

"And how much was the grant for?"

"We gave twenty-five thousand dollars to Spoons, though I think Neil donated the same amount to a charity. That's how we do it — we each pick a cause we want to support, then donate as we like. Why?"

"Just trying to keep everything straight."

Jake seemed ready to go, but Cam remembered that Rob had seen a document sitting in the dot matrix printer, and wondered if it had been left by one of the people who'd been there that day.

"Evangeline? Can we see the printer Rob looked at?" she asked.

Evangeline frowned. "I don't know which he looked at, but they're both in the same room." She lead them toward the office.

"And who have you seen in here recently?" Jake asked.

"Giselle uses the computer here pretty regularly to email — her kids are away. One is in college, and the other is a nanny in Europe."

"Right." Jake nodded. Evangeline was giving a lot more information than was necessary. "Unlikely she is very savvy if she doesn't have a computer at home," he said for Cam's benefit.

"Rob said he saw something printed on a dot matrix printer. Could we look at what that was?" Cam was growing impatient with Jake's disinterest in the printer. She wondered if he had even taken the note clue seriously.

"Of course." They reached the study, and Cam and Jake followed Evangeline in and began looking around.

Evangeline pointed at a late-model printer, "This one is hooked to the new computer, which requires a password. Guests use the other, at least if they don't ask for help logging on."

"Who has access to the new computer?" Jake asked.

"Just Neil and me."

Cam reached toward the dot matrix printer, but the page was blank. She shivered, sure someone had removed the document that had been there earlier.

With their list of questions exhausted, Cam and Jake returned to the police car, Jake hurrying and Cam wondering why.

"Who called you, and what did they say?" Cam asked.

"I can't really talk about it, Cam."

"Then why'd you bring me out here, if you didn't think I could help? Those interviews are the key. Somebody thought Rob was too close or they would not have tried to kill him."

"Okay," Jake said, giving in, "another pretty important clue. Did Rob tell you about that address? The cabin in the mountains?"

"Yes."

"Of course he did." Jake sighed. "Anyway, there was a match on an undeliverable UPS package — a box addressed to Jean-Jacques George at that address."

"What was in it?"

"Full of cash — the difference between what was withdrawn from the Patricks' account and what Evangeline claimed she donated to Spoons."

"So somebody was paying him to . . . what?"

"Based on the paperwork, I'd guess he was being paid to stay away from Evangeline Patrick. Neil Patrick sent it."

Cam tried to whistle, though she'd never been able to. "And what do we do?"

"I'd like us to talk to Samantha and Joseph for now — establish what time they were at the Patricks', but it's looking more and more like Mr. Patrick had something to do with the murders."

"It sure is," Cam agreed.

"Do you remember what Rob was asking about that might help with the interviews?" Jake asked.

Cam shuffled in her seat, suddenly uncomfortable. She figured it was time to finally come clean about some portion of her and Rob's suspicions. "You remember the picture from the party that showed Ian and Benny? It looked like Ian was giving Benny money?"

"Our money trail." Jake's expression was tired patience.

"We thought maybe Benny was selling drugs."

"Cam, I should take you back home right now!"

"No! Please! Samantha is fond of me! I'm more likely to get something from her than you are."

He sighed. "And that was why you followed Benny? You were looking for his drug connections?" His eyebrows had ascended nearly to his hairline.

Cam crossed her arms in front of her chest.

"So Benny is in first place," Jake said.

"Not anymore. My main reason fell through, and with all this stuff on Mr. Patrick . . ."

"Cam, investigations aren't solved on guesses."

Cam frowned. It seemed to her they must be. A logical guess was far more plausible a way to narrow options than having to know all the facts before even considering any of the possible solutions.

They arrived at Samantha's house and rang the bell. It was an elaborate ring, the kind impossible to not hear. Samantha, however, didn't answer the door.

"What does Samantha drive?" Jake asked as he walked across the driveway and peeked into the window of her garage.

"A Jaguar, usually."

"Anything else?"

"She has a convertible, I think — small. It might be a Mercedes. It's a little like Evangeline's, but red."

"No Volvo?"

"No. Joseph has a Volvo."

"So Joseph and Samantha are both here unless some third party took them somewhere."

As Jake said this, Joseph opened the door, disheveled and wearing a bathrobe.

"Can I help you?" he asked.

Cam gasped, then tried to call it back, but it brought a rather smug look to Joseph's face.

Jake took a few quick strides back to the front door. "Mr. Sadler-Neff, we came to talk to you and Ms. Hollister." He sounded ridiculously formal, considering Joseph's attire. A closer inspection suggested the robe was Samantha's, unless Joseph liked floral velour.

"I'm afraid that's impossible. Samantha's . . . well, not decent. If you'd come back in an hour or so?"

"Mr. Sadler-Neff, this can't wait," Jake said. "It's quite important." It was the most forceful Cam had ever heard Jake sound. She wasn't sure Joseph would respond well to his tone.

"Joseph? Maybe you could just talk to Jake for a few minutes, and I'll go in and write Samantha a note?"

"A note?"

Jake eyed Cam but didn't stop her. She looked at Joseph earnestly.

"So she knows how important it is we speak with her. I know where everything is." It was a lie. The hair on the back of her neck was prickling. She didn't know if Jake had detected her unease, but Cam knew Samantha would never allow a half-dressed Joseph to answer her door, and it was even more out of character for Joseph. She feared for Samantha's safety.

At last, Joseph said, "I guess you could leave a note."

"Thanks!" She rushed in, passing him,

trying not to let her fear show, though she hoped Jake had somehow sensed it.

She ducked left toward the office but then crept up the stairs as quickly and quietly as possible. Samantha's bedroom was empty except for Mr. Tibbles, or whatever his name was, sleeping at the foot of Samantha's bed. The office, the guest room, and the "day room," which to a normal family would have served as a fourth bedroom on that floor, were also empty.

She went down the set of steps at the rear of the house, moving through the main floor, but avoiding the kitchen and living room, which would require her to pass within Joseph's line of sight. There was no sign of Samantha.

Finally she went down another set of stairs and rushed through the basement, less careful about noise now, as she was starting to panic and knew she didn't have much time.

She found a locked room. She thought it might be the bedroom Jean-Jacques had stayed in. She knocked, quietly at first, then louder.

There was no answer.

Cam looked at the lock, just a hole in the door handle. She had a little sister who had liked to lock doors as a child and so knew how to handle a simple lock.

From the portable bar, the same one that had been rolled outside for the first *Garden Delights* party and which was now stowed in a basement corner, she took a corkscrew. The point was long enough, so she wiggled it in the hole until it sank farther, then carefully turned it clockwise until it clicked.

She rushed in and stopped, stunned.

Samantha looked like one of Joseph's fantasy princesses. She was unconscious, tied at her feet and wrists and laid across a baby blue satin comforter. She wore a regal white nightgown and robe and had flowers all around her. Thankfully, her chest seemed to be slowly rising and falling.

Cam began to hyperventilate but then heard shouting, so she ran upstairs.

"Jake! Arrest him! He's twisted!"

She heard a door slamming, footfall, and then Jake shouted, "Freeze, Joseph! Or I'll shoot!"

A screeching followed, and though there was then a gunshot, Cam felt certain Jake had shot wide. Joseph had gotten away.

As Cam reached the door and stepped out, Jake stood there, hands out, one holding his revolver, staring into the sky.

"I trusted you, Cam. This better be good, because I just shot at a man."

"If by good you mean repulsive, then yes.

This is very good." Her stomach continued to clench, and she was glad she'd only had one margarita.

Jake followed Cam downstairs, and she led him to Samantha. He felt her pulse, then called for backup. He put out an APB on Joseph and requested a police car and an ambulance at Samantha's home. When he hung up, he reassured Cam that Samantha's pulse was strong.

"It was Joseph, this whole time," Cam whispered.

"This is at least confirmation he must have drugged her both times, and the first drugging *does* seem related to the first murder."

"That and running. And putting her in Jean-Jacques's room? In that princess garb?"

"He looks guilty, Cam. I'm not arguing, but there are quite a few pieces still to fit together."

Cam sighed. It was true. She thought, though, that some of the other things she'd learned might help. She told Jake about Joseph's being protective of Samantha, and then what she'd learned was the true story about Benny's feelings for Evangeline and how that had reinforced in her mind the idea of the crush as a motive. She shared it all except for the apparent ruse regarding

Benny's deficits. She didn't feel comfortable blowing that out of the water. She believed Benny and his dad had their reasons.

CHAPTER 21

Cam was a little lost in the chaos that followed. As Jake barked orders and descriptions into his radio and cell phone, Cam returned inside to tend to Samantha. The poor woman was still out of it, but Cam thought if she woke up restrained, she would panic. Cam certainly would have.

She knew, however, it was a crime scene, so she didn't want to do too much. She found a camera in the kitchen and came down and took pictures from several angles, then donned a pair of the latex gloves she'd swiped from Jake. She used scissors to cut Samantha's wrists free, then heard the sirens arrive, followed by tromping down the stairs.

Cam had cut all the restraints by this time, but that was as far as she'd gotten. She answered the questions from the EMT about who she was, who Samantha was, how she'd found Samantha, and what appeared to have happened.

From a daze, she heard someone say something about pumping Samantha's stomach. Two men arrived with a stretcher, loaded Samantha onto it, and then Cam was left alone in this surreal room of princess nightmares.

She shivered and climbed the stairs. An officer had arrived to assess the crime scene, so Cam led him to it, again describing what she'd found. She gave him the camera and explained the pictures she'd taken.

"Glad you did that. I can dust for prints and all, but hard to prove what happened when the body is gone, if there are no pictures."

Cam shivered again. He made it sound as if Samantha was dead.

"Mind if I go?" she said.

"Leave your number?" the officer asked.

Cam pulled her card from her bag and handed it to him. He smiled sheepishly, and Cam left the basement, which was now making her skin crawl. She imagined slithery lizards and centipedes on the walls as she scurried out, completely itchy by the time she reached the kitchen where she realized that, once again, she was stranded with no car. Jake had gone after Joseph with another officer, and though he'd left his own squad car, she could hardly take that.

She swore under her breath and slowed at Samantha's countertops, and then noticed a few odd keys dangling from hooks next to a bulletin board. She didn't know what most of them went to, but the Mercedes key was pretty obvious. Samantha's convertible was nicer than anything Cam had ever driven. She smirked, opened a drawer for a pen and pad of paper, and wrote a note to Samantha about her need.

When she went to return the notepad, a letter from a lawyer named Schleigel tempted her. The letter was dated only a week earlier. She opened it and saw Samantha had been copied on a will. The will named Jonathan Jacobs Georges as sole recipient of the estate described, though Samantha was to be executor should Jonathan Jacobs be difficult to find. Cam guessed, based on their earlier conversation, this was the will of Jean-Jacques's father, and this meant Jean-Jacques had inherited everything. She raised an eyebrow but couldn't make any sense of it, so she put it back in the drawer and then tested a few house keys. She took the one that worked to the officer still in the basement, saying if he left the house with nobody there, could he please lock up and take the key to Samantha. He didn't pay a lot of attention, but she made a show of putting it on the dresser, and he nodded.

She then made her way to the garage, breathing a sigh of relief. It was over.

The car was the most fun she'd ever had at the wheel, though she was glad the Bug had acclimated her to German-made stick shifts, as she feared doing anything wrong in the expensive machine. She drove the long way, singing loudly with Patsy Cline, the only CD of Samantha's she recognized.

She considered driving another lap through Roanoke, but decided it was in poor taste to act too giddy after what had happened, so she went home.

She saw Annie's car in their driveway and sprinted up to Annie's apartment to tell her all was resolved.

The apartment, however, was a disaster. Not that it was ever particularly clean, but at least the furniture was usually upright.

The kitchen, where she entered, was disturbed only in the toppled chair and a broken glass that had been knocked across the room.

The living room, however, looked like a cyclone had blown through. Several pieces of furniture had been moved a fair distance, and many of the tchotchkes Annie normally displayed on walls or shelves had been thrown to opposite corners.

"Annie!" Cam called, nervous now.

There was no answer.

The bedroom seemed to have been clumsily searched, and upstairs, in what had once been an attic but now served as an office and darkroom, Annie's computer had been destroyed, as had much of her photo equipment.

"Oh no. Oh no." Cam's stomach knotted again as she descended and she sprinted down the short hallway, sure she'd be sick in the sink. She managed to hold it back by splashing water on her face.

She dialed Jake.

"Yeah, Cam?"

"He took Annie!"

"What?"

"Annie's apartment's been trashed. Her car is here, but she's gone!" Her sobs broke her off. She heard Jake trying to call to her, but she didn't understand him. She'd sunk to Annie's kitchen floor, barely aware of avoiding the broken glass, and she pulled her knees up and tucked her face between them.

She had no awareness of how long she was

there, but Rob found her.

"Come on, baby. Let's get you downstairs."

She shook her head and argued incoherently. Some part of her needed to be in Annie's space to draw her home.

"Jake will find her."

"No!"

"You don't want Jake to find her?"

"I do, but . . ." She let out a large sniff. "Jake? You think" — she gulped down a sob — "shouldn't we?"

"Cam, you're exhausted! You had a helluva day!"

"No! We need to figure it out."

"Come downstairs and we'll try, okay?"

Cam nodded; that made some sense. So she followed Rob to her own kitchen table and watched as he got out a notebook and pen.

Rob looked surprised when Cam pulled the notebook to herself and started grilling him.

"How long did you stay for the margaritas?"

"Just the one pitcher and nachos. Annie said I looked lousy and needed sleep, and I could tell she was drunk, so I drove her home — her car, obviously. I had to take a cab home, and then another one to get back here."

"Well . . . that's good. Better not to drive after that."

"Nice convertible, by the way."

"My need was great," she joked, gallows humor the only thing that might numb the pain. "What time did you get home?"

"Maybe eight. I made a protein shake, brushed my teeth, and was in bed by nine."

Cam rolled her eyes at the mention of the protein shake. Rob claimed they were healthy, but he only actually drank them when he feared a hangover.

"Then I woke up when Jake called."

"What time is it?"

"Midnight, I guess?"

Cam tried to make sense of that. She'd thought she'd left Samantha's at nine or ten, but time had probably morphed in the weirdness, and so it was certainly possible she hadn't left until later. It was probably why the officer had been so nice about it.

"So how do we find Annie?"

"You're going to be mad," Rob said, "but first we wait. Jake swore he'd call when he knew anything. Cam, you have to get some rest, and in the morning, when they know something, I'll help you with whatever we can piece together."

She tried to fight the idea, but her body rebelled. She was exhausted. She lay down, still dressed, on her bed with Rob. His phone was set loud, as she made him prove three different times, and he held her while she slept.

As promised, Jake called Rob at about three in the morning. A search of Joseph's apartment had revealed two toy Pomeranians, yappy and demanding, quite a rich fantasy life — though fantasy more of the swords and dragons variety than the *Penthouse* type — and five thousand dollars in cash that Jake thought meant he looked ready to leave town.

The clue Jake felt was most helpful, though, one he fortunately shared with Rob, was a stack of newspaper clippings about interest in a property south of Roanoke. Jake didn't know what to make of it, but Rob thought it might mean something, and so before he woke Cam, he turned on her laptop to search.

"Cam. Here. I think this is why he's so interested in that property."

Cam jerked herself awake, feeling oddly refreshed from her two-hour nap. Rob explained what Jake had found in Joseph's apartment, and then she joined Rob at her laptop to look at the article he'd pulled up from the *Roanoke Tribune*'s online version. It was in the archives, which, thankfully, Rob had access to because he was a newspaper employee.

Rob pointed out that he'd saved a number of related tabs, and Cam pulled the computer to her so that she could read through them. They described a series of lawsuits in the late 1990s against tobacco companies. Many local tobacco farmers had opted to sell their land, due, the article said, to the writing on the wall. Cam knew that had made Rob cringe — a reporter shouldn't resort to clichés.

The series, though, made it clear the landowners who'd sold before the court decision had mostly gotten fair money for their land. The sellers who had waited, however, had gotten only dimes on the dollar, nowhere near the true value for their land.

Joseph Sadler-Neff had been interviewed, one of a handful of landowners unwilling to part with family land for such a pittance.

"His elderly mother owns it. It's the reason my search didn't catch it."

"What search?"

"I ran a background search on everybody who was even a little suspicious. It's just part of the job," Rob went on, as though that shouldn't be news to Cam. "While he couldn't afford to farm it with all the increased financial burdens, he'd leased part of it to a man who raised sunflowers, and decided to just let the rest sit idle."

"That's where they are," Cam insisted.

Rob nodded. He'd drawn the same conclusion.

"Why does Joseph have it in for Annie?" Cam asked.

Rob opened a tab Cam hadn't gotten to yet.

Senator Alden Schulz expressed his sympathy for the farmers but said public opinion now sided against tobacco, and in good conscience, the state of Virginia couldn't legislate in a way that discouraged diversification.

"That doesn't sound like him — I mean according to Annie's grumbles. But what does it mean?" Cam asked Rob.

"Tobacco largely ruins the land for other crops. It has to sit a few years, recovery crops — that kind of thing. The state considered a parachute for tobacco farmers. Normally Schulz was all over stuff like that, but he voted against it, and took a couple other senators with him. It changed the outcome."

"Oh, geez. How fast can we get there?"

Rob looked up the address on a map. "Fifteen minutes, maybe?"

"Let's go."

"In what, babe? My Jeep is still in holding as evidence."

"Annie's car. The Mercedes probably shouldn't go on a rescue run, but the Bug is an old pro."

He grinned and followed her outside.

They weren't a bad team with Cam driving and Rob navigating — far better, Cam thought, than if the roles were reversed. Rob didn't trust her navigating, so refused to take her directions, and then offered being lost as proof she couldn't read a map. She knew, though, that the inability to ask for directions was a trait solidly bound to the Y chromosome.

This time they managed beautifully, up until they found themselves on a gravel road in the middle of nowhere. They parked and decided to walk the rest of the way so they didn't alert anyone to their presence.

Cam was starting to spook herself, and Rob found this amusing enough that he kept pointing out things to keep her on edge.

"Will you stop that? I'm scared!"

"You are not. Cam, this is just an old farmhouse with about three outbuildings — that satellite view showed nearly nothing out here."

She frowned irritably. She knew he was trying to calm her with his humor, and she, half hoped he was right, though she was also half waiting to shove his face in it if he was wrong, even if she didn't want to confront whatever would make him wrong.

The farmhouse, when they reached it, appeared to be abandoned, as did the shadowy buildings off to the side, though in the little bit of moonlight, the slatted design of the tobacco-drying barn made the structure look like something out of a horror movie. The spaces between the slats emitted only blackness.

"Look!" she whispered.

To the side, in the shadow of the tobacco barn, was an edge of white that Cam felt certain was the boxy corner of Joseph's Volvo. She was very glad he thought of himself as a white knight. A black car never would have been visible, and they might not have gotten closer.

Rob pushed a button on his cell phone.

"Jake? I'm pretty sure we found Joseph. The address you gave me south of town used to be his family's tobacco farm." He held up his phone toward the part of the Volvo they could see, transmitting a picture to Jake. When he hung up, Cam looked at him intently.

"Rob, I don't think we should wait. What if he's torturing Annie or something?"

"Torturing? Do you have any reason to think he would?"

"He killed somebody just to frame her."

"Allegedly, but good point. What should we do?"

"We need to get her out of there! I guess I don't know how we do that, but we could sure plan it a lot better if we could see what was going on."

Rob seemed skeptical, but he nodded, resigned to getting closer. "Seems like we probably want to come at it from the back, don't you think?"

Cam nodded and took Rob's hand so he could lead her around the edge of the property.

As the moon passed behind a cloud, they lost their only light source, making walking more difficult, but soon enough, they were near the barn. Approaching quietly from the rear, they could hear noises coming from within. It sounded like the scraping and the moving of something across boards.

"They're above us," Rob whispered. "I'm going up."

He indicated the pattern of siding at the back and a large window up above that indeed made the building look climbable.

Cam thought about arguing but knew she'd only hold Rob up — upper body strength wasn't her strong suit. "What do I do?"

"Show Jake where we are."

"Oh no!"

"Shhh."

He was right. It was not the time to make her case, but neither was it time to sit and wait for the cops. She wasn't sure what to do, but walking away from the barn where both her best friend and boyfriend might end up in trouble was not an option. She looked at her watch. They had called Jake ten minutes earlier, and he should be there soon, provided he'd left Roanoke immediately. She thought he probably had. That meant if she could somehow buy ten minutes, everything would be fine.

Rob wouldn't be at all happy with her plan, but she wasn't thrilled with his either, so she decided to go for it, creeping slowly toward the front of the building, and walking close to the Volvo as she did so.

There was a roll of duct tape on the seat, and gardening twine — visible because the driver's door hadn't been shut all the way, so the light was on. There was also a small gardening clipper, probably to cut the twine with. It was the sort that was sharp on the blade, to cut vines and small branches, but dull at the point — unlike the shears used to stab Jean-Jacques. If nothing else, she thought the clipper would be useful for cutting at any fingers trying to get too close, so she opened the door a little wider and grabbed it.

As she moved toward the front of the barn, she tried to listen more closely. She thought she heard Annie yelling, but muffled — she had something in or over her mouth. Joseph was talking calmly to her, though he was too far away for Cam to make out his words.

Cam edged around the front, peeking into the larger opening. The air coming from within smelled of dried tobacco, and she could make out some leaves still strung to the rows of clips that had at one time held up entire harvests to dry in the late summer heat.

The beam from a flashlight shone above

her head, but it was angled in such a way that she couldn't tell what it was illuminating.

She judged Rob had reached the level where Annie was right now, and what she needed to do was draw Joseph down so Rob could free Annie. She stepped into the doorway.

"Joseph!"

It took a moment, but then she heard scuffling.

"Miss Harris. You shouldn't be here. What do you need?"

"Just to talk to you. Can you come down?"

"I'm afraid I can't. I'm in the middle of something."

"Then I'll need to call the police." She pulled out her cell phone and started to dial.

"No! No need for that. Just give me a minute."

"I can't do that. I'm afraid you're going to hurt my best friend."

"Oh, Cam, this isn't personal."

"That's where you're wrong, Joseph. This is very personal. Annie and I have been best friends for twenty years."

He paused a moment. "Annie? What does Annie have to do with this?"

Cam didn't believe him. "Come down and talk to me and I'll tell you."

He sighed loudly, unhappy with this development, but he seemed resigned to having to talk to her. Cam did a little internal cheer, hoping her plan might work.

Joseph climbed down the ladder and walked toward her. She caught the glint of something shiny in his hand, and she realized he had a knife of some sort. He stuck it in a back pocket and pulled out a small box, though she couldn't make out what it contained.

"Now, Miss Harris. Why is it you think your friend is here?"

"She's disappeared, and I could tell there'd been a struggle at her apartment."

"Surely you've noticed she's not a reliable girl."

"She wouldn't disappear without her car, and she wouldn't go without telling me."

Joseph made a quick motion, and only then did Cam realize the small box was matches. He threw the tiny orange fireball behind him, and old straw and tobacco leaves blazed as though they'd had an accelerant poured on them.

"No!"

"It's okay, Cam. It's my own property."

"But Annie!"

"I assure you, Annie's not here."

"Rob!" Cam shouted. "Catch!" She tossed

the clipper she'd grabbed onto the loft and heard Rob scramble.

"Got 'em!"

"What?" Joseph looked angry and perplexed, pulling his knife again and heading toward the ladder.

Cam dived and grabbed his ankles, tripping him, but he turned with the knife. She scrambled backward out of Joseph's reach. He again headed toward the ladder and got partway up before Cam reached it, pulling with all her might. It didn't dislodge, but it shook enough to throw Joseph off.

"You little brat! Get out of here if you know what's good for you!"

"We're leaving, Cam! Run!" Rob's voice was sweet relief — she could stop fighting Joseph, because he couldn't hurt Annie or Rob anymore. She turned to sprint out, just clearing the doorway out of the barn when Joseph caught her ankle. She fell spectacularly but flipped onto her back and kicked. She was pretty sure she broke his nose as she backed the rest of the way out of the barn, trying to regain her footing.

Joseph rose, his face bloodied, and came toward her. She rolled, tried to run, then rolled again. Unfortunately, Joseph was like a madman, intent on taking her down. She scrambled for what she thought was her last time, and Joseph lunged at her. What happened next seemed in slow motion.

Just as Joseph reached her, a body flew toward them from the side of the barn at lightning speed, tackling Joseph. The knife spun away into the tall grass. It was only then Cam remembered how fast Rob could round bases. She gasped for breath, and Annie, following Rob from around the barn, reached her side, limping. She toppled down and pulled Cam into a hug.

Cam hugged back momentarily and then found her second wind and ran to the Volvo, fetching the duct tape. Rob had Joseph in a choke hold, and Cam and Annie finished binding his wrists and ankles just as they heard the sirens of arriving police cars.

Jake arrested Joseph and then proceeded to scold Cam and Rob on their recklessness.

"Annie would have been a roasted marshmallow if we hadn't been here!" Rob complained.

Jake sighed. "Okay, I get why you did what you did, but you also could have all three been roasted marshmallows. Wouldn't that have been worse?"

"No!" Rob and Cam shouted together, and Jake rolled his eyes. Apparently they were a bad influence.

"Fine. You don't believe me. Law enforcement needs to play its role. Rob, you should have called me when you first realized where Joseph was."

"We thought it was a long shot."

"Uh-huh. But don't you think this would have been a whole lot easier with police?"

Cam was growing more irritable. "Actually, we rocked. Rob saved Annie, and I took down the bad guy."

"I took down the bad guy," Rob argued.

"Only after I did."

Jake looked up at the sky, praying for patience. Cam winked at Rob, who grabbed her into a tight hug and laughed.

"Three-love!" Annie shouted, leaping at them, one-footed.

"We're a good team," Cam said.

"We are," Rob agreed.

"We still only have him for kidnapping Annie at this point," Jake said.

"And miles and miles of circumstantial stuff on the murders!" Cam protested.

"Cam, circumstantial is circumstantial."

"And drugging Samantha. Say, I bet Samantha can get the truth out of him!"

Cam drove Annie and Rob to the hospital, insisting they be checked for smoke inhalation. The accelerant had caused the flames and smoke to rise upward, rather than filling the space Cam and Joseph had tussled, so Cam felt okay, but worried for her friends. While they were waiting, Cam found her way to Samantha. Samantha came around about a half hour after Cam arrived and, after calling for something to stop her head from pounding, listened as Cam explained what had happened during the last several hours. Samantha was mortified with the facts of the day, not least because Joseph had apparently changed her clothes and set her up as a prisoner.

Midway through their conversation, a nurse came to administer ibuprofen. "A headache is pretty common after the large dose of ether you had." She smiled reassuringly and left.

Cam continued talking. "We are sure Joseph committed the murders, too. Can't you help us get him to admit it?"

Samantha looked at Cam curiously. "I think I can get him to confess." She sounded not only deeply angry but also so confident, Cam believed her.

It was only after leaving Samantha's room that the nurse's ether comment registered with Cam. She wondered why Joseph hadn't used the sleeping pills he had used the first time.

The next day, Jake initially refused to allow Cam to watch Samantha's meeting with Joseph from behind the interrogation room's one-way window, but given multiple reminders of all the help she, Rob, and Annie had provided, Jake finally yielded.

Now, peering through the glass, Cam watched as Samantha entered the interrogation room. She looked stately as she stepped toward the lone table at which Joseph sat, and seated herself purposefully at the chair across from him. "Hello, Joseph," she said icily.

Joseph seemed oblivious to her tone. "Samantha, darling! You came!"

Straight from the hospital, Cam mentally added, though she looked good, considering.

"You've never called me darling before." Samantha held herself stiffly, and Cam wondered if she would be able to coax anything out of Joseph when she looked so hostile.

"But you know I've always adored you!" Joseph was manic, twitchy and sweating. Samantha kept evading as Joseph reached for her hand, but she did so subtly, so as not to tip him off.

"I suppose I knew. You were only protecting me, then?"

Joseph looked thoroughly confused for a moment, the sheen of sweat Cam had seen in the photographs once again dampening his forehead and intensifying the unhealthy pallor created by the room's florescent lights. "Of course I was! I will always protect you!"

"So why did you kill Ian?"

"Who's Ian?"

"The man you hit with the camera."

"That was unfortunate."

"Joseph, look at me. What was unfortunate about killing Ian?"

"Samantha! I had to — you know why, don't you?"

"Of course not, Joseph. Can you tell me?" Her glare was menacing.

"He saw! And then . . . well . . . when they thought it was him. That senator's daughter was accusing him! I worried he'd break and tell them everything, even after all the money . . ."

Joseph leaned close to Samantha, whispering. But Samantha refused to stay close enough to hear if he didn't speak up.

"Why did you frame Annie?"

"They were *talking about you!* If it was Annie . . . don't you see?"

"No, and you're in trouble for taking her and doing what you did. You need to admit what you did, Joseph. They can see how upset you are."

"But . . ."

"Joseph, you need to admit to killing Ian . . . and Johnnie."

"Johnnie?"

"Yes, Joseph. You killed my nephew to protect me. You must have."

"What?" Joseph started to whimper. "But darling, you —"

Samantha cut him off. "But you did kill him." The statement held a sort of finality.

Joseph frowned. "Did I?" He stared around, upset at this news.

"It's okay, Joseph. I know."

He nodded but without admitting anything, then said,

"I love you, darling! Do you love me?"

Samantha leaned over the table and whispered something, and then kissed Joseph's cheek.

"You really want me to confess?"

"All this to protect me?"

Joseph nodded, resigned.

When Samantha came out, Jake went in and explained he still had a right to a lawyer.

"I know you wanted to speak with Ms. Hollister first, but it is still your right. Would you like to have an attorney present?"

"No. I know what I need to do," Joseph said.

Jake pulled out a notepad and began giving instructions to Joseph.

"Thank you, Samantha. You were amazing," Cam said.

"I just know how to handle him. Now if you'll excuse me, I feel rather violated and I'd like to go home and shower."

Samantha left, and Cam went out to the precinct room to see Rob. He hugged her, and they held each other until Jake came out of the interrogation room.

"You need to go let your nutty friend know she's in the clear," he said.

"So you like her?" Cam teased.

He grinned helplessly. "Yes, I like her. I just think maybe she has some things to work through."

"Well, who doesn't?"

"Touché, Cam. Touché."

CHAPTER 22

Cam's dad had said a friendly good-bye to Jane Duffy. They exchanged addresses and promises to stay in touch. Hannah and Tom also finally got to leave town. Cam thought they were glad their fiasco of a visit was finally over.

Cam had had mixed feelings about attending Jean-Jacques's funeral given all the trouble his life and death had caused, but she wanted to support Samantha and couldn't seem to help herself anyway. Joseph's confession had sat with her funny. There were some details that kept nagging at her, and this seemed a better place than any other to try to find answers.

She'd spent the fifteen minutes in the pews before the service trying to avoid Madeline's eye. Her boss wasn't happy, though Cam thought she appreciated Cam's efforts to spin the news so Joseph looked tragic rather than deranged, and the

Roanoke Garden Society looked heroic for having included him in spite of his eccentricities.

Rob's article about the murders in the *Roanoke Tribune* had only helped matters. Several Roanoke Garden Society members had come across as either sweet or smart for their compassion in the first case and their assistance in the second. None of it, though, had particularly flattered the dead men.

Rob was by her side, gripping her hand and rubbing her shoulders as necessary. She was grateful. Annie had declared plainly that she'd "had enough of those nuts," so Cam had worried she'd have to come alone.

She sat respectfully and listened, eyes scanning, but trying not to be too obvious. Most of the audience seemed to be part of Samantha's social network, but Samantha sat off to a side next to a poised woman with auburn curls. The woman appeared to be in her late thirties or early forties, and Cam thought it was most likely Margo, Jean-Jacques's sister.

Until she spotted Margo, Cam had planned to leave as soon as she'd paid her respects to Samantha, but now she felt that a few more puzzle pieces were begging to be slid into place. Samantha was clearly very fond of Margo. This woman seemed like she might be able to shed some light on where exactly those pieces fit.

Cam was thankful the service was not overly long and didn't dwell on any unbelievable saintly traits, because Cam knew better. Jean-Jacques was a user and a con artist. He'd not merited any real caring that she could tell.

Halfway through, another woman — about Samantha's age, but employing far more showgirl techniques with her makeup — arrived and stumbled up to the front of the church, throwing her body over the coffin and weeping. Cam quickly made the connection: the distraught woman was Margaret, Margo and Jean-Jacques's mother.

Margo rose, helped her mother to stand up, and returned to the pew with her.

The older woman's red hair was a shade too bright, making her daughter's look dull, and she continued sobbing loudly.

After the service, Cam approached Margo.

"Can I help you? I mean . . . I'm sorry; my name is Cam. I work with the Garden Society. I —"

"You figured out who killed my brother — thank you."

"Yes. I mean, though . . . with your mother."

"Oh, that's just Mother — ever the actress, looking for a few tears on her behalf and hoping somebody is carrying a flask to slip her a shot of bourbon."

"Oh dear. Are you sure?"

"Quite."

Cam was uncomfortable in the silence, so she looked for a safer topic.

"Samantha thinks quite a lot of you."

"Oh, she's wonderful! She's always been good to me. In fact" — Margo leaned in to whisper — "I almost worried she'd been the killer, after what Johnnie did to me!"

"What did he do?" Cam knew some portion of this but hoped Margo would share more.

"He embezzled a bunch of money from our dad, put it in my account, then blew the whistle. Dad was furious. Wouldn't listen to reason, and he wrote me out of the will."

"That's horrible!"

"It was sort of Johnnie's style — him and Mom."

"Why would you think Samantha killed him over that?"

"Just silliness on my part. Timing, I guess. I called her the night before the murder. I was a wreck when I told her about the will and how it had happened. Then when

Johnnie was dead, I worried even more what I might have set in motion. I'm so glad it wasn't . . . you know . . ."

"I completely understand. The first person the police investigated was my brother-in-law. It's horrible to consider a loved one doing such a thing."

"Exactly. You know, Cam, you've made me feel so much better."

Cam wondered, though, if Margo hadn't had quite the opposite effect on her.

Outside the church, she approached Rob and announced matter-of-factly, "I think there's something fishy."

"Fishy, how?"

"Call Jake. I'll call Annie. We need to put our heads together." She walked away from him, pulling her cell phone out of her clutch purse.

They met at Martin's again. It seemed to bode better for them than some of the other places they'd been.

"What's this about, Cam?" Jake asked.

Cam felt Rob shrug next to her.

"Pieces that don't fit."

"It's a closed case," Jake said, but in response to her glare, frowned and said, "Like what?"

She relayed Margo's story, then mentioned the different drugs used to sedate Samantha and the phrasing in Joseph's conversations with Samantha. "Why would Joseph use something sloppy like ether when the sleeping pills had worked so well?"

Jake frowned. "Forensics thinks the sleeping pills were not drunk from the cup at all. There was no residue on the sides of the cup, so they've concluded that somebody added the drug to the dregs rather than to the full cup before it was drunk."

"Shoot! I *did* give her that idea!"

When the others stared at her blankly, Cam elaborated. "Samantha wasn't drugged at all! She needed an alibi, and I gave her the idea!"

"So you think Samantha did all this?" Annie asked, her nose wrinkled in disbelief.

"Not all. Listen. Let's say you are a devoted aunt, and have a niece who is grateful and reciprocates your affection. And then a nephew who is a horrible ingrate."

"Jean-Jacques," Annie supplied, as if it weren't obvious.

"You're already having problems with the ingrate — in fact you have to basically blackmail him into doing something to pay you back. Then, on the night before this all starts, you get a letter that he's inherited a lot of money and a sobbing phone call from the worthy niece about how her father was tricked into changing his will."

"So she did do it," Annie said.

"Stay with me. You learn he is also trying to scam money out of a friend, and you go to confront him."

"And end up killing him," Rob added.

"But then you panic. You call your lapdog, who comes to help with the body, but he's seen — by Ian."

Annie and Rob gasped. It was a detail they'd apparently missed through the margarita haze.

"So Joseph dumps the body, gets money to bribe Ian, Samantha feels guilty and pays him back, but then Joseph decides it's his job to keep the focus off Samantha. He tries to accuse other people at first, then frame others because that isn't enough — Rob, I bet he heard us at the party talking about Samantha and that's why he tried to act like he'd been poisoned. But the fighting between Ian and Annie gave him the idea — he'd frame somebody solidly and kill the only witness all at once. It was a bonus that it would also frame the daughter of a man who'd caused him so much grief. Then Samantha would be safe. He finally even confessed for her."

"Wow," Rob said. "That's devotion."

"But why drug Samantha? What was that all about?" Annie asked.

"Maybe he expected some gratitude? That he would win her by saving her?" Cam suggested. "Maybe that was why that memory card was at her place, too — a present to prove his devotion."

"But when it didn't work," Annie said, "ewwww."

Jake chuckled.

Annie elbowed him since she had been the target of so much of Joseph's nastiness.

"So what about Mr. Patrick?" Jake asked.

"Just what we guessed. He was tired of Jean-Jacques pestering Evangeline about money, so he was trying to bribe him to get rid of him once and for all. I bet he really was trying to help Samantha by offering Jean-Jacques a different place to stay."

"Pretty impressive," Rob said.

"What will you do?" Cam asked Jake.

"Looks like we reopen the case, provided I can find some evidence to support these details, but I'm willing to bet you're right — there were several places the story was inconsistent, and this theory answers most of them. Good work, Cam. The killer almost got away with it."

Cam tried not to cringe. This turn of events might just mean she was out of a job.

TO: *Roanoke Tribune,* Living Section
FROM: Roanoke Garden Society
RE: National Media Event: Tragedy Turned Around. Roanoke, VA

Two months ago a great tragedy nearly ruined Roanoke's chances to display her floral glory to the nation via *Garden Delights,* America's premier magazine for gardening enthusiasts. [Details on the tragedy and ensuing investigation can be found in the April 25 edition of the *Roanoke Tribune.*] Thanks to local law enforcement and the hard work of a few key individuals, the magazine feature will be released as scheduled this week.

Garden Delights magazine came to Roanoke in mid-April for a feature centering on La Fontaine, the famous gardens owned by Roanoke Garden Society founder Neil Patrick and his wife Evangeline, a former Miss Virginia.

The Patricks graciously opened their home to the magazine staff, only to have tragedy strike. World-famous photographer Jean-Jacques Georges, who spent summers in Roanoke as a boy, was killed before the shoot ever started. Shortly thereafter, Ian Ellsworth, photo editor for the magazine, was killed as well.

Thankfully, local photographer Annie Schulz agreed to replace Mr. Georges and with the assistance of the *Garden Delights* staff, successfully completed the photo shoot.

The Roanoke Garden Society extends its condolences to the families of Jean-Jacques Georges and Ian Ellsworth.

CONTACT: Camellia Harris
camharris@rgs.org

The employees of Thorndike Press hope you have enjoyed this Large Print book. All our Thorndike, Wheeler, and Kennebec Large Print titles are designed for easy reading, and all our books are made to last. Other Thorndike Press Large Print books are available at your library, through selected bookstores, or directly from us.

For information about titles, please call:
(800) 223-1244

or visit our Web site at:
http://gale.cengage.com/thorndike

To share your comments, please write:

Publisher
Thorndike Press
10 Water St., Suite 310
Waterville, ME 04901

Ingalls